Pengu

FERREN AND THE

Richard Harland was born in Huddersfield, England, in 1947. He migrated to Australia in 1970. After several years as a singer, songwriter and poet, he became a university lecturer in 1987. He resigned to become a full-time writer in 1997. He now lives in Figtree near Wollongong, with his wife Aileen, plus a cat and an antique laptop.

His first book was the comic horror novel, *The Vicar of Morbing Vyle*, which has since become a cult classic. In 1997, he began the Eddon and Vail series, which combines a fantasy/ science fiction world with detective/thriller stories. The first novel in the series was *The Dark Edge*, followed by *Taken By Force*, then *Hidden From View*.

Ferren and the Angel, published in 2000, was his first book for Penguin.

Richard's homepage on the Web is at:
www.uow.edu.au/commerce/harland/hhome.html
Look it up if you want more information on angels!
Richard's e-mail address is:
richard_harland@uow.edu.au

RICHARD HARLAND

FERREN AND THE WHITE DOCTOR

BOOK **2** *IN THE* **HEAVEN AND EARTH**
T R I L O G Y

Penguin Books

> *For Linda, my first best reader*
> *and for Selwa, my first best agent.*

Penguin Books Australia Ltd
250 Camberwell Road
Camberwell, Victoria, 3124, Australia
Penguin Books Ltd
Harmondsworth, Middlesex, England
Penguin Putnam Inc.
375 Hudson Street, New York, New York 10014, USA
Penguin Books Canada Limited
10 Alcorn Avenue, Toronto, Ontario, Canada, M4V 3B2
Penguin Books (N.Z.) Ltd
Cnr Rosedale and Airborne Roads, Albany, Auckland, New Zealand
Penguin Books (South Africa) (Pty) Ltd
24 Sturdee Avenue, Rosebank, Johannesburg, 2196, South Africa
Penguin Books India (P) Ltd
11, Community Centre, Panchsheel Park, New Delhi 110 017, India

First published by Penguin Books Australia, 2002

1 3 5 7 9 10 8 6 4 2

Text copyright © Richard Harland, 2002

The moral right of the author has been asserted.

Cover photographs courtesy of IPL Image Group and Austral International
Design and digital imaging by David Altheim, Penguin Design Studio
Map by Cathy Larsen, Penguin Design Studio
Typeset in 11/15pt Sabon by Midland Typesetters, Maryborough, Victoria
Printed and bound in Australia by McPherson's Printing Group, Maryborough, Victoria

National Library of Australia
Cataloguing-in-Publication data:

Harland, Richard, 1947– .
Ferren and the white doctor.

ISBN 0 14 100511 4.

I. Title. (Series : Harland, Richard,
1947– Heaven and Earth trilogy ; bk. 2).

A823.3

www.penguin.com.au

BACKGROUND TO THE WORLD OF THE HEAVEN AND EARTH TRILOGY

Angels	Angels are the most important Celestials. Their spiritual power spreads out in an aura of light, which is protected by a transparent globe in the earthly atmosphere.
	Miriael is an angel who has become materialised because Ferren fed her human food when she was lying unconscious. She can no longer fly or return to Heaven.
The Bankstown Complex	The Bankstown Complex is one of many huge Humen military camps scattered across the Earth. The Bankstown Complex was once ruled by ten Doctors, who were overthrown in a great battle known to history as the Battle of Mowbray Park.
Humen	The Humen are artificial beings who have displaced the real human beings in the war against Heaven. They are led by the white-coated Doctors.
	The main foot-soldiers are the Hypers, who are clothed from head to foot in black

rubber. The Plasmatics are living muscles and organs built into Humen machinery. They obey mathematical orders.

The Millennial War | The Millennial War has lasted for a thousand years. It began when human medical scientists learned how to revive the brain of a corpse and discovered the real existence of Heaven. Aggressive scientific exploration led to conflict between Heaven and Earth.

The most single dramatic event was the Great Collapse, when large portions of Heaven's First and Second Altitudes crashed down onto the Earth. Nine hundred years later, in Ferren's time, the Burning Continents are still uninhabitable.

The focus of the war has now shifted to the east coast of Australia.

Morphs | As a result of the Millennial War, the souls of the real human beings are no longer allowed to enter Heaven. They congregate in sad lonely places as colonies of Morphs. Morphs are invisible except to the eyes of angels.

The People | Ferren comes from the People, a small isolated tribe of Residuals. With the help of the angel Miriael, the People constructed a special shelter and survived the Battle of Mowbray Park.

Residuals | Residuals are the real human beings. They have regressed to a primitive state, partly because the Selectors take away their more

	clever members. The tribes scarcely know of one another's existence.
The Selectors	The Selectors are Hypers who pay an annual visit to each tribe and select one or two for military service. As Ferren has discovered, those selected are actually 'processed' in Pits to produce a kind of psychic jelly. The jelly is injected into Hypers as a mental fuel, while the leftover bodily organs are used in the making of Plasmatics.
The War Council	A War Council of great archangels has governed Heaven ever since the Supreme Trinity of Father, Son and Holy Ghost withdrew, following the Great Collapse. The Supreme Trinity remains hidden behind clouds on the Seventh Altitude.

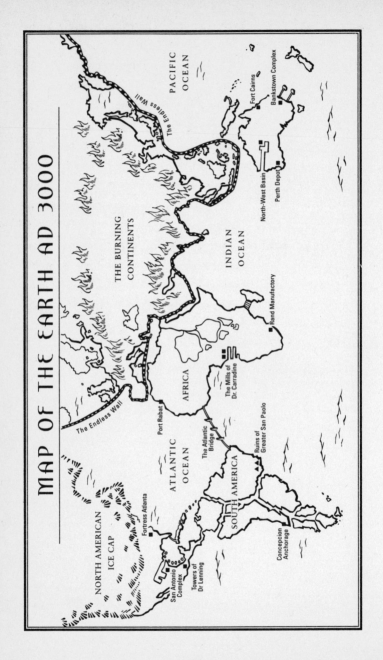

MAP OF THE EARTH AD 3000

1

The NESTERS

1

'This is the most important decision of your lives! Already there are twenty-nine tribes in the alliance. The Nesters will be the thirtieth. We need you with us!'

Kiet watched the speaker as he addressed the assembled Nesters. He was impassioned. She had never seen anything like it. In physical appearance, he was not unlike many of the males of her own tribe: black hair, solid muscular build, dark eyes. But there was a flash in his eyes and a forcefulness in his stance that was completely different. This speaker – this Ferren – seemed to burn with an inner fire.

'Ours is an alliance of free and equal tribes!' he cried. 'Not made in fear, like your old alliance with the Humen. The Humen only want to use us. You don't know what they are – but I do. I've seen inside their Camp. Break away from them! Break away from fear and oppression!'

The Nesters listened in silence. They were drawn up in their four Stocks, spreading out behind the four Guardians. Each Guardian sat behind a carved wooden Stockstump. Sunlight percolated through the trees and fell in bright patches on the banks of the Bowl. The branches had been bent and tied together to create a continuous green canopy of foliage.

'Let me tell you about the Humen,' he went on. 'They are artificial beings, not natural human beings at all. *We* are the only natural human beings. That's why they have to trick us into what they call military service. So they can steal our bodies and our minds!' He lowered his voice dramatically. 'Think about it! Did any member of this tribe ever come back from military service?'

Kiet hung on every word, every gesture. She could swear he was no more than her own age – and she was only sixteen. Yet he could travel far away from his own tribe, he could address a whole assembly of people. How could he be so confident?

He rotated to face each Stock in turn, standing on the high platform at the bottom of the Bowl. The angel stood lower down, on the grass beside the platform. When the pair of them had arrived last night, everyone had wanted to stare at the angel. It had been the greatest sensation in living memory. But Ferren was now the focus of attention.

'The Humen always told us they were defending the Earth in the great war against Heaven. We thought we needed their protection. Then came the great battle half a year ago. You saw it, didn't you? The lights and explosions in the sky?'

The four Guardians nodded in response. They made the decisions and represented the views of the Nesters as a whole.

'Well, my tribe was there in the middle of it. We saw

the Humen *defeated*. The ten Doctors who led them were all wiped out. The Humen have stayed hidden in their Camp ever since.'

He paused to let the idea sink in. Kiet felt as though the world was spinning under her feet. It was hard to comprehend, even harder to believe. And yet she did believe it.

'For the last half year, the Celestials could have attacked our tribes whenever they wanted. But they didn't, they haven't. The last half year has been the most peaceful time we've ever known. Even the nights are safe and quiet. Why? Because Heaven doesn't *want* to attack us!' He directed an arm towards the angel, bringing her in as support. 'Tell them, Miriael.'

The angel stepped forward and addressed the Nesters. 'It's true. Heaven doesn't regard Residuals as evil. Tribes like yours, all the surviving tribes across the Earth, are called Residuals. Celestials don't hate you, don't love you, don't even think about you. Heaven only fights against the Humen.'

Her voice was beautifully melodic. Whether she was also beautiful in appearance, Kiet couldn't decide. She was tall and slender and long-legged, with eyes as blue as deep water and hair like falling gold. From her shoulder-blades at the back sprang two small white feathered wings. From Kiet's point of view, she was too strange and striking to measure against ordinary beauty. She conveyed an impression of purity and serenity which was simply alien. The only thing which wasn't immaculate was her long yellow robe, stained from travel and repaired with many stitchings.

She stepped back and Ferren took over the speaking again. He was as intense and urgent as Miriael was cool and composed.

'Now is our chance,' he cried. 'The peaceful time won't last for long. The Humen will rebuild their forces. Then it'll all start again – the Selectors, the terror, the military service.'

His eyes shot glances in every direction – shooting out, making contact. To Kiet, it seemed they kept making contact with her. An answering intensity stirred in her blood. Her pulse was racing, her face felt hot.

'We have to make an alliance to resist their demands!' His voice rose to a crescendo. 'No more military service! All the tribes together, we can do it! An alliance of our own! *We can do it*!'

His final cry echoed around the Bowl. There was a long silence. Green leaves moved in the faint breeze overhead, winking in and out of the sunlight. Small flies and other insects hummed through the air. The four Stocks waited for their Guardians to speak.

Berwin of Heartstock was the first to stand up. Heartstock was the Stock to which Kiet herself belonged.

'Why does it matter what the Nesters do?' he asked. 'We're not important.'

'Yes, you are!' Ferren's response came back quick as a whip. 'You're one of the biggest tribes. There must be, what, two hundred of you? Now you can be part of something even bigger. Our Residual Alliance is almost two *thousand*!'

The Nesters shook their heads in wonder. Such huge

numbers of people were almost inconceivable.

Then Dunkery stood up. She was the only female Guardian, the leader of Headstock. When she spoke, her voice was shaky but her tone was sharp.

'You talk about a Residual Alliance. An alliance of our own. But if it's an alliance of our own, what's *she* doing here?'

Her bony finger was aimed at Miriael. A slightly sad smile appeared on the angel's face.

'I'm not with Heaven any more,' she answered. 'They no longer communicate with me. If you'd seen another angel close up, you'd know I've lost the radiance of true spiritual existence. I need food and water, just as you do. I've undergone a change which makes me physical and condemns me to live here on the Earth. My destiny is linked to yours.'

'You can trust her,' Ferren confirmed. 'She saved my tribe in the great battle half a year ago. Her knowledge can help us.'

Spiddal of Bloodstock rose up from behind his Stock-stump and went across to talk to Dunkery. Berwin joined them, then Clemmart of Bonestock. Kiet watched with bated breath. Surely they had been moved by the appeal? It seemed so obvious to her. Couldn't they be swept away by something for once?

But the Guardians weren't going to hurry into a decision.

'We shall need to ask further questions,' said Berwin at last.

'Privately,' added Spiddal.

Dunkery turned to the assembled Nesters. 'There will

be no new share-out for today. All tasks remain the same as yesterday.'

Each Guardian made the same formal announcement to their own Stock.

'The meeting is concluded. Let the day's work begin.'

2

Apart from the Bowl, there were few large open spaces in the Nesters' territory. Instead there were the tunnels, green tunnels which ran this way and that through a vast jungle of lantana bushes. The tunnels crossed hills and valleys and creeks, always hidden below the surface of the foliage.

Kiet was looking for someone to talk to. For Heart-stock, yesterday had been a day of home duties – so today again, there was cleaning and mending to be done in the family nest. But all of that could wait. She felt she would burst if she couldn't share her feelings about the meeting with someone.

Every twist and turn of the green tunnels was familiar to her. She knew the location of every nut tree and fruit tree, every patch of grain-grass and every animal trap. For five minutes she jogged around in vain.

It seemed that the young members of her own Stock had all gone back to their nests. Old members of other Stocks eyed her suspiciously, as though she might be planning to hunt and gather on their allocated day. The

Stocks were very possessive about their rights and entitlements.

Then she came upon Tadge and Flens. They were in a recess at the side of the path, under a clump of tea-trees. As usual, Tadge was collecting something – in this case, the spiky fallen seed-pods from the tea-trees. Flens grinned as Kiet approached.

'Tadge is inventing a new game,' he told her.

Tadge was Kiet's younger brother, twelve years old. Flens was the same age as Kiet and a member of Headstock. Friendships across Stocks were generally frowned upon, but allowances were made for someone as young as Tadge. As for Flens, he was a loner whose own Stock had given up trying to correct his behaviour. Kiet had a sneaking liking for him.

'What did you think?' she demanded. 'Wasn't it amazing, about the Humen being defeated?'

Flens nodded. 'I didn't understand a lot of what he said, though. Did you?'

'Not all of it,' Kiet admitted. 'Why didn't the Guardians ask more questions at the meeting? I wish I could've asked questions.'

Flens shrugged. He was tall, thin and gangling, with pale eyes and hair like straw. His face was remarkably ugly, dominated by a monster of a nose.

'Questions about what?'

'About all those things he was talking about. Doctors and Camps and stuff. I bet he could've answered. He must know so much. You can tell from just looking at him. He's been through all kinds of experiences. I wish – I wish I could live like that.'

Flens whistled. '*You?*'

Kiet understood his surprise. Compared to him, she was known as a dutiful member of her family, Stock and tribe. She was even surprised at herself.

Tadge added one final seed-pod to his collection, and leaned back on his heels. The collection was set out in military formation on a bare patch of ground.

'Finished!' he announced proudly. 'That's my Residual army!'

Flens inspected over his shoulder. 'Tadge's new game,' he explained to Kiet. 'Now it's a Residual army instead of a Humen army.'

Kiet was curious. 'Who do they fight against?'

Tadge frowned thoughtfully. He was small for his age, with spiky brown hair and prominent buck-teeth. His knees and elbows seemed to stick out at all angles.

'I haven't decided yet,' he said. 'Maybe Heaven. Maybe the Humen. Maybe both.' He pointed to the largest seed-pod. 'That's me at the front, see?'

Flens grinned. 'Yesterday you were leading the Humen army.'

'I thought they were still winning then. I didn't know they'd been defeated. And I didn't know there's no real military service.'

'You heard him say that?'

'Yes. They trick us.' Tadge readjusted the pods on the left wing of his formation. 'I never *liked* the Humen anyway. The Residual army is going to smash 'em to pieces.'

Kiet turned away. Was Tadge ever going to grow up?

Her mother said he'd mature in another year or two – but Kiet had her doubts.

Flens laughed. 'Doesn't take Tadge long to swap sides.'

'He doesn't understand how serious this Residual Alliance is,' said Kiet. 'It'll change everything.'

'You think we ought to join?'

'Of course. I *want* everything to change. We'll get to know about the world beyond our tunnels. We'll meet those other tribes. I'm sick of being closed in and having to do the same boring duties all the time.'

Flens raised his eyebrows. 'Ah,' he said.

'What do you mean, *ah*? Is that all you can say? Don't you want everything to change?'

'Maybe.'

Kiet scowled. 'Then why aren't you more excited?'

'I am. Only not as much as you.'

'No, because you never do what you're supposed to do anyway. You've never had proper habits. Everyone says you don't do your duties . . .'

Her voice petered out as she became aware of a difficulty in her argument.

'Don't blame me,' Flens protested. 'You want everyone to stop doing their duties. So you can't blame me for not doing them.'

Kiet's scowl deepened, then suddenly lifted. 'Yes, I can.' She burst into laughter.

Flens stood watching her laugh. 'You don't do that very often,' he commented.

Before she could answer, someone else appeared around the corner of the tunnel.

'Kiet! There you are!'

It was Rhinn. As usual, there was a worried expression on her face. She counted herself as Kiet's best friend.

'I've been looking for you everywhere,' she said as she hurried up. 'Your mother needs help with your baby sister.'

She addressed herself to Kiet as though Flens wasn't there. Like Kiet and Tadge, she belonged to Heartstock. She had a very low opinion of those who were born into any other Stock.

'Same boring duties,' Flens remarked to no-one in particular.

'Enough,' Kiet told him. 'I'm coming,' she said to Rhinn.

She set off running in the direction of her family nest. Behind her, she could hear Rhinn speaking sternly to Tadge. It seemed there was a home duty for him too.

3

Miriael lay stretched out comfortably on the ground. She had composed herself to patience. The questioning by the Guardians had finished long ago. Now the Guardians were discussing their decision in some other nest. Two hours of questioning followed by six hours of discussion . . .

Ferren was far from patient. For the hundredth time he rolled over to peer out through the entrance-hole. For the hundredth time he clicked his tongue in frustration. Miriael watched and said nothing.

The nest where they waited was the same in which they had slept the previous night. Like all the Nesters' nests, it was a hemispherical structure woven out of lantana twigs. The inside walls were moulded with smooth grey clay. It was a recently constructed nest, relatively bare and not yet occupied by any family. The clay smelt fresh and earthy.

'This is going to be the most difficult tribe so far,' said Ferren. 'I have a bad feeling about it.'

'They've all been difficult in different ways,' Miriael

responded calmly. 'We haven't failed yet.'

'But this organisation into Stocks. It's like four separate tribes in one.'

'True. But they're not as backward as the People, for example.'

'The People changed quicker than anyone.'

Miriael half-smiled to herself. He could still be surprisingly loyal to his own tribe.

'Yes, but they *had* to change quickly,' she pointed out. 'Or they'd have been annihilated in the battle.'

Ferren scuffed at the ground. 'It's the waiting I hate,' he said.

She studied his face in the dim light from the entrance-hole: the compressed lips, the forward thrust of the jaw. How much he's changed in the last six months, she thought.

There was silence between them again. She looked away – but she didn't stop thinking about him.

It must be the commitment, she decided, the commitment to the cause of a Residual Alliance. Six months ago, he'd still been bound up in himself and his own uncertainties. Now his thoughts were directed towards a larger goal. His skills as a speaker seemed to increase with every new tribe he addressed. He'd become remarkably capable and competent.

And she'd encouraged him to take over as far as possible. It was much better for the Residual tribes to be addressed by one of their own kind. They didn't have the same belief in the words of a Celestial. They goggled at her in stunned wonder until often she felt like some kind of a freak.

Only Ferren wasn't in awe of her. Over the past six months, he'd begun to speak to her more as an equal. But there was a problem there too.

She'd always been aware of Ferren's feelings for her. In the past, he'd made sudden blurted confessions about her beauty and how he adored her. She'd taken such confessions in her stride, though she hadn't much liked them. But now that he spoke to her more as an equal, she couldn't afford to give him any encouragement.

She had to force herself to maintain her distance. Sometimes she caught the look of devotion in his eyes, but it remained unspoken. She would have loved to share everything with him, reveal her loneliness, draw on his support. But she didn't want him to think she returned his feelings.

So she kept her loneliness to herself. There was no-one for her to talk to, not as she had once talked with her fellow warrior-angels in Heaven. She had never imagined her destiny on the Earth would be so hard. A solitary destiny . . .

'They're coming!'

Ferren's call interrupted her reverie. She raised herself into an upright sitting position. The roof of the nest was too low for standing. Ferren moved across from the entrance-hole and took up a position beside her.

One by one, the Guardians entered on their hands and knees. They were all very old, with leathery skin and deep sunken eye-sockets. The three males were grey and grizzled around the chin. The female, Dunkery, wore a dozen massive wooden bangles on her arms, a dozen more around her ankles.

They sat in a line facing Miriael and Ferren.

'Well?' Ferren spoke first. 'Will the Nesters join the Residual Alliance?'

'The issue remains undecided,' said Berwin.

'Neither a yes nor a no,' said Dunkery.

Ferren frowned. 'I don't understand.'

'It could only be a yes if we were all in favour,' explained Clemmart. 'And only a no if we were all opposed.'

'So you were divided,' said Miriael. 'Was there a majority either way?'

The Guardians exchanged glances.

'Should we tell them?' asked Berwin. It wasn't so much a question as a proposition.

'Yes,' said Clemmart.

'No,' said Spiddal.

'No,' said Berwin.

'Yes,' said Dunkery.

'Undecided.' Berwin turned back to Miriael and Ferren. 'We can't tell you and we can't not tell you.'

Ferren uttered an angry growl. 'Why don't you just say *no* and have done with it? It comes to the same thing.'

'No, it doesn't,' said Dunkery. 'A *no* would disadvantage the Guardians who said *yes*.'

'I couldn't allow the views of my Stock to be ignored,' said Clemmart.

Ferren shook his head in disbelief. 'This is so petty!'

Berwin puffed out his chest like a frog. 'Are you saying that the interests of Heartstock are petty?'

'Or the interests of Bonestock?' demanded Clemmart.

'Especially the interests of Bloodstock!' Spiddal jumped in.

'No, Heartstock!' cried Dunkery.

'Can we get back to the original issue?' suggested Miriael.

The Guardians stopped eyeballing one another.

'What was the original issue?' asked Clemmart.

'You wanted to know if there was a majority one way or the other?' asked Berwin.

'No.' Miriael remained patient. 'We want to know if there's any hope you'll ever decide to join the Residual Alliance.'

The Guardians looked thoughtful.

'It could be decided at a Summoning,' said Dunkery.

Ferren came back into the discussion. 'What's a Summoning?'

'A special ceremony,' answered Dunkery. 'At the City of the Dead.'

'What's the City of the Dead?'

But the Guardians were already on their hands and knees, already heading towards the entrance-hole.

'Very well then,' said Berwin over his shoulder. 'Our next Summoning takes place in seven days' time.'

'Seven days!'

Miriael could see that Ferren was ready to explode.

'We'll wait,' she said quickly.

4

The sun shone down on another glorious day. In the green tunnels, it filtered through leaves in a lacy texture of light and shade. There was a sweet lemony fragrance in the air.

Ferren ambled along, inhaling deeply. In spite of yesterday's frustrations, the world didn't seem so bad. It wasn't the first time that he and Miriael had had to wait while a tribe made up its mind.

He waved or nodded to Nesters as he passed. They returned his salute, then became very busy with their work again. As soon as he'd gone by, they stopped and stared after him. Clearly, it was no use trying to talk to them yet.

Then one Nester joined him on his walk. Or at least, she emerged from an intersecting tunnel and stepped along five paces ahead of him. She neither hurried to get away nor slowed to let him pass.

She held her head slightly bowed, in the manner of all the Nesters. Her hair was a thick mass of dark red, her skin somewhat paler than his own. She wore a wraparound garment of stitched hides and pelts. Unlike most tribes, the Nesters made their clothing from the animals they trapped.

He gained ground on her little by little. She threw a half-glance backwards. Was she encouraging him to catch up?

He lengthened his stride and came level. He looked into her face – a sharply modelled face, almost severe, with straight heavy eyebrows, wide mouth, strong white teeth. A beautiful face in its way, though not with the beauty of Miriael, of course.

'Hi, I'm Ferren,' he said.

'I know.' Her eyebrows were drawn down in a scowl. 'I'm Kiet.'

They walked on for a while in silence. *Handle with care,* he thought to himself. There was a strange smouldering quality about her. This was his first chance to talk with an individual Nester. He waited for her to speak.

'You must be disappointed in us,' she said at last. 'That we're not ready to join the alliance.'

'You heard?'

'Of course. At work-meet this morning.'

'Were *you* disappointed?'

'Me?' She snorted. 'What does it matter what I feel? I'm too young. I don't count.'

He was surprised at the bitterness in her voice. 'Only the adults count?'

'The adults agree with whatever the Guardians decide. Except the Guardians hardly ever manage to decide anything.'

'Mmm.' Ferren made a non-committal noise. 'You think we're wasting our time here then?'

'No.' She halted and swung towards him. 'You have to persuade them! You *have to*!'

There was a fierce light in her dark brown eyes. More than ever, he had the sense of something pent up inside her.

'We're waiting for the Summoning,' he said. 'Whatever that is.'

'It's when the ghosts of the Old Ones answer our questions.'

'Ghosts? Old Ones?'

She sucked at her lip. 'If you haven't been told, it's not for me to tell you.'

'Why not? Is it forbidden knowledge?' He took a gamble. 'I already know that the ghosts of the Old Ones live in the City of the Dead.'

'Ye-es.'

Plainer than words, her expression told him she was caught between social obedience and her desire to help. He took another gamble.

'Take me to the City of the Dead.'

She looked both shocked and excited. Her voice sank to a whisper.

'You can't ask that! Don't you have any sense of right and wrong?'

'I don't know what your tribe sees as right or wrong. I'm an outsider here, remember.'

She nodded slowly, as if making a new discovery. 'Yes, you are, aren't you? You *can't* know. You just want things.'

'I want you to take me to the City of the Dead.'

'No. Impossible. We'd be seen.'

'When there's nobody about, then.'

'You mean, at night?' Her eyes were round, her cheeks flushed. 'In the dark?'

'Do you want to help me?'

'Yes. But it would be a hundred times scarier in the dark.'

'What's to be scared of?'

'Hearing the sounds of the ghosts.'

'Miriael could come along with us. She can deal with anything.'

Kiet stared at him. 'No.'

'No?'

'Not her. If I do it, it's just the two of us.'

'Okay.'

'But I haven't said I'll do it yet.'

'I'll keep it a secret. If that's what you want.'

'Secret from *her* too.'

'From Miriael? But this might be –'

'She's a Celestial. She's different. I don't trust her.'

'You should.'

'Her too. Promise.'

'Okay. I promise.'

'And *mean* it!' Her voice was very intense, almost a hiss.

'I do. I promise. So you will take me to the City of the Dead?'

'Yes. Tonight. Meet me – here.' She indicated the spot where they were standing. 'When the moon rises.'

He grinned. 'I'll be here.'

For a moment, he thought she was going to grin back. Then the scowl came down even heavier than before.

'Good,' she said.

She turned on her heel and left him standing.

5

A light breeze rustled through the leaves and branches. Small patches of moonlit sky were visible overhead – sometimes brighter, sometimes darker, as clouds passed across the face of the moon. The ground underfoot was lost in shadow.

The tunnels seemed endless. Ferren walked along one step behind Kiet. He concentrated on the path and where he was putting his feet. He had long since given up trying to remember the route.

'Nearly there,' she announced after several kilometres.

Ferren came up closer. 'Tell me about the Old Ones.'

'They built the City of the Dead. Now only their ghosts remain.'

Ferren had been thinking about the Old Ones during the day. He believed he had worked out who they were.

'Did they live many hundreds of years in the past?'

'Yes. They had beautiful cities with streets and buildings.'

'Ah.' Ferren nodded, his guesses confirmed. 'The Good Times.'

'The what?'

'The time when they lived. That's what my tribe calls it. Maybe you call it something else?'

'The Age of Peace.'

'Right. Same thing. A great civilisation. Millions and millions of human beings all over the Earth. They had moto-cars and electrics and flying machines.'

'Yes.'

'And your tribe is descended from them.'

'Yes. How did you know?'

'It's the same with every tribe we've visited. Different names and details, but every tribe worships the memory of the Ancestors. That's the name for them in my tribe. The Ancestors, who ruled the Earth in the Good Times.'

'The Ancestors.' Kiet repeated the word, trying it out.

'We had special totems handed down from our Ancestors. Do you have anything like that?'

'Like what?'

'We had an Alarm Clock, a Flyspray Can, a Lighter and a Ma-ma Doll. Small precious things made out of metal and plastic.'

She shook her head. 'All we have are their ruined buildings. The City of the Dead.' She touched him on the elbow, slowing him down. 'We're coming to it now.'

The tunnel opened out and they emerged onto an outcrop of rock, looking across a valley. Over the floor of the valley ran a network of rivulets, threading through a rubble of broken brick and concrete.

Ferren peered towards the other side of the valley. The scene appeared in a weird contrast of black-and-white, as the clouds cleared momentarily from the face of the moon.

The black was the blackness of vegetation – dense clumps of bushes and trees. The white was the whiteness of pale walls, rising above the bushes, rising among the trees. Not crumbled remnants but the perfectly preserved walls of whole high buildings. Ferren could even see the rectangular holes of windows.

He whistled softly to himself. 'Incredible!'

'This is where we stand for the ceremonies,' said Kiet, indicating the rock beneath their feet. 'We stand and watch the Guardians go across to the other side.'

She had lowered her voice to a whisper. This must be a place of solemn religious awe for her, Ferren realised.

'Only the Guardians go into the City?'

'No, the Guardians stop outside the walls. Nobody goes into the City any more.'

'But they did once?'

'Before the ghosts came.'

'What sort of ghosts?'

'Scary noises. Nothing to see, just scary noises.'

They stood very still, listening intently. But there was only the rustling of the leaves, only the plashing of the water below.

Ferren needed answers. 'Let's go across to the other side,' he proposed.

Kiet shook her head. Ferren put on his most persuasive voice.

'It's no use here. You said you'd take me to the City of the Dead.'

'I have.'

'I thought you meant more than this.'

Kiet scowled. But Ferren sensed a yielding.

'Please. This really matters to me.'

Suddenly, without a word, she turned and led the way. They followed a narrow trail down to the valley floor.

The trail petered out when they came to the rubble of brick and concrete. Kiet picked a route across the rivulets. Cold water splashed against their ankles.

The trail started up again on the other side. They had to push through clusters of lush flowering plants. Higher and higher they scrambled, until they climbed up onto a kind of concrete platform.

Ferren stood gazing in wonder. The platform ran to the foot of a massive wall. The wall was made of pre-cast blocks, all exactly the same shape and size, all with identical mouldings and projections. He couldn't even imagine the techniques behind such a construction. The stony material of the blocks seemed to glitter in the moonlight.

Kiet stayed on the very edge of the platform. 'This is where the Guardians stand.'

But Ferren wasn't satisfied. 'Just a little further.' He pointed to a place where the wall ended. There was a gap of a few metres before another wall began. 'We could go in there.'

'I've already come a little further,' Kiet hissed indignantly.

'But I haven't heard the ghosts yet.'

'I'm not going in there.'

'Are you afraid?'

'No.'

Her answer was contradicted by her wide staring eyes and the tension in her body. But Ferren chose to take the answer he wanted.

'Come on then.'

He walked off slowly along the platform. Would she follow? After a dozen paces, he heard her footsteps hurrying to catch up.

The gap turned out to be a kind of lane between tall buildings. It was clogged with a tangle of thickly growing bushes. Ferren had to get down and crawl on his hands and knees.

Kiet crawled after him. A snapping and cracking of twigs accompanied their progress. For a while, it was even darker than in the tunnels.

When they finally emerged, they had left the lane behind. Now they were in a wide street. They rose to their feet and looked around.

The sudden silence was overwhelming.

The street was as if transported from the time of the Ancestors. Shopfronts and housefronts, doors and windows, pavements and gutters. Almost all the buildings were still intact, in spite of the zigzag fissures running across their facades.

Only the pavements and roadway were shattered. Whole trees had sprung up, bursting through tarmac and concrete. Root systems had buckled the surface and heaved up slabs like a sea of choppy waves.

Ferren walked along in a dream, trying to take it all in at once. He felt he was actually living in the time of the Ancestors. He could imagine crowds of people thronging the pavements, moto-cars moving along the roadway, overhead electrics making the night as bright as day. He hardly noticed how Kiet walked behind with lowered head, holding herself in, clenched rigid.

He wondered what lay behind the windows and doors. Peering into the glass of the windows, he could make out only a kind of grainy darkness.

'Let's see,' he said aloud.

He stopped at one of the doors, seized the door-handle and pulled. It took him a minute to work out how to turn the handle.

Kiet uttered an inarticulate sound that might have been a 'No!'

But Ferren kept pulling. The door snapped suddenly off its hinges, toppling outwards. Behind it was a solid mass of earth.

With a small avalanche, some of the earth slid forward and poured out onto the pavement. Ferren jumped back. A dusty mouldy smell filled his nostrils.

'Nothing but dirt!' he exclaimed.

He walked on again, thinking of the strange impenetrable rooms behind the outer walls. Now when he looked at the windows, he could see the texture of packed earth behind the glass.

He came towards a corner where the street opened out onto a square. Then he realised that Kiet was no longer with him.

'Kiet?' He swung around. 'Why have you stopped?'

She stood as if frozen in mid-movement. She had advanced only a few metres beyond the avalanche of earth.

Reluctantly, he went back to her. She was trembling all over, breathing in tiny rapid breaths.

'What's the –'

'Listen!'

He listened but heard nothing.

'It's *them*!' she gulped. 'The ghosts of the Old Ones!'

'Where?'

She pointed ahead, towards the square from which he had just returned.

Ferren listened again. Was that a faint sighing of the breeze? Or something else?

'Let's go back now,' she said.

Ferren cursed to himself.

'I have to go closer,' he said. 'I have to hear them properly.'

Kiet shook her head and stayed where she was.

'Don't be frightened. Just as far as the square. You can't ask me to stop now.'

But Kiet didn't move. It seemed she couldn't move.

'My legs,' she said through gritted teeth.

He took her by the arm and pulled. He could feel the trembling all through her body. But there was no time to think about that now.

'You can do it,' he urged.

For two paces, she resisted passively, a mere dead weight as he dragged her along. Then she exploded.

'You jerk! Don't tell me what I can do!'

She flailed her arms and broke away from him. He reached out to grip her again. But the fury in her eyes made him change his mind.

'Okay, then. I'll go on by myself. You wait here and I'll come back for you. Okay?'

'Not on my own!' She could hardly get the words out. 'That's not fair!'

'You'll be all right. Just wait here.'

'You selfish, selfish, selfish jerk!'

Suddenly she sprang at him. She was like a whirlwind. She slapped at his head and lashed out with her feet. One swinging blow caught him in the eye, another caught him painfully on the shin.

'You *know* I'm terrified!' She shouted full in his face. 'You saw I couldn't even move my legs! That's how terrified I am! But because *you're* not terrified, you don't care about anyone else!'

He drew away without hitting back. Somehow he had the feeling that he was in the wrong.

In the next moment, she spun on her heel and ran back the way they had come. Ferren was stunned.

Damn, damn, damn her! And yet it was true what she said. He *had* known how terrified she was, only he hadn't wanted to think about it. It was a strange jolt when her experience had leaped right out at him, out of her blazing eyes.

He set off running after her. She was already almost back at the place where they'd entered the street.

He didn't catch up until he emerged from the lane and the bushes. She was sitting on the concrete platform, cross-legged, with her face in her hands.

He approached warily. Her shoulders were hunched and heaving with emotion – whether tears or rage, he couldn't tell.

'I'm sorry,' he said. 'I wasn't brought up believing in the ghosts of the Old Ones. It's easy for me to be brave. I should've thought about you.'

She lowered her hands and looked at him. She was swollen around the eyes.

'Yes, you should've. Especially after everything I've done for you. I took a risk just bringing you here.'

'I'm sorry,' he repeated. 'I owe you. I won't forget again. Do you want to go back now?'

She nodded and rose to her feet. She rubbed at her nose with a loud aggressive sniff. Then she led the way back towards the nests.

6

'It's time to finalise the arrangement,' said Berwin of Heartstock.

'Yes,' agreed Clemmart of Bonestock. 'It's been seven years now.'

'She's ready,' said Nettish. 'Look how well she's grown!'

Kiet remained motionless as they inspected her legs, hips and breasts. Her mother, Nettish, had been grooming her for this all morning. A dozen carved wooden ornaments were fastened in her hair, a dozen more dangled around her neck. She couldn't move a muscle without clattering.

She hated being inspected, but she endured it without protest. This was normality, this was the way things were. She'd always known she'd eventually be mated with Bross. She couldn't even think to question it.

And wasn't it good to be normal? Last night she'd gone against the rules – and look what had happened! She'd never been so terrified in her life. Hadn't she got what she deserved?

Yet it was somehow pleasing to remember what she'd done last night. In spite of the terror. Memories of her adventure with the strange boy kept passing through her mind. She had to hold back from grinning even as they examined her.

Finally they sat back. Kiet's representatives were her mother Nettish, Grandfather Niot, and Berwin as Guardian of her Stock. Bross's representatives were his mother Idris, his father Trebb, and Clemmart as Guardian of his Stock. Bross himself wasn't permitted to be present.

For a while there was only the sound of the rain drumming steadily on the roof of the nest. Then Clemmart turned to Bross's parents.

'What do you think?'

'She's grown well,' said Idris. 'But not as well as our Bross.'

'He's the biggest strongest lad of his age,' boasted Trebb. 'No-one can run as fast or jump as far as Bross.'

'It's true, you couldn't do better than Bross,' said Clemmart, turning to Berwin.

'Kiet has good qualities too!' Nettish broke in, pleadingly. 'Really she does!'

Berwin quietened her with a motion of his hand. Kiet's mother was forty years old, but her complexion was like a baby's, smooth and pink. Sometimes her manner was like a baby's too.

'Our Bross is special,' said Idris firmly.

Grandfather Niot frowned. 'So is our Kiet. We don't have to have this mating.'

'Oh, don't say that!' cried Nettish.

'We don't have to have this mating,' he repeated. 'Kiet is a great help to her family.'

He winked across at Kiet. Masses of small wrinkles spread out around the corners of his eyes and the corners of his mouth. He had tufty white eyebrows and white tufts of beard.

Kiet couldn't help smiling. There were times when she felt much closer to her grandfather than to her mother. It wasn't that Nettish didn't love her. Nettish was as fond and proud of Kiet as could be. But her fondness showed itself in a kind of perpetual fussing and nagging.

And now she was so eager to lose her daughter to Bross. All Nester mothers wanted to see their daughters well matched and mated – so Nettish naturally wanted the same. It would be a wonderful success for her. But what will you do without me? Kiet wondered. How will you ever manage the family on your own?

Kiet often wondered if she'd inherited her personality from her father. It was hard to believe a mother and daughter could be so different. But she couldn't remember much about her father. The Selectors had taken him away when she was only three years old.

Meanwhile, the negotiations continued.

'I don't know,' said Clemmart. 'She's a risk.'

'She's been very dependable for a long time now,' Berwin insisted.

'Yes. But how do we know the problems won't come back?'

'What problems?' Grandfather Niot was indignant. 'She's always been a fine girl!'

'Temper problems,' said Clemmart.

'Unpredictable outbursts,' said Idris. 'With other children, when she was young. Twice with adults, when she was ten or eleven.'

'I don't remember that. What I remember –'

'You remember only the good things, Grandfather Niot.' Clemmart cut him off abruptly. 'We know, we know. You'd think she was a fine girl just because she kept growing taller every year. That would be enough for you to admire.'

Berwin coughed sharply. 'The important thing is, she's been quietened down now.'

'Yes, with good habits.' Nettish clapped her hands. 'We've quietened her down with good habits. We've worked so hard on it, haven't we, dear?'

She bent encouragingly towards Kiet. 'What would you do if an adult dropped food on you? What would you do?'

The question related to a famous occasion in the past, when Kiet had thrown a bowl of hot soup into old Mevan's face. Kiet answered automatically.

'I'd ask for something to wipe it off.'

Her mother uttered a tiny sigh of relief. 'You see?' She swung round to Trebb and Idris. 'Totally changed! Totally trained!'

Yes, trained to give the correct answer, thought Kiet. But not totally changed. Not after her fury against Ferren last night. She'd almost forgotten she could be like that.

It was true, she'd been quietened down with good habits. Her tempers had seemed like a thing of the past.

She'd been nagged for so long that now she could never act without thinking first. Until last night!

And she didn't even feel bad about it. She'd been right to let fly at Ferren's selfishness. She'd made him realise, she'd made him apologise. So now it could be left behind. Wasn't that better than bottling it up?

The negotiations moved on to the stage of practical details. Bross's representatives had raised doubts only in order to improve their bargaining position. Four mats or three mats, six pelts or seven. Boring, boring. The voices became a background drone as Kiet followed the train of her own thoughts.

The negotiations concluded half an hour later. The two Guardians linked little fingers to seal the pact. Then Nettish spoke up, blushing behind her hand.

'When shall we bring them together for First Intimacies?'

'Before the next Summoning,' said Trebb.

'Two days from today,' said Berwin.

'Four days,' said Clemmart.

'Three,' said Berwin.

'Agreed.'

Again they sealed the pact by linking fingers. Kiet listened to the rain on the roof, falling less heavily now. A plan had formed in her mind – and it had nothing to do with Bross or First Intimacies.

As soon as this meeting was over, she'd go and tell Ferren about it. She waited impatiently for the representatives to leave.

7

'I think it's stopped raining,' said Ferren.

He moved across to look out through the entrance-hole. Then discovered that someone was starting to crawl in from the other side.

'Kiet!' he exclaimed. 'Hi! Are you paying us a visit?'

Only Kiet's head and shoulders appeared. Straight heavy eyebrows, wide mouth, dark red hair.

'No. I have to talk to you.'

'Come in and tell us.'

Kiet kept her eyes averted from Miriael. '*You*,' she said. 'Outside.'

Ferren exchanged glances with the angel. Then he followed Kiet as she backed out through the hole.

Outside, the sun was already shining. The air was hazy and the ground was steaming. Everywhere was the patter of water dripping from the leaves.

Kiet said nothing, only beckoned with one finger and set off at a jog. She led the way through the green tunnels, first one path, then another. Finally she left the path altogether and plunged straight in among the bushes.

There was no track, but she knew where she was going. Wet grass wrapped around their ankles. She passed between two closely growing tree-trunks and headed towards a flowering rhododendron bush.

The bush was like a natural umbrella. They ducked under the leaves and found themselves in a relatively dry and very cosy space. There was even a length of log that had been dragged across to make a seat.

'This is one of my private places,' said Kiet. 'Good, isn't it?'

She sat down on the log and Ferren sat beside her. Fallen rhododendron petals lay on the ground like stars. The rain had brought out the dark frowzy smells of earth and vegetation.

'You haven't talked about last night?' she demanded. 'To *anyone*?'

'No. I made a promise.'

'I'm not going to take you back to the City of the Dead. You know that, don't you? Not after what you did. And you'll never find the way by yourself.'

Ferren shrugged.

'But I've got another plan. *My* way of helping. I can organise the young Nesters to come and hear you speak.'

'About the Residual Alliance? But I've already spoken about the Residual Alliance.'

'Not just that. About the world and your own experiences, everything. You can turn us into your supporters.'

'Mmm.' Ferren considered. 'But you said yourself. Only the adults count.'

Kiet snorted. 'Things can change!'

Ferren glanced at her, surprised by her sudden vehemence.

'It's not as though we don't think for ourselves,' she went on after a moment. 'Maybe we think more for ourselves than the adults. We haven't been so worn down with habits. Look at you.'

Ferren was bewildered by the new twist in the conversation. 'Me?'

'How old are you? Sixteen, seventeen?'

'Sixteen.'

'Yet *you* make your own decisions. I'd trust you to make good decisions more than I'd trust the Guardians.'

'I've made some bad decisions too.'

'At least you've made them. At least you've *lived* your life.'

Her dark brown eyes were fixed upon him in a way that he found almost unsettling. There was a moment of silence before he broke the intensity.

'Okay,' he said. 'I like your plan. If you can organise the young Nesters.'

Kiet nodded. 'Tomorrow. But it has to be a secret, right? I don't want the adults to know. Promise.'

'I promise.'

Again her eyes fixed upon him. Then suddenly she sprang up, seized a branch overhead and gave it a violent tug. The rainwater gathered on the leaves cascaded down over Ferren.

'Hey! What's that for?'

'For last night! Payback! Now we're equal again!'

The expression on her face had changed completely – as though the inward smouldering had suddenly burst into a warm bright flame. She laughed and darted out from under the bush. Ferren jumped up quickly to follow.

8

Miriael awoke from a beautiful dream. She'd dreamed that an angel came down to her in the middle of the night. An angel of great power, a six-winged Seraph, with the light of his aura streaming out from his globe. So pure and bright and awesome!

And then? She seemed to remember that he'd knelt down beside her, his light falling across her body. It was as though he was watching over her. Perhaps he'd even folded his hands in prayer?

Then she opened her eyes – and of course he wasn't there. Reality was the dark clay-lined nest, the earthen floor. The first streaks of dawn were creeping in through the entrance-hole.

She tried to hang on to the dream. Already it was slipping away. Why, oh why couldn't it be true?

But she knew it was only her own yearning that created it. She was so desperate for contact with Heaven. Even though she could never return – yet she longed to hear about the state of the war, the doings of her own troop, the gossip of the Heavenly Halls. Just to listen to the music of a Celestial voice again . . .

There had been a time when angels had visited her on the Earth, when they still hoped she might be able to return to Heaven. They had come down only to reproach and speak sternly to her. But at least they had come down. Anything was better than being cut off like this.

She had felt it more and more over the past six months. The initial physical euphoria had left her. She no longer wanted to dance with delight at her new state of being. Bodily movement had become second nature. It was her first nature that continued to haunt her.

She had lost almost all of her spiritual powers, but none of her spiritual memories. Her mind was woven out of earlier scenes and personalities, interests and experiences. She would willingly forget them if she could. But instead they pulled and pulled at her like a hook.

Was this her everlasting curse then, to be neither one thing nor the other?

Her thoughts flashed back to the visit of that female Nester . . . *Kiet,* Ferren had called her. It was the usual reaction, the usual awe and suspicion. Kiet was eager to talk to Ferren, but not in the presence of an angel.

She wondered if there was any closer connection between the two of them. Kiet was certainly very attractive. If Ferren was attracted to Kiet, that would remove one of her own problems.

She turned her head to look at him. He had shifted position in his sleep, so that the top of his head was now almost brushing against her calves. She frowned and moved her legs away.

Yes, she hoped there was a connection growing between Ferren and Kiet. As long as Ferren didn't start to exclude her too. Over the past two days, she'd had the impression that he wasn't telling her everything. For long periods he'd been off on his own, with no explanation afterwards.

But she couldn't blame him. Of course he was closer to his own kind. Whereas she wasn't close to anybody. She was the only one of her kind in the entire universe.

She blinked away the moisture in her eyes. What was the use of her existence? She felt detached and irrelevant, like a loose thread . . .

She looked towards the entrance-hole again. The light was coming in more strongly now. Another day was beginning on the Earth.

But it was a pale and paltry light compared to the glorious light of the angel in her dream.

9

It was a trees-and-traps day for Heartstock. Kiet had the task of picking up fallen nuts from the various scattered nut-trees in the Nesters' territory. She had plenty of opportunity to talk to young Nesters about the gathering with Ferren.

She tried to invite people from all four Stocks. Most of her friends were in Heartstock, naturally. But she didn't want the gathering to be associated with any one Stock above others. She wanted to get beyond narrow Stock-loyalties.

So she sought out Flens and Cubbert from Headstock, Elvet and Ethamy from Bonestock. They were all very willing to attend. But who could she ask from Bloodstock?

Then she came upon Tadge and Gibby playing together. Of course, she'd always intended to ask Tadge, who'd been in favour of the Residual Alliance from the very beginning. Now she could also ask Gibby as a member of Bloodstock.

Gibby was twelve years old, the same age as Tadge,

with small dainty features and fair curling hair. She looked very pretty – until she started pulling faces. She had a reputation as a pest.

She was being a pest to Tadge right now. Tadge's idea of playing was to move a squadron of six plum stones across an obstacle course of twig barriers and tiny trenches. Gibby's idea of playing was to keep flipping the plumstones into the trenches when Tadge wasn't looking.

As Kiet approached, Tadge had the crinkly expression which foretold a flare-up of anger. Gibby was pretending innocence, not very convincingly, in the face of his accusations.

'Hold it!' Kiet called out. 'Listen up, both of you.'

They forgot their quarrel and listened as Kiet told them about the gathering. They promised to come almost before they understood what it was about. Then Kiet turned to Gibby.

'I need at least one more person from Bloodstock. Can you think of anyone?'

'Miffa! I'll ask her!'

Miffa was Gibby's older sister. Kiet nodded approvingly.

'Okay then. We meet after family dinner by the abandoned nests.'

'Why after family dinner?' Gibby wanted to know.

'Because it's the best time. The adults will all be sitting around talking.'

'Why the abandoned nests?'

'Because no-one else will come there.'

'Why?'

'Why what? Don't be silly, Gibby. And don't be silly at the gathering either.'

''Course not!' Gibby stuck her fingers into the corners of her mouth and pulled an enormous clown-like grin.

Kiet gave her a warning scowl and strode off. Even as she went, she could hear Tadge's voice rising in protest over another plum stone which had fallen mysteriously into a trench.

The very last person she invited was Rhinn. In some ways, Rhinn was her closest friend – but she had serious doubts about asking her at all. Rhinn had a very strong sense of what was right and proper. How would she react to the idea of a gathering not approved by the Guardians?

As it turned out, Rhinn hardly thought about the lack of approval. What bothered her was the fact that Kiet had included people from other Stocks.

'It ought to be kept within our own Heartstock,' she objected. 'We're the natural leaders. Our *hearts* tell us what to do.'

There was a disapproving look on her long bony face. Rhinn was solidly built and had a way of standing planted on the ground like a bull. She accepted without question all the old prejudices about the different qualities of the different Stocks. In her opinion, the members of Heartstock were special and unique. They were more courageous, more honest and more generous, with longer necks, better teeth and stronger ankles.

Kiet refused to fall in with Rhinn's prejudices. But she saw a way of turning them to advantage.

'If you don't attend, Heartstock will be one member less,' she said. 'The other Stocks combined might be able to outweigh us.'

'Outweigh us? Never!' Rhinn huffed indignantly. 'Of course I'll come! Did I ever say I wouldn't?'

Kiet flung an arm around her and gave her a celebratory hug. 'Wonderful! I knew you would!'

Rhinn didn't withdraw from the hug. But she seemed puzzled. When Kiet dropped her arm, she studied her curiously.

'You're very pleased with yourself,' she commented. 'I've never seen you so happy before.'

'No?'

'What's got into you?'

'I don't know. Organising this gathering.'

'No. It's more than that. You've changed.'

'Have I?'

'Is it because you're going to be mated with Bross?'

'I've hardly even thought about Bross.'

'You're very lucky to get him. Everyone says so. You *ought* to be happy.'

Kiet laughed. 'Right then. You say I ought to be happy and I am happy. No problem.'

But Rhinn continued to look troubled. Kiet thought about it afterwards. What Rhinn said was true. Whatever the cause, she hadn't felt as happy as this for years.

10

Fifteen young Nesters were present at the gathering. Everyone who had promised to come was there. Kiet was delighted at the turn-up.

She got them to sit on the stretch of grass between the abandoned nests. There were five nests, all tumble-down, with gaping holes in their walls.

At first the young Nesters divided out automatically into four Stocks. They were in the habit of always sitting separately. But Kiet insisted that everyone had to join together in a single bunch. There was much joking and giggling as they rearranged themselves.

Rhinn frowned at the rearrangement. But she was a great help in hushing the audience to silence. She bossed and bullied and stamped her feet. Soon they were all sitting still and attentive.

Then Kiet brought Ferren forward. Nervously, she cleared her throat and addressed the gathering.

'We're here to listen to Ferren of the People. He's going to tell us about things he's experienced. Things that are beyond our experience. So we have to try and imagine. Okay? Use your imaginations.'

Then Ferren began to talk. He started with his own life in his own tribe. He described what it was like to live in the Home Ground, and the fear, every year, when the Selectors came around.

'It's the same for every tribe,' he said. 'The only difference is how many people they select.'

'Three for the Nesters,' Kiet put in.

He nodded. 'Because you're a bigger tribe.'

He went on to tell how he'd only just escaped being taken away for military service himself. He described the overbridge he had walked along and his first sight of the vast Humen Camp called the Bankstown Complex. Then his secret entry into the Camp itself.

Fifteen pairs of eyes were fixed on his face in fascination. Over the past six months, Ferren had become an expert in painting pictures with words.

He told them about the three kinds of Humen he'd seen inside the Camp. There were the white-coated Doctors who gave orders to the Hypers, the rubber-suited Hypers who gave orders to the Plasmatics. He didn't need to describe the Hypers, because everyone had seen Selectors, who were an example of the type. But their mouths fell open when he described his discovery of the Plasmatics.

'They were inside the metal engines. Bits of muscle and tissue, nerves and brains, working the machinery.' He paused dramatically. 'And where do you think they come from?'

He had given the overall facts before, when he'd addressed the whole tribe in the Bowl. But now he turned it into a story. The young Nesters lived through it as if they were actually there and seeing it with their own eyes.

He spared none of the details. The enamel baths at the bottom of the Pit, the selected Residuals packed into the baths, the transformation process that extracted a kind of psychic jelly from them. Then the bloody business of slicing up the leftover bodies, preparing the various organs to be made into Plasmatics.

The young Nesters shuddered in horror. And shuddered again as he went on to explain what happened with the psychic jelly. He gave them a picture of the Hypers lying back on the stretcher, the plug unscrewed from their foreheads, the nozzle inserted and the 'dose' injected.

'That's what the Hypers feed on!' he cried in conclusion. 'Our memories, our lives! The Plasmatics are made from our bodies, the Hypers are fuelled from our minds! The Humen are all parasites! Now do you see? We *have* to resist them!'

There was a long silence. No-one doubted the truth of his story. But they needed time to absorb it.

Then the questions began. Ethamy was the first to raise a hand. She was a roly-poly girl with a habit of breaking into uncontrollable laughter. But she wasn't laughing now.

'Weren't you scared at all?' she asked.

Ferren nodded. He told them of his terror every night after leaving his own tribe. He described the plain of dried blood, the incandescent hills, the Forest of the Morphs. By the time he'd reached the Humen Camp, he was almost used to being scared.

Then Miffa, Gibby's older sister, had a question.

'How did you get out of the Camp?'

So Ferren explained about the mechanical monster where he'd made his hiding place. When the monster started moving, he'd been carried along with the army on its way to the great battle. He'd been trapped in his hiding place while the muscles of Plasmatics heaved and twanged all around.

By the time he'd finished answering, another half dozen hands were raised.

'Where do they keep the jelly?'

'When did you meet the angel?'

'How did the Humen get defeated?'

And so on and so forth. Ferren did his best to answer, but the questions became more and more demanding. Until finally:

'How did the war between Heaven and Earth begin?'

Ferren spread his arms in a helpless gesture. 'You want the whole history of the Millennial War?'

'Yes!' 'Yes!' 'Yes!'

Eager voices cried out on all sides. Kiet could see it was time to step in.

'Do you *know* the whole history?' she asked him.

'Yes. But it'll take more than a few minutes to tell.'

'Okay.' Kiet was decisive. 'We'll have another gathering. A much bigger assembly. Will you tell us then?'

When Ferren nodded, she turned to face the audience. She had lost her earlier nervousness. She felt that the event had been a great success. The young Nesters had reacted even better than she'd expected. Her confidence now was like an inner glow.

'A much bigger assembly,' she announced. 'So everyone has to ask their friends to come. Okay?'

'I'll bring dozens!' Gibby piped up. 'Everyone from Bloodstock will be here!'

'No more than everyone from Heartstock,' Rhinn responded immediately. 'Heartstock won't be left behind.'

'But no adults,' Kiet warned. 'We don't want anyone older than sixteen.'

'Where?' 'When?' 'What time?'

Kiet was bombarded with questions. She considered for a moment.

'Same place, same time,' she told them. 'We'll meet here after family dinner. The day after tomorrow.'

'Why not tomorrow?'

'Because we'll need more than a day to organise. The day after tomorrow.'

They accepted her decision. They were all buzzing with excitement. They looked wide-eyed at one another.

'The whole history of the war between Heaven and Earth!' they breathed. '*Wow*!'

11

'It's only difficult at the start.'

'Everyone gets used to it.'

'You'll see, it'll soon become a habit.'

Kiet's family was trying to sound encouraging. Nettish flustered all around her, Uncle Abnel nodded firmly, Grandfather Niot smiled his many-wrinkled smile. Naturally, they thought she was reluctant about First Intimacies because she didn't like to be intimate with anyone outside her own Stock. But Kiet was only reluctant because she had more important concerns. These mating rituals were taking up valuable time.

'Now, you know what to do, don't you?' Nettish handed her the oil. 'And how long for?'

'No longer, mind,' warned Uncle Abnel.

'There you go,' said Grandfather Niot, and propelled her forward with a gentle pat on the back.

Bearing the small bowl of oil, she crawled in through the entrance-hole on her knees. There at the back of the nest was Bross, sitting in semi-darkness. He wore the special ritual garment, the loose moleskin wrap round his waist.

Kiet knew what to do, but she didn't know how to begin doing it. Did she just go straight up to him? But he'd have to move away from the wall first.

'Hi,' she said. 'Why don't you come and sit here?'

Bross shifted forward to the middle of the floor. He was big for his age, with powerful arms and a well-developed chest. Compared to his hard muscular body, his face was mild and pleasant-looking, sprinkled with freckles.

Kiet eyed his chest thoughtfully. There was a long silence.

'Are you going to do it then?' he asked at last.

'Ye-es.' Kiet put the bowl of oil down on the ground. 'You want me to, don't you?'

He shrugged. 'It's what they expect.'

'You don't want me to?'

'It seems strange to me. Why would I want to be rubbed with oil?'

'I don't think it's the actual oil. It's the touch of my fingers.'

'What's so wonderful about your fingers?'

'Search me. They're meant to make you feel all soft and squishy.'

'I don't want to feel soft and squishy. I'm going to be wrestling Stoggett in a week's time. If I beat him, I'm the best in the tribe.'

'Stoggett? He's ten years older than you.'

'I'd be the youngest ever, if I could win.'

He was hopeful but not boasting. Kiet looked at him with grudging respect.

'So this mating is at a bad time for you?'

'The worst.'

Kiet swivelled towards the entrance-hole. 'They don't look in, do they?'

'No. But they'll be watching when we come out.'

'What if I just drop some oil on you? You could spread it around. Then we could tell them we'd done it.'

He pondered the suggestion. 'They'd never know.'

'Especially if you could act a bit soft and squishy.'

'Sounds good to me.'

She picked up the bowl and poured a trickle of oil over his left shoulder, a trickle over his right. He spread it over his chest and around his back. Kiet dipped her hands in the remaining oil and rubbed her palms together.

'They'll expect me to have oily hands,' she explained.

'Right. What now?'

'Now we wait a while. As long as if we were really doing it.'

They sat facing each other. Bross grinned and Kiet grinned back at him.

'I was told you'd be really wanting to touch me,' he said.

'I was told you'd be really wanting to be touched,' she answered.

'And instead, we neither of us care.'

'Mmm. You've got the wrestling with Stoggett on your mind. And I've got this assembly to organise.' She looked at him thoughtfully. 'Have you been invited yet?'

'No.'

'You have to keep it a secret.'

'I'm already keeping our other secret.'

Kiet laughed. 'Okay, you can come. I'll tell you what happened at the first meeting. It'll help pass the time.'

For the next five minutes, she repeated everything Ferren had said about the Humen and their Camp. By the time she'd finished, Bross was very enthusiastic about coming to the next assembly.

Then they crawled out through the entrance-hole and submitted to the admiring inspection of Kiet's family. Kiet decided it would be appropriate to act a bit soft and squishy herself.

12

The day of the assembly dawned bright and sunny. Ferren had nothing much to do. Miriael was in a silent withdrawn mood, as often lately. Ferren couldn't understand how such a wonderful perfect being could be unhappy about anything. But he decided to leave her in peace.

So he wandered around watching the Nesters at work. He knew the nests of most of the families now, and the storage huts, the Guardians' nest, the Firepit. At the Firepit, he discovered the adult members of Heartstock squatting in small groups on the ground. Smells of smoke and roasting food hung in the air.

He searched for Kiet and found her in one of the green tunnels nearby. She sat with two other young Nesters, grinding seed-grains between smooth stones.

'Hi!' she said as Ferren approached. 'Today's our day for food preparation duties.'

'Can I watch?'

She shook her head and turned to her fellow-workers. 'Will you cover for me?'

'Why?'

'Very important things to talk about. For the meeting tonight.'

'Oh.' The two young Nesters looked suitably impressed. Obviously they knew all about the meeting. 'All right then.'

Kiet jumped up. Before Ferren could ask what they had to talk about, she seized him by the hand and led him off along the tunnel. Only when they had rounded a corner did she release his hand. She was grinning from ear to ear.

'I just wanted to get away.'

'So there's nothing important?'

'No. But let's talk anyway.' She thought for a moment. 'I'll take you to my most special private place.'

It was a private place much further away than the rhododendron bush. The tunnels grew narrower as they passed beyond the core area of the Nesters' territory. Finally, they left the path and zigzagged around rocks, through creepers and vines.

It was a pool of water, clear and brown. A shelf of rounded sandstone encircled it on one side, a bank of soft grey clay on the other. Rays of light descended through the foliage and danced on the tranquil surface.

Ferren whistled. 'Amazing!'

Kiet skirted the water's edge, stepping lightly on the exposed roots of trees. She lay down on the shelf, flat on her stomach. Patches of sunshine dappled the mellow-coloured stone. Ferren lay down beside her.

'It's warm!' he exclaimed.

She turned to face him, resting her head on her arm. 'Mmm.'

'What shall we talk about?'

'You.'

'Me? What about you?'

'You're the interesting one.'

'I talked about me at the last meeting.'

'Yes, your adventures. But I want to hear more about your ordinary life. How you grew up. Your tribe.'

'The People? I didn't get on with them so well when I was growing up.'

'Because you were different?'

'I suppose. But now they're different too. New attitude, new leader. They have the youngest leader of any tribe anywhere.'

The image of Zonda flashed before his mind. Zonda with her plump well-developed figure, her bouncy confidence, her temper. A temper similar to Kiet's . . . though probably not so fierce, he decided.

'What about your family?' she asked.

Ferren stared down at the sandstone. He didn't want to talk about his family. But Kiet was still waiting for an answer.

'I don't have a family,' he brought out at last. 'They were taken by the Selectors.'

'What, both of your parents?'

'Taken away before I was three years old.'

Kiet shook her head sadly. 'Same as my father. I was three years old when they took him away. I hardly even remember what he looked like.'

'I remember what my parents looked like. At least, I think I do.'

'My mother mated with another man later on.

Then *he* was taken by the Selectors two years ago.'

'That's the same time . . .' Ferren began, then stopped. It was too painful.

'Go on,' said Kiet gently.

The lump in his throat was almost choking him.

'Did you lose someone else?' she asked.

The words came out in a rush. 'My sister, Shanna, she would've been eighteen by now.'

'Tell me about her.'

He blinked furiously as the long-repressed memories welled up inside. Things that Shanna had said to him, things that Shanna had done for him. Her stern firm jaw, her sympathetic smile . . .

'She was like a mother to you, wasn't she?'

He nodded miserably. 'Like a mother and a father, both. She took care of me.'

Kiet waited to hear more. After a while he began to talk. He had countless stories of Shanna's wisdom and determination. He was immensely proud of her. He was even proud of the times when she'd been harsh to him.

'That was her kind of love,' he explained. 'She didn't say much, but what she said you had to listen to. She made me act sensibly. She knew we were different and she knew we had to hide it. Until she gave herself away.'

He told Kiet about Shanna's ingenious plan for building a roof over the shelter where the People slept. How she'd suggested it to the old leader of the tribe, and how the old leader had rejected it. Then when the Selectors next came around, it was Shanna they had picked for military service . . .

On and on he talked, until he'd completely talked

himself out. Kiet said little, only the occasional comment or prompt. When he finally fell silent, she stayed silent too.

It had done him good to share his memories of Shanna. He lay for a long while watching the sparkles of light bouncing off the surface of the pool.

It was very calming, very peaceful. The whole world was composed of green leaves, golden light, brown water. From time to time, dragonflies darted into view, hovered and glittered in mid-air, then darted off again.

'Listen to the rock,' said Kiet. 'You can hear the water through the rock.'

Pressing his ear against the rock, Ferren could hear it too. The sandstone carried the vibrations of the water lapping at the side of the pool. It was a constant steady sound like an echo.

'Everything's doing something,' he said.

He meant the activity of the water, the activity of the light, the activity of the insects. Kiet didn't answer, but he had the impression she knew what he meant. Everything was in motion while they lay motionless in the centre of it all.

The afternoon wore on. Behind the foliage, the sun moved slowly down the sky. But time seemed to stand still in Kiet's private place.

It was hardly necessary to talk. The current of their thoughts ran on in silence, only occasionally surfacing in words.

One time Kiet asked, 'Can you feel the coolness on your face?'

'Mmm, coming off the water,' said Ferren.

Another time she said, 'I always thought you were a very restless person. I never thought you could be so still.'

'What about you?'

'I'm always a quiet person.'

'I don't think so.'

'You don't know me. You don't see the way I am normally.'

Later again she said, 'Do you believe, if you control one kind of feeling, you lose your other feelings too?'

'Like how?'

'For instance, if you control your temper.'

'I don't know.' He looked at her curiously. 'That's not *your* problem anyway.'

'Yes, I control my temper.'

'Not with me, you don't.'

Kiet laughed. 'So think yourself honoured!'

They lay side by side without touching. Again he noticed that the colour of her skin was paler than his own. Yet she no longer seemed like a member of a different tribe. He felt wonderfully relaxed in her company.

But at last it had to end. The rays of the sun were slanting in at a much lower angle now. Kiet sat up with a sigh.

'It's almost family dinner time,' she said.

'Do we have to go?'

'*I* have to. You don't. You can stay here if you want. I'll come and collect you in time for the assembly.'

'Sounds good to me,' said Ferren lazily.

'Wait a minute.'

She stood up from the shelf and disappeared into the bushes. A few moments later she was back, bearing half a dozen yellow pears.

'From my secret tree,' she announced.

He reached out and she poured the fruit into his cupped hands. The pears were small but ripe and fleshy. He sniffed the smell appreciatively.

'That's for your dinner,' she told him.

13

This time there were at least fifty young Nesters at the assembly. They sat tightly packed on the grass. The late-comers had to stand among the bushes.

Ferren was impressed. He hoped he'd be able to live up to expectations. Miriael had told him the history of the war between Heaven and Earth, but there were many details he didn't fully understand.

He began with the Ancestors – or Old Ones, as the Nesters called them. He sketched a picture of advances in science and technology up to the start of the so-called 'Twenty-First Century'. The Old Ones had almost ceased to believe in Heaven or angels or an afterlife.

Then came the famous Venables-Hirsch experiment. Ferren described the crucial breakthrough which had enabled medical scientists to resuscitate a human brain after death.

'They couldn't believe it!' he cried dramatically. 'They called back souls from the afterlife and learned that there really was a Heaven! A realm outside of Earthly space and time!'

Next came Project Olympus and the scientists' attempts to explore the new realm with psychonauts. Finally, the Heavenly forces had turned on the invaders and destroyed them. When they also expelled all recently arrived souls, Earth suffered the terrible murdering rampages of the Rising of the Undead.

Ferren couldn't exactly explain about separate nations or the formation of the United Earth Congress. But his audience didn't ask for exact explanations. They listened intently as he told them about the period of negotiating between Heaven and the United Earth Congress, and the secret activities of the scientists under cover of the negotiating.

'The Celestials were very innocent and forgiving in those times,' he said, almost repeating the words that Miriael had once used to him. 'They even allowed the expelled souls back into Heaven. They never guessed that the scientists were secretly pulling down Heaven into Earthly space and time.'

There were puzzled expressions on the faces of the young Nesters.

'I thought the Old Ones believed in peace and harmony,' someone objected. 'Are you saying they wanted war?'

'Only some of them. Only a small elite who wanted to conquer in the name of science. The ordinary people just wanted to look upon the beauty of Heaven.'

Then he described the second invasion of Heaven, when hundreds of terrestrial flying machines had carried millions of people up onto the lower Altitudes. In the Great Collapse, huge chunks of Heavenly ether

66

had fallen away, causing catastrophic fires and destruction over the Earth.

'From then on, the Millennial War became a fight to the death,' said Ferren. 'And the forces on each side changed too.'

He explained how changes on the Heavenly side became necessary when the Supreme Trinity withdrew to the Seventh Altitude. A War Council of archangels had assumed direction of the war. On the Earthly side, it was the Humen who had gained control, under the rule of the Doctors.

There was a question from the audience. 'Where did the Doctors come from?'

'Miriael thinks they came from the original medical scientists. Either the same or descended from them. They're all incredibly old. It was the Doctors who invented the Hypers and Plasmatics.'

The young Nesters nodded. 'You told us about them.'

'Yes. And the artificial life-forms took over the fighting against Heaven. So then they could do without real human beings, except as raw materials.'

'Why did they want to do without real human beings?'

'Because they never trusted people like us. Hypers and Plasmatics have no souls, so they *have* to fight against Heaven. But we have the power to choose one side or the other.'

'And we are choosing!' someone cried out.

'What are souls?' cried someone else.

Again Ferren borrowed a phrase that he'd heard from Miriael. 'A soul is the spiritual part of a human being which keeps on experiencing after death.'

'What about us? Have we got souls?'

'Yes.'

'Now? Have I got one in me now?'

'Yes.'

There were giggles and whispers all round. The idea of having a soul both delighted and embarrassed them.

'The natural inclination of the soul is towards Heaven,' Ferren went on. 'In a natural state of the world, our souls would go up to Heaven after death. But because of the war, they're locked out. They become Morphs and settle in quiet lonely places on the Earth.'

'Have you *seen* them?'

'Not seen them. They're invisible, except to the eyes of angels. But there are ways of talking to them. Miriael and I talked to a colony four weeks ago. One of them was the Morph of a Nester.'

The young Nesters were agog. 'Who? Who was it?'

Ferren shrugged. 'They don't use names. They prefer to leave their old names behind. But this Morph told us how to find your territory. Otherwise we'd never have known to come here.'

Kiet stepped forward to address the audience. 'We understand, don't we? The Morphs are *our* Morphs! Because we have souls! And the Humen don't have souls! So we're better than them!'

The audience muttered its agreement.

'We're the real human beings and we're better than them,' she repeated. She turned to Ferren. 'Go on with your history. Tell us about the rest of the War.'

Ferren went on with his history of the War. He told them all he knew about the Weather Wars in North

America and the great South American offensive by Doctor Mengis and Doctor Genette. Every time, Heaven had used its control of the air to beat back the Humen. Centuries of stalemate, centuries of attack and counter-attack.

He brought the story up to date, up to the end of the Third Millennium. Then stopped. He had been talking for nearly half an hour. Already the light was fading fast.

Kiet glanced up at the sky.

'No time for any more questions,' she said. 'It's time to make decisions. What do we think about the Humen?'

Hisses and boos from all sides.

'What do we think about the Residual Alliance?'

Cheers and hurrahs from all sides.

'Will we support Ferren and help him any way we can?'

'Yes! Yes! Yes!'

'How can we help?'

'Tell us what to do!'

Kiet swung around to Ferren. But Ferren had no answer.

'I don't know yet.'

'We'll do whatever you ask,' said Kiet.

'Thanks for your support,' said Ferren. 'I'll have to think. Let's wait until the Summoning.'

'Tomorrow,' said Kiet.

'Yes, tomorrow.'

He wished he had some plan to put forward. But there was no time for further discussion. The young

Nesters had to get back to their family nests before nightfall. They jumped up from the grass and began to disperse. They chattered among themselves as they hurried off along the green tunnels.

In a matter of moments, the crowd had melted away.

14

Half the night had gone, but Kiet couldn't drop off to sleep. Her mother and baby sister Twy lay on one side of her, Tadge on the other. She was thinking, thinking, thinking . . .

What would happen after the Summoning? What would Ferren and Miriael do if the ghosts of the Old Ones gave a negative answer? And they usually did give a negative answer. In fact, Kiet couldn't remember a time when they'd given a positive answer.

Surely Ferren and Miriael wouldn't just give up and go on to the next tribe? How could the Nesters be the only tribe left out of the Residual Alliance? She refused to accept it. She didn't want her life to go back to boring normality. She liked this excitement. She *wouldn't* let it end!

Her thoughts slid back to the afternoon by the pool. The brown water, the dancing light, the dragonflies. Why was it all so strange and magical?

It wasn't as if they'd said anything very important. And they certainly hadn't done anything except lie side by side on the warm sandstone. Yet the whole afternoon seemed somehow charged and thrilling. She went over every tiny moment, every tiny detail. It was almost an addiction to keep going over it.

What was it, about sharing it with him? Was it a friendship thing? But it wasn't at all like being friends with Rhinn, for example. What sort of friendship could give her this light-headed feeling, this exhilaration?

So was it a male-and-female thing? But the male-and-female thing was what she was supposed to be doing with Bross. She tried to imagine Ferren in the ritual of First Intimacies. She would enter the darkened nest with the oil, she would rub oil into his back and shoulders . . . No, that wasn't it at all. Ferren belonged by the pool . . . his back and shoulders dappled in the patches of sunlight. She had no desire to go through First Intimacies with him.

Had anyone ever got this way just from lying side by side before? She'd never heard anyone speak of anything like it. Perhaps it hadn't even existed until now.

I shall have to give it a name, she thought to herself. I shall call it *lying-by-the-pool-ish-ness*. She had to hold back an impulse to giggle.

She propped herself up on one elbow and stared round in the darkness. There were the dim humps of her mother, brother and baby sister. And the storage baskets, the waterbags, the animal hides on the floor. All so very, very familiar . . .

The giggle rose again as a crazy idea occurred to her. She wanted to do something against all the rules. So unexpected, so completely out of the ordinary. Far more outrageous than the way she'd spent the afternoon.

She got up on her hands and knees and crept towards the entrance-hole. She wanted to see how Ferren looked when he was sleeping.

15

Ferren and Miriael ate breakfast in their nest: flat cakes of grain roasted with honey. The morning was well advanced and there was a great deal of activity going on outside. The Nesters were making ready for the Summoning.

Then a figure blocked the light in the entrance-hole. One of the Guardians come to call them for the Summoning? Ferren licked the honey from his fingers.

It was Kiet. She darted a glance at Miriael, then focussed on Ferren.

'Come quick,' she said. 'I have to tell you something.'

Ferren hesitated. He didn't want to be late for the Summoning.

'It's *urgent*,' she hissed.

So Ferren shrugged and followed her. When he tried to question her outside the nest, she shook her head and glanced warningly back towards the entrance-hole. It seemed she particularly didn't wish Miriael to hear.

He was forced to follow her all the way to the rhododendron bush. Kiet's private place looked very different in the morning sunshine. The pink and white flowers were opened wide, the waxy leaves were almost glittering. Kiet ducked in underneath and plumped herself down on the log.

'Guess what!' she began.

'What?'

'I came visiting your nest last night. Guess what I saw!'

'Why did you come visiting our nest?'

'It doesn't matter why.'

'But why –'

'Don't worry about it. Listen to what I saw. There was an angel in your nest!'

'Of course. Where else do you think she sleeps?'

'Not *she*! *Him*! It was another angel!'

'*What?*'

Ferren's exclamation was almost a shout. Kiet put a finger to her lips.

'It was scary,' she went on. 'Scary and wonderful. He was filled with light. I can't describe it. And golden light spreading out around him. He was inside a kind of globe, like a circle of glass.'

'Yes, that's their protection against the terrestrial atmosphere.' Ferren nodded. 'All angels need a globe outside of Heaven.'

'Miriael doesn't.'

'She's different. She changed. What was he doing?'

'Hovering above her. Then he sort of knelt down in mid-air. He put his hands together, like he was praying over her. It was so beautiful.'

'And Miriael?'

'She was fast asleep. You too.'

'What colour robes did he wear?'

'What colour? Purple. Why?'

'Different colours stand for higher or lower Orders of angels. Miriael wears yellow for a Junior Angel.'

'What's purple?'

Ferren knitted his brows, but in vain. 'I forget. Something much higher than a Junior Angel.'

'Do you think he knew I was there?'

'Did he look at you?'

'No. I'd have died if he'd have looked at me. But I was afraid he could tell without even looking. I only watched for a minute. Then I ran off.'

Ferren was silent, busy with his own thoughts.

'What do you think?' she asked at last.

'I'll have to tell Miriael.'

'What does it mean?'

Ferren couldn't even guess. They came out from under the rhododendron bush and headed back towards the nest. But they were already too late.

Young Ethamy almost ran into them, hurrying along in the opposite direction.

'Come on!' she cried. 'The Summoning! Everyone's gone to the City of the Dead!'

Ferren cursed under his breath.

'Okay,' he decided. 'We'll catch up with her out there.'

16

For Kiet, it was like all the other Summonings she'd attended. The Nesters were drawn up along the outcrop of rock, looking very nervous and very solemn. They had separated into their four Stocks, facing across the valley towards the City of the Dead.

Kiet spotted Miriael one second before Ferren.

'There!'

'Right.'

The angel was alone on a rocky spur. It was obvious that none of the Nesters liked to stand too close to her.

Ethamy had already gone off to take up position with her own Stock. Kiet knew she ought to do the same. But when Ferren began pushing though the crowd in the direction of Miriael, she made up her mind to follow.

They threaded their way through Bonestock, then Headstock. Kiet could hear the whispering: 'What's she doing?' 'Why isn't she with her own Stock?' But she looked straight ahead and kept going.

Miriael turned as they came up.

'There you are! I think it's about to start.'

Before Ferren could reply, there was a barrage of noise from the other side of the valley. The Guardians stood on the platform outside the walls of the City of the Dead. They were banging on instruments of carved wood and stretched animal skins.

Two hundred Nesters leaned forward intently. So did Miriael, so did Ferren. The buildings of the City stood out, sharply etched in the morning sunlight.

Kiet wondered if Ferren would try to tell Miriael about the visiting angel. But he seemed to have decided that now was not the time. He swung round with a question.

'What are they doing?'

'Summoning the ghosts of the Old Ones,' said Kiet. 'Listen!'

The Guardians had protective symbols painted all over their skin. No part of their bodies had been left undefended. Louder and louder they beat on their instruments.

'The ghosts of the Old Ones,' Miriael repeated. 'Are the Old Ones who I think they are?'

Kiet hung back, keeping on the safe side of Ferren, away from the angel. It was Ferren who answered.

'Yes, the same as the Ancestors. Human beings of the old civilisations, before the Millennial War.'

'Mmm. But why would they have ghosts? Don't you see the problem?'

'Because their souls were allowed up into Heaven?'

'Yes. It wasn't until after the Great Collapse that human souls were permanently locked out.'

'So they can't be ghosts.'

78

'Or they can't be the Old Ones.'

Kiet frowned as she tried to follow the conversation.

'Why not?' she demanded aggressively. 'What else are they then?'

For the first time she spoke directly to Miriael. She refused to flinch, even when Miriael's piercing blue eyes fixed upon her.

At that moment, the ceremony moved on to another stage. The Guardians began yelling at the tops of their voices.

'Old Ones! Old Ones!' cried Clemmart.

'The Nesters ask for your instruction!' cried Spiddal.

'Shall we abandon the Humen alliance?' cried Dunkery.

'Shall we join the Residual Alliance?' cried Berwin.

The banging of the instruments rose to a thunderous crescendo, then stopped. Everyone froze.

In the silence could be heard a faint wailing sound. It came from deep within the City of the Dead. It was like a sad sighing music, infinitely mournful.

Ooh-oh-ooh-oh-ooh-oh! Ooh-oh-ooh-oh-ooh-oh!

Kiet saw Ferren and Miriael exchange glances. They nodded, as though the sound meant something to them.

Ooh-oh-ooh-oh-ooh-oh! Ooh-oh-ooh-oh-ooh-oh!

The Guardians interpreted a meaning in their own way.

'It's a *No*,' they shouted. '*Noo-no-noo-no-noo-no*!'

But Ferren threw his hands up in the air. 'It's not a *No* at all!'

Dunkery glowered across at him. 'You have your answer,' she cried. 'The answer is negative.'

Miriael spoke up. 'There was no answer!'

The Guardians merely turned their backs and bowed their heads in homage to the ghosts of the Old Ones. Ferren whirled to face the Nesters on the rocky outcrop.

'You didn't hear words!' he appealed. 'But you can! They *can* speak to you!'

The adult Nesters growled disapprovingly.

'What does he know?'

'That's the sound they always make.'

'He's spoiling the ceremony.'

Kiet was totally confused. What did Ferren and Miriael think the ghosts of the Old Ones really were?

'We'll show you!' Miriael raised her voice. 'We'll go right in and talk to them!'

Looks of panic appeared on the Nesters' faces.

'What does she mean?'

'Go into the City of the Dead?'

'They must be mad.'

Ferren scanned the crowd.

'Who'll come with us?' he demanded. 'Who'll be a witness?'

There was no response. His gaze roved across everyone, but it was the young Nesters that he focussed on.

'Who'll come?' he repeated. 'Who'll help?'

Kiet felt her stomach turn over. He was appealing for the support they'd all promised at the assembly. She stared across at the City of the Dead. Did she dare? It didn't look so scary by daylight . . .

'I will!' a voice called out.

It was Flens from Headstock, with his pale eyes, big nose and gangling frame. Daredevil Flens, who seemed to have been born without a nerve in his body.

Kiet was annoyed she hadn't been first. Of course she dared!

'So will I!' she declared.

'Me too!' cried Gibby, Tadge's friend.

She was pulling a comical face even as she spoke. In the next moment, Tadge himself joined in.

'And me, and me!'

Soon there were young Nesters volunteering from all sides. They pushed forward through the crowd to join Ferren, Miriael and Kiet.

'I'll lead the way across,' Kiet offered.

The adults gaped at the small young bodies pushing past them. There were a few half-hearted attempts at control: 'Where are you going?' 'You can't!' 'Come back here!' But the adults seemed more stunned than anything else.

The Guardians on the platform were equally bewildered.

'What's happening?' Berwin shouted across.

Ferren raised an arm and pointed towards the ruins.

'Forward into the City of the Dead!' he cried. 'Now we'll find out the truth!'

17

When they came to the concrete platform, they marched past the four Guardians without stopping.

'Come with us,' Miriael called out over her shoulder.

And the Guardians did come with them. Angrily, unwillingly, complaining every step of the way – but they came. They held their arms high in the air, warding off danger with their protective symbols. They walked along at the back of the young Nesters.

Ferren took over the lead when they came to the gap between the walls. He crawled through the tangle of bushes in the lane. Everyone followed in single file.

Out on the other side of the gap, the street looked very different to the way Kiet remembered it. Sunlight beat down on the facades of the buildings and the tilted slabs of roadway. Lizards scuttered suddenly on stone and vanished into zigzag cracks. The stone itself tick-ticked as it warmed in the heat.

Kiet could still hear occasional wailing sounds: *Ooh*! *Oh*! *Ooh*! But they were much quieter now, as though most of the voices had fallen silent.

The procession continued along the street. Ferren and Miriael walked in front, engaged in serious discussion. Kiet walked at the head of the young Nesters, with Flens and Rhinn alongside. Gibby and Tadge followed, then Bross and Ethamy.

They had to detour around the door that Ferren had pulled off its hinges. All eyes turned to the spill of earth and the solid earth packed up behind. Kiet couldn't resist displaying her knowledge.

'Every building's the same,' she said. 'They're filled full of dirt.'

She was rewarded with Rhinn's look of astonishment. Even Flens was impressed.

'You can see the dirt through the windows too,' she added airily.

She felt more and more confident all the time. She strode forward without hesitation as they approached the square at the end of the street.

Then Ferren stopped and swung around, hand raised. The procession came to a halt.

'We have to be quiet from now on,' he said. 'No sharp movements, no loud noises, no calling out.'

'Why not?' asked Gibby.

'Because they're very shy. They hate to be disturbed. We don't want to frighten them.'

'The ghosts of the Old Ones?' Rhinn was incredulous. '*They're* afraid of *us*?'

'Yes,' said Ferren. 'Except they may not be the ghosts of the Old Ones.'

He turned again. Miriael had advanced alone to the

corner of the square. The wailing sounds had ceased completely.

'Can you see them?' Ferren called in a low voice.

'Yes. Over a hundred. It's what we thought.'

'What? What?' Kiet was bursting with impatience. 'What is it you thought?'

'It's a colony of Morphs,' said Ferren.

There were gasps of surprise from the young Nesters. At the back of the procession, the Guardians raised their voices in protest.

'Nonsense!'

'It's the ghosts of the Old Ones.'

'Never heard of Morphs.'

But the young Nesters had heard of Morphs.

'They're the souls of the dead!'

'Locked out of Heaven!'

'Since the time of the Great Collapse!'

Ferren nodded. 'Many of them are probably the Morphs of Nesters. Not so far back in the past. Maybe your grandparents or great-grandparents. We're going to speak with them.'

There was a hubbub of excitement. Ferren shushed for silence. They waited until Miriael beckoned them forward.

'We walk where Miriael walks,' Ferren told them. 'So we don't knock into any Morphs by accident.'

Miriael moved out across the square. The procession followed in a long curving crocodile.

The square was a wide flat space covered in concrete flagstones. All around stood silent blank-faced buildings. There were loose bits of rubble and dry grass sprouting in the cracks between the flagstones.

Everything was very still. Yet Kiet felt the hairs standing up on the back of her neck. She had a definite sense of invisible presences.

Miriael halted in a spot that looked exactly the same as the rest of the square. Ferren halted a pace behind. Kiet peered over Ferren's shoulder. There was nothing to see but scattered rubble.

'Where are they?' she whispered to Ferren.

'Between the bits of rubble.'

Miriael herself glanced around at the question. 'And the grass. And the corners of the flagstones.'

'Miriael has special perceptions,' Ferren explained. 'Angels have the power to see Morphs.'

Miriael smiled sadly. 'One of my few remaining spiritual powers.'

She pointed to a particular chunk of rubble.

'Do you see that pyramid-shaped piece of stone? Right? Imagine a line from the point at the top across to the corner of that flagstone, there. Now, see that blade of grass? Another line from the corner of the flagstone to the tip of the grass. Then across to that lump of brick, there, where it sticks out at the side. Then back to the piece of stone.'

'That's it?'

'Yes. That's the Morph I'm going to talk to.'

'Like a pattern of lines?'

'Morphs exist in the patterns between things. I see them as faint structures in the air. This one is trembling. Stay very still, or it'll detach and float away.'

She lowered herself slowly onto her knees. Kiet

hardly dared draw breath. Miriael's way of talking to the Morph was a kind of singing. She turned her sentences into a gentle musical chant.

'Please don't be afraid,
Please don't go away.
We only want to question you
And hear what you say.'

Ferren whispered to Kiet behind his hand. 'Morphs like music. That's how we communicate with them.'

'You can do it too?'

'Yes, but not as well. Miriael can invent new tunes as she goes along.'

Miriael changed into a new tune now, with a different rhythm matching a different kind of utterance.

'Tell us, tell us, who you are.
Speak out loudly, who you are.'

A tiny voice piped up out of nowhere. The response itself wasn't musical, but fluting and mournful.

'We are the Morphs of the City of the Dead!'

Miriael turned to Ferren. 'Bring the Guardians forward,' she whispered.

Ferren passed the message back along the crocodile. Very reluctantly, the Guardians came forward. Miriael indicated a place for them to stand. Then she sang to the Morph again.

'Louder, louder, tell us so.
Are you Old Ones, yes or no?'

The tiny voice responded with a hint of peevishness. 'No, not the Old Ones, we are Morphs.'

The Guardians frowned thoughtfully, but said nothing.

'When you had a body,
When you were alive,
Where was your dwelling?
What was your tribe?'

The first response was a thin pitiful wailing: *Oh-oh-ooooooh!* But finally words came forth.

'My tribe was the Nesters, eighty years ago. I was Guardian of Bonestock, but now no more.'

Other pitiful voices took up the refrain. 'No more, no more! No more, no more! We are lost and forgotten, no more, no more!'

Berwin, Clemmart, Spiddal and Dunkery looked at one another in amazement.

'Guardian of Bonestock?'

'Eighty years ago?'

'It must be Cadwin!'

Ferren silenced them with a stern gesture. Miriael still had the most important question to ask.

'You come from the Nesters
And your tribe needs instruction.
Should they join with other tribes
Or stay with the Humen?'

A kind of twittering sound spread across the square. 'Not the Humen! Not the Humen! Do not trust them! Not the Humen!' The voices were still mournful, but also shrill with anger.

'What do you know of them?
Why don't you trust them?'

The twittering became a clamour. Dozens of voices called out one after another.

'No souls, no Morphs, from those who are selected!'

'What happens to the soul on military service?'

'How do they die? We do not know the answer!'

Kiet spoke into Ferren's ear. 'It's what you said! Doses for the Hypers! That's what happens on military service!'

Then the Morph of Cadwin piped up above the rest. 'Here in our colony, many tribes together! Let the Nesters do the same, join the tribes against the Humen!'

Miriael turned to the Guardians. She didn't need to ask if they'd heard. Their faces were grim, almost haggard.

'You were right,' said Dunkery.

'We'll tell the Nesters,' said Spiddal.

'We'll support the Residual Alliance,' said Clemmart.

Miriael faced the Morphs once again. She held her arms wide and made slow soothing gestures.

'Thank you for your answers.

Now no more disturbance.'

But the Morphs were not so easily soothed. 'We are disturbed! We are! We *are*!'

Miriael spoke to Ferren. 'Go back the way we came. I'll sing until they're peaceful.'

Ferren signalled to the young Nesters. The crocodile reversed direction and retreated back along the same curving route across the square.

Kiet grinned at Ferren. 'You've won!'

Ferren returned the grin. 'We've all won.'

Behind them, sweet strains of melody filled the air. Miriael was singing a hymn to the Morphs, pure and clear as a peal of bells.

18

With the Guardians in favour of the Residual Alliance, it didn't take long to convert the adult Nesters. It was as though they had always been eager to join. Miriael and Ferren explained how meetings would be organised with representatives from every tribe.

The Nesters had more difficulty adjusting to the idea that the ghosts of the Old Ones were actually ghosts from recent times. They accepted it as a fact, but they were still confused. Miriael made the whole tribe promise that the Morphs would be left alone and undisturbed.

The joining of the Alliance was sealed with an impromptu ceremony. Ferren and the four Guardians formed a circle and linked little fingers. Miriael tactfully stood aside. She knew that no Residual would want to touch fingers with an angel.

Then the Guardians decreed a night of feasting and dancing. The Nesters, rapidly recovering from all the shocks of the day, set about making preparations. The nests and tunnels were soon stirring with hustle and bustle and shouting of orders.

For Miriael, the biggest shock of the day was still to come. When Ferren told her about the *other* angel, she instinctively clasped her hands together in prayer.

'He's the one in my dream,' she breathed. 'It wasn't a dream at all.'

Ferren wanted to fetch Kiet and have her describe what she'd seen. But Miriael shook her head. Instead, she made Ferren go over and over every tiny detail. Outwardly calm, she was tingling with inner intensity.

'I wonder how often he comes?' she said, more to herself than Ferren. 'Every night? Tonight? I *have* to see him!'

They went on to discuss plans for visiting further tribes, but Miriael's attention kept wandering. She could hardly wait for night to arrive.

First, though, there was the feast to attend. It began an hour before nightfall and took place in the Bowl.

It was a feast to remember. Course after course was served. There were stews with herbs and nuts, meats roasted on skewers, peppers, marrows, sweet potatoes, stuffed braised onions, grain-breads, honey-rolls, purees of fresh fruit and a dozen other delicacies. Miriael ate without tasting a thing.

The Nesters sat on the grassy slopes, circulating the bowls from hand to hand. Inevitably, they divided out into their four separate Stocks. But no-one thought to object when the young Nesters moved round in the company of their friends. The sharp divisions gradually melted away.

Darkness had fallen by the time the feasting came to an end. Then the dishes were cleared and the musicians came forward to the platform in the centre of the Bowl. They carried hollow wooden tubes and gourds filled with loose dry seeds. There were eight musicians, including Grandfather Niot and Uncle Abnel.

'I don't know much about Morphs and Alliances,' said Uncle Abnel. 'But so long as someone else understands –'

'We know all about music and dancing!' Grandfather Niot concluded.

They took up positions on the platform. They made music by hammering on the tubes and shaking the gourds. Grandfather Niot sang bass and Uncle Abnel sang baritone.

Miriael decided it was time to slip quietly away.

19

Ferren and Kiet didn't dance together at the start. The dancing was in two long lines, which curved and swirled up and down the slopes. Ferren came opposite Nesters of all ages. He grinned at the younger ones he knew and recognised.

The music wasn't very melodic but the rhythm was irresistible. Ferren just wanted to keep dancing and dancing.

After a while, the rhythm speeded up. As many of the older adults retired, the two lines broke apart into separate circles. Ferren was in the same circle as Kiet. He found himself repeatedly facing her, catching her eye, matching his dancing to hers.

Faster and faster went the rhythm. Eventually even the circles broke apart. Now Ferren was dancing with Kiet, the two of them alone. She flung out her arms, gyrated her hips, flexed from the waist. Her skin was shiny with sweat, her mouth was wide with laughter.

Sometimes she looked at him, sometimes she looked

away. But it wasn't her face, it was her whole body imprinted on him. She was sheer flowing motion, an undulating sea. There was amazing muscular strength and energy in her slight figure.

How long had they been dancing? Ferren had lost all sense of time. More than half the dancers had fallen away. The driving rhythm went on without a pause.

He couldn't take his eyes away from Kiet. She began swinging her head from side to side, so that her dark red hair flew out like a banner in a storm. She was showing off to him.

He showed off to her too. He jumped and sprang, whirled his arms, kicked out with his legs. But he couldn't compete with her furious grace.

He took the lead from her movements. Her face was wild – almost as wild as when she'd raged at him in the City of the Dead. But now it was wild with a kind of savage joy.

Everything became a blur. There wasn't a thought in his mind – only liquid flickering movements. It seemed impossible they could move so far between every beat of the rhythm. He rose as she rose, sank as she sank, higher and lower, further and further . . .

Until finally he lost his footing and fell. Even as he fell, it seemed that the rhythm still bore him up, leaping and turning in slow motion. And she fell too, gliding with him through the air. They hit the ground almost simultaneously.

Side by side they lay, gasping and panting. The blood pounded in Ferren's ears, so loud that the music seemed suddenly far away. It was as though a nest had formed in the darkness, enclosing Kiet and himself and a small patch of grass.

She struggled to speak.

'It's – it's – it's – it's –'

Every time she began, her lungs demanded another gulp of air.

'What – what?' Ferren was panting too.

'It's *lying-on-the-grass-ish-ness*!' she brought out at last.

She burst out laughing, and Ferren laughed too.

'Like *lying-by-the-pool-ish-ness,*' she added eventually.

Ferren didn't understand, but it didn't matter. He reached out to take hold of her wrist. She didn't pull away.

'Your pulse is running wild,' he told her.

'What about yours?'

'Don't know. Maybe it's mine I'm feeling.'

They laughed again as though it was the greatest joke in the world. Kiet used her free hand to wipe the sweat from her forehead.

'This is the best,' she said.

'You're the best,' said Ferren. 'I wish I didn't have to leave.'

She withdrew her hand instantly. 'Leaving? When?'

Somehow he had spoiled the moment. But it was too late to call back the words.

'Tomorrow.'

'*Tomorrow*!'

'We have to continue expanding the Residual Alliance,' he went on in a flat voice. 'Me and Miriael. We travel to a tribe called the Sea-folk next.'

There was a long silence. Kiet looked away from him, looked up at the interwoven branches overhead.

'I'll come back to the Nesters,' said Ferren.

'When?'

'I can't say. A month perhaps?' He said it more as a question than a statement. 'I promise I'll be back.'

Kiet seemed indifferent to the idea. 'Things change.'

'Why? How?'

'You don't understand our tribe. You don't understand my duty to my family.'

'Tell me.'

'I'm going to be mated to Bross.'

'Oh.' Ferren considered. 'Is that –'

'Yes.'

'But it doesn't stop us being friends?'

She flashed a sharp look at him. 'Friends. Yes. That's what we are, isn't it?'

'What's the matter?'

'I don't want to talk about it right now.'

'I'm only –'

'I said I don't want to talk about it!'

She jumped suddenly to her feet. She seemed angry, yet she grabbed him by the hand.

'Let's dance some more!'

She pulled fiercely on his arm, jerking him up into a sitting position.

'I'm exhausted,' he protested.

'Come on! Now!'

Her body was already swaying to the rhythm of the music. She gave him another jerk, half lifting him off the ground.

'I can't.'

'Yes, you can!'

And she was right – he could. Back on his feet, his exhaustion vanished. Once more, the rhythm swept him away. Once more, he gave himself up to the movements between them. Stamping and swirling, spinning and swerving . . .

20

Miriael was determined to stay awake all night. She lay motionless on the floor of the nest, eyes closed as if asleep. She was filled with an immense yearning, pulled out tight like stretched elastic. Hour after hour she waited . . .

The first thing she experienced was a soft golden glow on her eyelids. Then a warmth on her skin. As she lay there motionless, the warmth penetrated into her skin until she seemed to be glowing all through.

It was unutterable bliss. She felt that her heart would burst. Then the light changed. The golden glow became a pure white radiance. The radiance grew stronger and stronger. She opened her eyelids the tiniest fraction.

'I know you're awake, Miriael,' said a firm, gentle voice. 'You can look when you're ready.'

Her eyelids flew open – then snapped shut again. He was so incredibly bright. Her first image was only of a hovering globe with rays pouring forth like a wind. Her sight was no longer attuned to the intensity of spiritual light. She had spots behind her eyes.

It took many attempts and many blinkings before she could form a better impression. She saw a purple robe, sixfold wings, a silver circlet around his brow. He carried a kind of wand, a long clear cylindrical tube. The light spilling from the edges of his robe was like light spilling out of a crystal. Even without moving, he seemed to shimmer.

'I am the Seraph Asmodai,' he told her. 'Also known as the Tenth Angel of Strategy.'

She gazed in awe. She had seen male angels of greater power, but never one so beautiful. His face was dominated by great lambent eyes, his hair was like fine spun glass. The curls of his hair streamed out in the light.

'I've been visiting you,' he said. 'Did you know?'

She hardly heard the words. She was thinking of moral beauty, the special celestial beauty which was so superior to mere beauty of appearance. His heart was the very centre of his light, she knew. The centre of goodness, love and care . . .

Then she realised he was waiting for her to speak. She went back over his question and produced an answer.

'I knew in a dream. And someone observed you. But I was never awake myself.'

'No.' Asmodai understood why she was puzzled. 'I didn't want to wake you. This isn't an official visit.'

'Heaven didn't send you?'

'Nobody in Heaven knows about it. I'm sorry. I wish I could bring you an official message of reconciliation.'

Miriael was too full of joy to feel disappointment. 'But *you've* come anyway!'

'Yes. And in myself, so far as I can, I represent the love and mercy which Heaven *ought* to offer.'

'Thank you.' Miriael blinked, not solely from the brightness of his light.

'I've been watching over you,' he said. 'As often as I can get away.'

'Have you seen what I've been doing?' she asked eagerly. 'Gathering the Residual tribes together? Getting them to turn against the Humen?'

'Yes. It could be a significant new development.'

'Even more than you know. I've learned some things about Plasmatics and Hypers. Plasmatics are constructed from Residual body parts. And Hypers are fuelled by the psychic deposits taken from their brains.'

'Ah!' His eyes were glowing with interest. 'Go on.'

'The Residuals are the raw materials. The Humen take them away for what they call military service. But if the tribes refuse to contribute to military service –'

'Then no raw materials!'

'No new Plasmatics, no fuel for the Hypers!' Miriael was triumphant. 'How about that!'

'Very important. It should be built into Heaven's strategies.'

'You can report it back to them.'

'I will. But I don't know what use they'll make of it.'

Miriael's face fell. 'Wouldn't it give them a huge advantage?'

'It would. But perhaps you've forgotten how Heaven operates?'

Miriael's face fell even further. 'Traditional. Unchanging. Stuck in the past.'

Asmodai nodded. 'They like to keep to established strategies. They don't welcome new ideas.'

'They'd have won the Millennial War long ago if they did.'

'Very true, I'm afraid. It's frustrating for those of us who can see more clearly.'

'Can't you persuade them? You speak so beautifully.'

He smiled. 'Unfortunately, I'm only a Tenth Angel of Strategy.'

'But . . .'

'A Tenth Angel of Strategy is no more than a quartermaster. I arrange supplies and equipment in accordance with the battle-plans. But I don't make the plans.'

'They don't listen to you?'

'I've tried. I've developed new techniques and suggested new methods. But what I say is always disregarded.'

Miriael looked at him, so beautiful, so radiant. Surely he deserved a far higher position than Tenth Angel of Strategy?

'Heaven hasn't treated you very well,' she said. 'Perhaps that's why you're able to sympathise with me.'

Asmodai moved a little closer. His expression was gentle and tender.

'My problems are small compared to yours,' he said. 'Would you like me to try to change Heaven's attitude towards you?'

'Yes! More than anything! Is it possible?'

'I can't promise. But I can do my best.'

Miriael could hardly believe the offer. 'Just to be trusted! Just to be forgiven!'

Asmodai shook his head. 'What do *you* have to be forgiven for? You haven't done anything wrong.'

'That's what Uriel said too. But he still cut me off from Heaven.'

'Mmm. Even though you haven't *done* wrong, yet in his eyes you *are* wrong. You know the prejudice against the physical. Everyone in Heaven thinks like that.'

'But not you.'

'No, not me. I see you as a being in a very interesting state.'

'Not a corrupted state?'

'Not at all. A uniquely in-between state. Who knows what it might mean? Who knows what we might be able to learn from you?'

'I never thought of that.'

'No, and Heaven hasn't thought of it either. But I shall try to change their attitude.'

Miriael had to stifle a sob as an immense feeling of gratitude welled up in her chest. Asmodai bowed his head in thought.

'Unfortunately, I can't approach Uriel myself. I'll have to talk to other angels and see who I can influence in your favour. Can you be patient?'

'Yes, now I know there's someone on my side. I can have patience enough for anything.'

'Good.' He smiled. 'I'll start immediately. I'll visit again when I have progress to report.'

'When?'

'Patience!' He raised one hand. 'When I have progress to report.' Even his hand was beautiful, with long slender fingers. 'In the meanwhile, I think you should get some sleep. You've been awake all night.'

'I couldn't sleep now.'

'Yes, you could. Let yourself relax.'

The light of his aura began to change. The rays of pure white light were replaced by a softer glow, a golden haze. Miriael felt herself becoming drowsy.

'Is this why I slept through your other visits?' she murmured.

'It is. A very simple technique. I could teach any Celestial how to do it.'

'One of your new techniques?'

'Yes. Don't speak any more.'

A wonderful golden slumber crept over her. She felt sure that everything was being put right, everything would turn out well in the end. It was only a matter of time . . .

2

The SEA-FOLK

1

Miriael and Ferren left quietly the next morning. The Guardians escorted them as far as the edge of the Nesters' territory, where the trees and lantana bushes came to an end. Ahead was a wide plain dotted with mounds of ruined stone. Miriael and Ferren made their final farewells and went on alone.

Miriael moved in long graceful strides, almost springing over the ground. Ferren trudged along with lowered head. His legs were like lead, his muscles sore from dancing. He was absorbed in his own thoughts.

Most of all, he wondered about Kiet. He remembered how they'd danced themselves into total exhaustion, danced till they'd dropped. Then slept side by side on the grass. But when he awoke in the morning, she'd gone.

She wasn't in her family nest either. Neither Tadge nor Nettish had seen her all night. He'd had to leave without saying goodbye. He felt somehow unsatisfied.

They walked on until they came to a slow winding river. Miriael consulted the sketch-map she'd made from information given by previous colonies of Morphs.

'We follow the river downstream,' she announced.

It was difficult walking: the ground was soft and their way was often blocked by stagnant scum-covered ponds. The scum was so thick it was like yellowy-brown leather. Huge air-bubbles rose from deep under-water and bulged in blisters under the scum. When the blisters became large enough to burst, they spattered foul matter far and wide.

There were creatures in the water too, though never fully visible. They revealed themselves only in sinuous snaky ripples. They made long humps under the surface of the scum.

Ferren held his nose against the disgusting smell when the blisters burst. But there was no avoiding the gnat-like insects which descended upon them in clouds. Buzzing and biting, the tiny pests flew into nostrils and eyes. Beaten away a thousand times, they were always back again a moment later.

It was many hours before they passed beyond the ponds and approached a different landscape. They saw it ahead as a band of whiteness.

Ferren suggested a break for lunch. They unslung their packs and sat cross-legged. The Nesters had refilled their packs with grain-breads and honey-rolls left over from the feast.

Ferren was thankful to rest his aching limbs for a while. Miriael was strangely silent, smiling to herself. Ferren eyed her curiously as she ate.

He could guess the reason for her smile. She'd already told him that she'd spoken to the other angel. He was a beautiful Seraph and his name was Asmodai. But she seemed reluctant to say more. It was as though she preferred to keep him to herself.

All too soon, it was time to move on again. They advanced towards the band of whiteness, which turned out to be a forest of dead trees. The trees were set out in neat rows like an orchard. Their trunks and branches were dry as bone.

Ferren pointed. 'What's that?'

He went up close to inspect. Implanted between two branches was a tiny silvery box. It had no projections or openings of any kind. Looking around, he noticed similar implants between other branches.

'They're on all the trees,' said Miriael. 'It must be some old Humen experiment. Probably trying to torture the trees into a new way of growing.'

Ferren nodded. In their travels, they'd come upon many such experiments. It seemed that this particular experiment had failed, since the trees were dead.

All afternoon they walked through the forest parallel to the river. Every once in a while, the silvery implants gave out a sudden loud *click*! At first Ferren was startled, but soon he got used to it.

The sun was low in the sky by the time they came out into the open again. Now they could see what the trees had masked. Cutting across their route was a Humen overbridge. It looked like a straight black line running along the horizon.

'Does it lead to the Humen Camp?' asked Ferren.

Miriael nodded. 'Certainly. The Bankstown Complex is south-west of here.'

They continued on towards the overbridge. Coming

closer, they could see the huge black pylons and criss-cross girders holding up the deck. The river wound its way between the pylons.

Then the ground changed suddenly underfoot. The grass stopped and the entire surface was covered with a light-brown glaze. It was as though rock and soil had fused to form a hard semi-transparent coating.

Ferren didn't need to ask Miriael to explain. He knew that such effects had been caused by the Great Collapse, when portions of Heavenly ether had fallen onto the Earth. This was a only a small fall, where the fires had gone out long ago. Elsewhere, especially in the Burning Continents, the fires were still raging.

They had to walk more and more carefully. The light was fading and the smoothness of the glaze made the surface treacherous.

'It'll be dark soon,' Ferren commented.

Miriael came out of her inward daydreaming. 'Yes. We'll need a place to spend the night.'

'I slept under an overbridge once.'

'Mmm?'

'Between the concrete blocks.' He pointed to the massive cubes of concrete at the base of the pylons. 'It's a sort of shelter.'

She raised her eyebrows, smiling. 'So you want to relive your past?'

'It's an idea.'

'And I don't have a better one. Okay. Let's do what you did.'

It was the longest conversation they had had all day.

2

'Wake up! Wake up! *Wake up*!'

Someone was shouting at him, pushing and prodding at him. He half-resisted, half-opened his eyes.

It was daylight and there was grey concrete in front of him. Ah yes, he remembered. He had slept through the night beneath the overbridge. With Miriael.

But it wasn't Miriael who was shouting at him. He rolled over and looked up into a familiar face. Wide mouth, white teeth, dark red hair.

Kiet.

It didn't make sense. Kiet had been left behind with the Nesters.

'Why are you here?' he mumbled.

Kiet stopped pushing and prodding. Her face came even closer.

'Get up! You have to see this! Quickly!'

'You can't be here. You were –'

'Get up! *Listen* to me!'

Ferren was lost in his own bewilderment. But Miriael was now awake.

'What is it, Kiet?'

Kiet turned to appeal to her. 'Something coming! I don't know what! Out there!'

She gestured frantically towards the side of the overbridge. In the next moment, there was a flash of yellow robe as Miriael hurried past. Ferren shook himself and rose on one elbow.

'You too!' yelled Kiet.

She seized him by the hand and dragged him upright. Then propelled him forward from behind.

'Move! Move!'

Ferren was still struggling to understand. 'Did you follow us? Is that what you did?'

Kiet kept driving him forward. She didn't bother to reply. He staggered out beyond the pylons.

'*There*!' she cried.

Then he saw. It was an ominous cloud of dust in the distance. It was approaching along and beside the overbridge. Huge black shapes of machinery loomed through the cloud.

'Must be the Humen,' muttered Miriael grimly. 'Get back. Out of sight.'

They retreated behind the shelter of the pylons.

'I was sleeping close by,' Kiet explained. 'The vibrations woke me up.'

'It's a Humen army,' said Miriael. 'But not like anything I ever saw before. Some of those machines are gigantic.'

Ferren was finally fully awake. 'What do we do?'

'Run?' suggested Kiet.

But there was no cover on the bare glazed plain. They

would be clearly visible as soon as they left the shelter of the overbridge.

'No, we'll stay and hide here,' said Miriael. She raised her eyes to the deck of the overbridge, like a dark roof high overhead. 'Up in the struts and girders.'

Kiet shuddered. 'And let them roll right over us?'

'As long as they don't see us, we'll survive.'

She led the way to the nearest pylon. She leaped up onto the concrete base and began to scale the massive iron pier. Kiet and Ferren followed. It wasn't a difficult climb, thanks to the many projecting bolt-heads.

Twenty metres above the ground, they swung off the pylon and onto the underframe supporting the main deck. It was a strange dim world, a crisscross forest of struts and girders. The slatted plates of the roadway were directly above them. They had to bend and crouch to keep from hitting their heads.

Then Miriael looked down – and gasped.

'Our packs!'

Ferren and Miriael had used their packs as pillows during the night. The packs still lay on the ground between the concrete blocks.

'They'll be seen!' cried Ferren. 'I'll get them!'

In an instant, he was back at the pylon and shinning down as fast as he could go.

The army had advanced with amazing speed. The front row of machines was now only a few hundred metres away. They made a thunderous sound, a rumble of innumerable wheels and engines.

Half-sliding and scraping his chest on the bolts, he dropped to the concrete block. Then turned and jumped down to the ground. The glazed surface thrummed under his feet.

He snatched up the packs and slung the straps round his neck. He had to keep his hands free for climbing. But the packs hung down awkwardly at his sides.

Crack! Crack! Crack!

Sharp sounds rang out like shots. He stared and saw the glazed surface breaking up under the vibrations. Small chips flew high in the air, zinging in all directions.

He clambered back onto the concrete block. The front row of machines seemed to be racing towards him. They rose up from the ground as high as the top of the overbridge.

He began to climb. But the packs hindered his movements and slowed him down. Desperately he fought his way up from bolt-head to bolt-head. Twice he almost lost his grip. He willed himself not to panic.

He reached the underframe just in time. In the next moment, the machines came surging past. They moved in a tidal wave of their own dust. Ferren watched from behind the outer struts and girders.

The machines in the first row were huge cylindrical shapes shrouded in black material. They were mounted on roller-bogies, each pulled by three or four snub-nosed traction engines. The engines gave out terrible screechings and roarings, like animals in pain.

'Ferren! *Quickly*!'

It was Miriael and Kiet calling. They had started to come across to him, arms reaching to pull him in. He waved them back, turned away from the side of the overbridge. He made his way through the underframe and joined them in the middle.

'Get a safe hold!' shouted Miriael.

The vehicles coming along the roadway were almost on top of them. Loose dirt and flakes rained down from the slatted plates. All around, the stressed metal squealed under the strain.

They took up positions on the widest girders, arms wrapped around the most solid struts. The din was earsplitting. Booming and clanking, grating and grinding . . .

Everything was going blurry around the edges. They looked at one another, faces white and clenched. Even their faces were going blurry around the edges.

Closer and closer and closer. The pounding and battering seemed to beat directly onto their skulls. Their teeth rattled.

And then the slats in the plates went dark. Mighty wheels and caterpillar tracks passed over inches above their heads. They prayed and hung on.

3

For what seemed like hours, the nightmare continued. The incessant grinding friction heated the metal of the overbridge.

Miriael's expression grew increasingly grim. From where she was sitting, she could glimpse the army going past on the ground, while the slats overhead gave a limited view of the army going past on top.

It wasn't merely the size of the army that troubled her. Even more worrying were the many new devices and unknown types of weapon. She had seen concertina-like bags with nozzles, multiple batteries of hexagonal cells, mobile arches strung with shining wire and monstrous skeletal structures which moved by folding up and opening out, like insects on jointed legs. Did anyone in Heaven know that such things existed?

There were new types of being as well. Most of the Hypers riding on the machines or marching overhead were normal Hypers in their normal rubbery black suits. But she had also glimpsed what looked like Hypers of some specially tall and augmented breed.

They moved in bounding five metre strides and carried weapons like spiral pipes.

Most extraordinary of all was the being that passed over at the very end. The machines on the ground had finished going past a few minutes ago. Then mighty footsteps approached along the top of the overbridge: *Thrungg*! *Thrungg*! *Thrungg*! The roadway plates sagged under the weight. A couple of rivets popped out completely.

The hairs stood up on the backs of their necks. It was like an evil presence passing over.

'What's that?' breathed Ferren.

Miriael didn't respond. She could see only the vast shape of feet shadowing the slats overhead. But she had a sense of some enormous intellect humming with a million calculations.

As the footstep went away, she rose from her sitting position.

'I'm going to take a look.'

She crossed to the side of the overbridge and peered through the outer struts. The army was gone, the cloud of dust diminishing into the distance. Still she couldn't get a clear view of the thing that had passed over.

She climbed up on the outside of the underframe, as high as the level of the roadway. Ferren climbed after her. They stared in the direction of the retreating footsteps.

'It's a *Doctor*!' Ferren whistled.

Lumbering along the top of the overbridge was a Doctor in a medical coat. But very different to the original Doctors of the Bankstown Complex. Whereas they had been shrunken and dwarfish, this was a colossal figure, fifty metres tall. The coat which hung down to his feet was a vast expanse of dazzling white.

They watched in stunned silence. The giant looked like a tower against the sky. His head was hunched into his shoulders, half-hidden by the collar of his coat. But, unlike the original Bankstown Doctors, he seemed to have no wires running from the back of his skull.

'What is it?' Kiet stuck her head out at the side of the overbridge but made no attempt to climb up.

'A totally new kind of Doctor,' answered Miriael. 'New army, new weapons – and a new kind of Doctor to lead them.'

'Heading towards the Humen Camp,' added Ferren.

Miriael shook her head in disbelief. 'A whole new force coming in. I never anticipated this. I thought they'd build up with gradual reinforcements. But this is a takeover. The new force will incorporate what's left of the old and become stronger than ever.'

'Where do they come from?' asked Ferren.

'Who knows? Perhaps the North-West Basin or the Perth Depot. They must have been developing their powers in secret.'

'So we're under threat sooner than expected. What does the Residual Alliance do?'

'Set up the meeting with representatives from all the tribes.'

'You mean, we don't go on to the Sea-folk?'

'I'll need to think.' Miriael knit her brows. 'Let's get down from here first.'

Kiet led the descent to the ground, then Ferren, then

Miriael. The ground was unrecognisable. The once glossy surface had been scoured with abrasions, shattered like ice.

Kiet was very shaky on her feet after all the noise and pounding. But she spoke up firmly enough.

'Wherever you decide to go, I'd like to go with you.'

She addressed both Ferren and Miriael. But Miriael was busy with her own thoughts. Ferren stared at Kiet curiously.

'You *did* follow us, didn't you?'

'Yes. You never saw me. I came up closer in the night.'

'But why leave the Nesters? Why leave your family?'

Kiet snorted and made no reply. But after a while she said, 'Because they were going to mate me with Bross.'

'Ah.' A look of understanding dawned on Ferren's face. 'And you don't like Bross?'

'Yes, I like him. He's all right. That's nothing to do with it.'

Ferren looked puzzled again. Kiet glared at him, then swung around to Miriael.

'I'd like to go wherever you decide to go. Is that okay?'

Miriael glanced up and shrugged. 'I don't have any objection.' Her eyes flicked across to Ferren. 'Do you?'

Ferren had no objection either.

'Good,' said Kiet, with satisfaction. 'So where do we go?'

Miriael took a deep breath. She hoped she had come to the right decision.

'I see it like this,' she said. 'Even when the new force

117

gets to the Bankstown Complex, it'll take them time to reorganise. They can hardly pose much danger for a while yet. I think we should give ourselves another month for drawing more tribes into the alliance. Then we'll set up the meeting.'

It was a decision she was later to regret.

4

As a party of three, they continued their journey on the other side of the overbridge. They were still walking parallel to the river. Several tributaries added their flow to the river, which grew steadily wider.

Later again the land began to tilt upward. The river wound on in a gorge between steep walls of grey shale. As the gorge deepened, the walls closed in and the banks almost disappeared. They were forced to stumble over loose scree and negotiate landslips. Their progress slowed to a crawl.

Kiet was fascinated by the fossils in the rock. There were dozens of them in some layers of shale. They appeared as outline shapes of white on grey, like drawings in a gallery.

'Why do they look like skeletons lying down?' she asked.

Miriael and Ferren had seen similar fossils elsewhere in their travels.

'Because that's what they are,' answered Miriael. 'The mineralised remains of the old human beings. The people you call the Old Ones.'

Kiet was thunderstruck. It made her uneasy to be so close to the Old Ones. She tried to give the fossils as wide a berth as possible.

There were other signs too. In many places, underground pipes of concrete and lead had been exposed. In one place, a whole latticework of plumbing spanned across the gorge. Kiet goggled at these remnants of a lost civilisation.

It was late in the afternoon when they first heard the sound of the sea.

'What's that?' asked Kiet.

Ferren had no answer – he'd never seen the sea either.

'You'll find out,' Miriael told them.

They pressed on through the last twisting loops of the gorge. The walls rose to their greatest height, plunging the river into darkness. Then, suddenly, the walls fell away. Ahead was a great U-shaped cleft.

The smell of the sea came to their nostrils. Salty, tangy and alluring. Ferren and Kiet sniffed in wonder. They made haste to scramble over the final stretch of scree.

Then there it was in front of them: the sea. The vast openness took their breath away.

'Yieee!' cried Ferren.

'Whoo! Whoo!' whooped Kiet.

They had came out onto a curving beach, a crescent of sand between cliffs and sea. The sea was in bands of colour: a greeny-grey close to the shore, a greeny-blue further out, then silvery pearl along the horizon.

Immediately, they had to race down to the water's

edge. Even Miriael had only ever seen the sea from a distance. They stood and watched the endless rhythm of the breakers breaking. It was hypnotic: the long rolls swelling and building, peaking and toppling, crashing and seething.

They stayed for almost half an hour. Ferren and Kiet jumped around in the hissing frothy tongues that rushed and retreated up and down the slope of the beach. They dipped their hands in the water and splashed cold droplets at each other. The breeze off the sea blew into their faces and lifted their hair. They felt the sand sucked out from under their toes in the backwash.

But, finally, Miriael called a halt. Once more she consulted her sketch-map and notes.

'We follow the beach to the left,' she announced.

Luckily, they were already on the left of the river, which entered the sea by a long lagoon. They set off across the sand.

The cliffs were in shadow, the sun was sinking behind them. The twilight sky had darkened to mauve. The moon stood forth faintly as a pale sliver above the horizon.

The beach ended where the cliffs came forward to meet the sea. At the foot of the cliffs was a rocky promontory and a jumble of enormous boulders. They clambered over the boulders, passing placid rock pools, slipping on green slime. The salty tang was stronger than ever.

Beyond the promontory was another beach, which curved around to another rocky promontory. How much further to the dwellings of the Sea-folk? They trudged on across the sand. Their calf muscles were starting to ache.

Then they began to hear a different sound above the crash of the breakers. It was a vast clamour in the distance, harsh and threatening. The cause was revealed when they passed around the next promontory and onto the next beach.

The third beach was a replica of the previous ones, with yet another promontory at the far end. But this promontory extended out to sea in a series of reefs and islands. Circling above the islands was a flock of at least a thousand screaming seagulls.

'What are they doing?' asked Kiet.

'They seem to be attacking something,' said Miriael.

'Look!' Ferren pointed. 'There are people on those islands.'

'It must be the Sea-folk!' cried Kiet.

They shielded their eyes to peer into the distance. There were about twenty islands, some large and some small, connected by ropes. Most of the islands supported various ramshackle human structures.

It seemed that a full-scale war was going on. The Sea-folk were clustered on the two largest islands. As they watched, the gulls wheeled and swooped down in squadron after squadron.

'The Sea-folk are in trouble!' Ferren exclaimed.

'Let's help!' cried Miriael.

Without another word, they set off running along the beach.

5

They could see more clearly when they came to the promontory. Between the two largest islands was a long sagging rope. The gulls were trying to peck through it and the Sea-folk were trying to defend it.

Some of the Sea-folk were shaking the rope in order to stop the birds from landing. But they themselves were under attack from the squadrons diving down. Other Sea-folk attempted to shield the rope-shakers by waving sticks above their heads. Others again threw bits of stone and shell.

Yet still the attackers kept coming. The actions of the Sea-folk were inexplicably clumsy. It seemed that the birds were winning.

Ferren, Miriael and Kiet stood on the final rocky shelf at the point of the promontory. They considered the rope that connected to the first tiny island. How to get across?

The rope was about ten metres long, made of strands of seaweed interwoven with strands of human hair. Projecting lumps of rock had been cut and grooved to anchor its loops at either end. In the middle, it hung down until it was barely skimming the waves.

'We'll have to pull ourselves across hand over hand,' said Miriael.

Kiet shivered. 'What, dangling in the water?'

'Yes.'

Ferren was already shrugging his pack from his shoulders. Miriael followed suit. Then, one by one, they lowered themselves over the edge of the shelf. Holding fast to the rope, they pushed off and swung out above the waves. Ferren was in the lead, then Miriael, then Kiet.

As the rope arced down, their feet dangled in the water. Soon they sank in up to their knees, then their waists. The water was cold, and floating seaweed slithered against their legs.

'Ugh!' cried Kiet.

Hand over hand, they hauled themselves across. They were almost halfway when a single seagull flew down. It perched on the rope ahead of Ferren.

Cark!

It fixed a beady eye upon him. It looked vicious and aggressive, blocking their way. Ferren continued to advance.

Cark! *Cark*!

As the rope swayed, the gull gripped more fiercely with its red webbed claws. It extended its wings and drew back its neck to strike.

But Ferren struck first. He was less than an arm's length away. He flung himself up out of the water and swung at it with his balled fist.

The blow knocked the bird's head sharply sideward. It tumbled into the sea with a squawk and a splash. In the next moment, it righted itself, paddled backwards and took off with a furious beating of wings.

Ferren, Miriael and Kiet resumed their progress. As the rope arced upwards again, they rose higher and higher out of the water. The island was sheer-sided rock, with brown seaweed hanging down. Ferren was almost there when Kiet yelled a warning.

'Look out!'

Above their heads, the sky was dark with wings. It wasn't just a few birds sent to drive them away. The entire flock was intent on their destruction.

Even as they gaped, the first squadron came hurtling down.

Ferren leaped into action. With two great lunges, he pulled himself up onto the flat top of the island. He knelt and leaned out towards Miriael, extending his hand.

The birds focussed their attack upon Kiet. A snow-storm of wings descended over her. She was helpless. Beaks and claws ripped at her hands as she tried to maintain her hold.

She let go of the rope and fell back floundering. With no experience of swimming, she thrashed and spluttered and swallowed water in mouthfuls.

'Catch hold!' cried Miriael.

She was three quarters out of the water. She stretched back with her long slender legs. Kiet got the idea when her thrashing arms made contact with Miriael's left foot. She clung on for dear life.

Miriael towed her in closer to the rock. The birds whirled around and turned against Miriael too. Without thinking, Miriael spread her wings.

That was what saved them. Miriael's wings were purely ceremonial, useless for flight – but they were still far larger than the wings of any seagull. As the white feathers fanned outwards, the birds swerved aside in a sudden flurry. If not panicked, they were at least disconcerted.

There was a brief lull as the attack drew off. It was just long enough. Miriael pulled Kiet in to the rock, then lifted her until she was able to take hold of the rope again. Ferren helped them both up on top of the island.

They stood there dripping water, gasping for breath. In the next moment, the gulls returned to the attack.

This time it was a more calculated attack. The birds came in horizontally in successive waves, first from one direction, then another. Their beaks were their weapons and they were going for the eyes.

The top of the island was only a few paces wide. Miriael, Ferren and Kiet stood back to back in a defensive triangle. They whirled their arms and yelled at the tops of their voices. Trying to keep the beaks from their eyes, they were stabbed, slashed and buffeted. Blood ran down their arms and the sides of their faces. The sight of blood drove the gulls into a kind of frenzy.

Kiet staggered backwards under the buffeting. Her shoulders hit against Ferren's shoulders. She recovered her balance as he lost his.

'Aaaagh!'

He toppled off the island and into the water. He came up spluttering. Kiet and Miriael rushed to the edge of the island and peered over. Ferren clutched onto a spur of black rock.

Already the gulls were massing to attack. They hovered in a spiralling column over the sea. Clearly they were going to pick Ferren off first. The column swirled closer.

'Climb up! Climb up!' shrieked Kiet.

He lifted his face and shook his head. There was no rope on this side of the island. It was too sheer for him to climb unaided.

The column of seagulls exploded outwards at the bottom. A stream of birds skimmed over the waves, aimed like projectiles straight at Ferren's head.

There was only one thing he could do. He took a deep breath of air and vanished below the surface. For one second, Kiet and Miriael glimpsed his hands on the spur of rock underwater, his dark hair floating upwards like a mop.

Then the gulls arrived. They blitzed the surface with their webbed claws, they tried to dive and peck at his hands. But he was so close to the side of the island, they couldn't get a proper shot at him. For five metres around, the sea was a cauldron of spume and spray.

Kiet and Miriael knelt and flapped uselessly with their arms. They couldn't reach low enough to create a distraction.

After half a minute, the gulls changed tactics. They stopped diving and began to sweep around in circles. As the spume and spray died down, the top of Ferren's head became once more visible under the water. The gulls were waiting. They knew he would have to come up for air.

Two minutes later, he rose. Mouth wide, eyes popping.

'No! Don't!' cried Kiet.

The flock came at him immediately. They landed on his head and shoulders, scrabbling and gabbling. When he tried to submerge again, two birds had their webbed claws caught in his hair.

Then Kiet had a flash of inspiration. The seaweed hung down in brown straps from the top the island. She ripped off a strap and rose to her feet. It was two metres long and she wielded it like a whip.

Swack!

The tip of the lash cut into one of the two birds on Ferren's head. The other seemed stunned by the sharp clap of sound. They tore their claws free from his hair. He sank back into the water trailing blood.

Miriael saw what Kiet had done. Immediately, she began ripping up more straps of seaweed. She passed one length to Kiet and kept two for herself. They stood on the edge of the island, each holding a strap in either hand.

Ferren couldn't stay under for long. His lungs were only half-filled with air. As soon as he resurfaced, the gulls flew in again. But Kiet and Miriael were ready for them.

Swack! Swack! Swack! Swack! Swack! Swack!

The flicking tips knocked the birds aside, the whip-cracking sounds disoriented them. Kiet swung her straps in a fury, Miriael was more controlled. They were both equally effective.

The gulls drew off, discouraged. They seemed to have lost their bloodlust. Some attempted to attack Kiet and Miriael, again flying in at their eyes. But Kiet and Miriael lashed out and picked them off in mid-flight. The birds couldn't even get close. Most swerved and managed to stay airborne, a few crashed and knocked themselves out on the rock.

The attacks grew less and less determined. Almost the entire flock was now wheeling high in the sky. Their cries were raucous and bitter with disappointment.

Ferren had remained above water. With Miriael standing guard, Kiet tied her two lengths of seaweed together and cast one end down to him. He wrapped the strap round his wrists and began to climb. Kiet heaved backwards, dragging him up. He came to the top and sprawled face-down.

'You – saved – my life!' he gasped.

Kiet grinned. 'Aren't you glad I came along?'

Miriael was watching the gulls in the sky. A thousand flickers of grey and white against a violet backdrop.

'They're going,' she announced.

The birds streamed away into the distance, their cawings increasingly faint and faraway. They were returning to their nesting places in the cliffs. Soon they had vanished completely into the shadows.

Ferren wasn't watching the gulls. He was still coughing up water. But when he raised his eyes, he saw something in the opposite direction.

'Look!' he said. 'The Sea-folk are coming!'

6

The Sea-folk had tanned golden skin and pale bleached hair tied up in knots. Clothing for both sexes consisted of a patchwork of many different materials wound round with horizontal belts. They wore necklaces of stringy seaweed from which hung coloured shells and oddments of metal, plastic and glass.

They walked over the ropes balancing like tightrope walkers. Only half a dozen made the final crossing to Miriael, Ferren and Kiet. There was no room for more on the island.

They spat three times in the water as they crossed. While they talked, they fingered their necklaces, touching a particular shell, a particular ring, a particular button or bent nail. They touched item after item in a deliberate sequence.

Miriael, Ferren and Kiet found them difficult to understand at first. They spoke with a strange accent, drawing out their vowels and rolling their 'r's. But their feelings were obvious in the tone of the their voices: immense gratitude and overwhelming wonder.

One woman held up a small container of oily paste. It smelled strongly of fish – as did the Sea-folk themselves. The woman collected paste on her fingertip and dabbed at Kiet's many small cuts and scratches. The paste soothed the pain and staunched the flow of blood.

Then the woman dabbed at Ferren's wounds in the same way. But she was naturally afraid to touch the skin of a real-live angel. She passed the container to Ferren, who passed it to Miriael, who applied the paste with her own fingertip.

By now the two groups were adapting to the difference of accents. Speaking slowly, Ferren explained why they had come to visit the tribe. But even when the Sea-folk understood, they still shook their heads.

'Tell it to the Mothers,' they said.

It seemed that the Mothers were the elders of the tribe, on one of the larger islands. The Sea-folk pointed the direction. But Miriael, Ferren and Kiet couldn't walk on the ropes as the Sea-folk did.

After much discussion, a solution was found. The Sea-folk produced new lengths of rope which they held up like safety rails on either side of the main rope. Miriael, Ferren and Kiet shuffled along the main rope holding on to the side-ropes.

The method was repeated as they made their way from island to island. On every island was a group of Sea-folk, fingering their necklaces and smiling a welcome.

Finally they arrived at the largest island, a wide rocky platform. There were shelters on the island, but only around the edges. A huge outspread net occupied the centre.

Their escorts took care not to step on it. Miriael, Ferren and Kiet were led around the side to a fire at the far end of the island. It burned in a kind of metal sieve, producing a great deal of smoke and a smell of fish-oil. On one side was a neat stack of dry driftwood. On the other side sat three old women.

They too fingered their necklaces, muttering rapidly under their breath. Their faces were lined with creases, their cheeks seamed with scars. They nodded at Miriael, Ferren and Kiet.

'Thank you,' they said, simply and sincerely.

They gave their names as Gweir, Lorne and Krye. The other Sea-folk had gathered in a circle all around the net. Gweir spoke first.

'The birds are our enemies. They think we steal fish from them.'

'For many years, they have been trying to conquer our islands,' said Krye.

'If they can break our ropes, they can divide and destroy us,' said Lorne.

'You saved us in a time of great peril,' said Gweir.

Miriael smiled. 'Well, you saw how we did it. Whips of seaweed. Now you can do it yourselves.'

The Mothers shook their heads.

'No,' said Lorne. 'Taboo.'

'Taboo?'

'The changing of hands rule.'

Miriael, Ferren and Kiet exchanged puzzled glances.

'Your luck is probably different,' said Krye. 'You

have different taboos to obey.'

'For our tribe,' explained Lorne, 'it would be unlucky to repeat the same act with the same hand. We have to keep changing hands.'

Ferren remembered the seemingly clumsy efforts of the Sea-folk fighting against the gulls.

'So that's what you were doing? That's why the gulls were winning?'

'Yes,' sighed Gweir. 'It is difficult for us.'

'But better than breaking the taboo,' added Krye.

Ferren was incredulous. 'You'd rather risk getting wiped out?'

'Ah, we would never have been at risk if we hadn't lost our luck,' said Gweir. 'We must have broken a taboo. Otherwise the birds would never have attacked.'

Ferren could hardly help treating it as a joke. 'The birds attacked because someone forgot to change hands?'

'No, it could have been any one of our taboos,' Krye answered very seriously. 'We have seven hundred and thirteen altogether.'

'Look at the net behind you,' said Lorne.

'It is the diagram of our luck,' said Gweir. 'It shows our total system of taboos and pay-ups. It helps us to remember.'

Looking more closely at the outspread net, Miriael, Ferren and Kiet observed that the weave was amazingly irregular, with unequal strands and strangely placed knots.

'Do you know what taboo you *did* break?' asked Miriael thoughtfully.

'Not yet,' said Lorne. 'But we shall find out. Then we shall do pay-up for at least a week.'

'But it will not disturb you,' added Krye. 'You are our honoured guests, as long as you wish to stay.'

'We weren't planning to stay long,' said Ferren. 'We've come to ask you to join the Residual Alliance.'

The Mothers waited in silence for further explanation.

'It's an alliance of many tribes similar to this tribe,' Ferren went on. 'All giving help to each other.'

'As we gave help to *you*,' Miriael pointed out. 'When we drove off the seagulls.'

'We are in your debt,' said Gweir. 'We would surely want to help you in return.'

'But first we must finish pay-up,' said Lorne. 'We can do nothing until we have regained our luck.'

'It doesn't matter –' Ferren began.

'You would not seek alliance with unlucky people,' said Lorne firmly. She seemed to think that Ferren was only being polite. 'But please explain about the alliance. So that we can know what to do, when we are able to join.'

Ferren was eager to start explaining there and then. But Miriael held up her hand.

'It is late and we are tired,' she said. 'Why don't we tell you tomorrow morning? It'll take at least an hour to explain properly.'

Kiet nodded agreement. She could hardly stop from yawning. The three Mothers rose to their feet, deeply apologetic.

'Of course, of course.'

'Forgive our lack of thought.'

'You must sleep in our very best shelters.'

Lorne addressed the surrounding circle of Sea-folk. 'Who will offer our guests the hospitality of their homes?'

Everyone crossed their arms over their chests. It was evidently their signal for willingness. Lorne stepped forward and selected three families.

'We're going to be split up,' said Kiet, disappointed.

Ferren answered out of the side of his mouth. 'We fit in with their customs. It's the only way.'

Kiet was too weary to argue. When one of the three families approached her, smiling and nodding, she followed without a murmur.

7

There was a salty fishy smell in the morning air. Kiet woke up on a narrow shelf of rock, facing a wall of stones. Her mattress was a mat of dried seaweed.

She remembered being brought to the smaller island where the family had its shelter. All the islands had individual names – this one was Fia Mor. She had been too tired to bother with food. She had fallen asleep to the lap-lap-lap of the waves.

The same sound came to her ears now. The wall of stones was a shield against the sea-winds, with each stone so cunningly matched and fitted that no draft could penetrate. On the other side of the wall, the waves gurgled constantly around the base of the island.

She rolled onto her back. Her sleeping-shelf was roofed over with woven green seaweed. Various items of sea-treasure were incorporated into the weave: fish-bones, pieces of glass, scraps of transparent plastic.

She rolled over again, towards the seaweed curtain which divided her shelf from the main part of the shelter. Someone was speaking.

She parted the strands with her fingers and peeked out. The main part of the shelter was a square space surrounded on three sides by curtained shelves similar to her own. The fourth side was wide open to the morning sunshine. There were no furnishings, only a few spears and baskets stored in corners.

She recognised the speaker: Moireen. She also recognised the audience: Jike and Jorika. She'd been briefly introduced to them all last night. There was no sign of their parents.

Moireen was telling Jike and Jorika a story. She sat facing them on the sand-sprinkled floor.

Moireen was about the same age as Kiet, big-boned and solidly built. Even sitting cross-legged on the floor, she managed to appear ungainly. Against the deep tan of her skin, her knotted hair was white and her lips were pale and pink.

Jike and Jorika were twins, a year or so younger than Tadge. Both had wide faces, snub noses, jughandle ears. They nudged and elbowed one another constantly. But they were still listening to the story.

Kiet began to listen too. It was a story about a time when birds nested in the cities of the Lords of the Earth. And when the birds were ordered to stop doing their dirty droppings, they refused.

'So what do you think the Lords of the Earth did then?' Moireen paused dramatically.

'I know!' exclaimed Jike.

'So do I!' cried Jorika.

'No you don't!'

'I know as much as you!'

'Hush, and I'll tell you,' said Moireen. 'The Lords of the Earth created huge flying machines with metal wings.' She spread her arms. 'A hundred times bigger than any bird. A hundred times faster than any bird. They flew those machines round and round in the sky until the birds begged for mercy.'

The twins cheered.

'Drive them off!' cried Jorika.

'Wipe them out!' cried Jike.

'No, they didn't need to wipe them out,' Moireen went on. 'The Lords of the Earth were so clever and strong, the birds didn't frighten them at all. They *forgave* them. And then they fed them.'

'Fed them?' The twins' mouths were wide with amazement.

'They put out crusts and leftovers for them. That's how powerful they were! The birds were grateful to be allowed to eat their leftovers!'

'Eat their leftovers,' Jike repeated, in an awed whisper.

Kiet swivelled and poked her head out through the curtain. 'The Old Ones had flying machines too,' she said. 'Lords of the Earth, Ancestors, Old Ones – they're all the same. The original human beings.'

Moireen and the twins looked round.

'Ah, you're awake,' said Moireen. 'Do you want breakfast?'

Kiet nodded, suddenly aware of how hungry she was. She stretched and rose with a yawn. She sat on the edge of her sleeping-shelf with the curtain swept back over her shoulders.

Moireen smiled. She had beautiful sea-green eyes. 'I'll get you some.'

She lumbered to her feet and disappeared out of the shelter. The twins looked aggrieved.

'You've done it now,' said Jike.

Kiet raised her eyebrows. 'What?'

'Ended our history time. Now she'll make us do learning of rules.'

'Boring, boring, boring,' said Jorika.

'I was distracting her,' explained Jike.

'I was too,' said Jorika.

'I was doing it more.'

'You were more sticking your elbows into me.'

As if falling back into an old groove, they resumed elbowing one another. Kiet listened idly to their 'Were-were-were's' and 'Weren't-weren't-weren't's'.

After a few minutes, Moireen returned with a bowl of hot fish broth.

'Hardly spilled a drop,' she announced.

It was a strange breakfast, but Kiet was hungry enough for anything. She tilted the bowl and drank, almost burning her throat in her hurry.

Moireen took Jike and Jorika off to a corner and handed each of them a necklace similar to her own.

'Practise from number sixty to number ninety-nine,' she ordered. *'If one person steps on another person's shadow . . .'*

The twins began to chant in low sing-song voices.

'If one person steps on another person's shadow, that is taboo.

If one person's shadow passes over another person's shadow, that is taboo.

If one person's shadow falls across the sharp end of a spear, that is taboo . . .'

They fingered the objects on their necklaces as they chanted. The chant was so automatic, they continued their elbow-jostling at the same time. Moireen turned back to Kiet.

Kiet raised her head from the bowl. 'That's a lot of taboos you have to remember,' she commented.

Moireen nodded glumly. 'I know all the rules, but my great lump of a body keeps forgetting them. I can't seem to control what I do. I break so many taboos, I spend half my life doing pay-up.'

'What does it mean, pay-up?'

'It means, when you break a taboo, the things you have to do to put it right. For example, if you step on someone else's shadow, you can put it right by blinking fifty times.'

'That stops the bad luck?'

'Yes. Today, I'll have to do pay-up for breaking the changing of hands rule. When I spooned out your broth, I used the same hand three times. So now I'll have to wash my hand three times in the sea.'

'Doesn't sound so difficult,' said Kiet.

'Doing it three times on every island!' Jike piped up from the corner.

Moireen whirled around. 'Keep on with your practice!'

'Now you broke the half-circle rule!' crowed Jorika.

'Oh, damnation!' Moireen seemed more resigned

than angry. 'There's a taboo against turning round more than a half-circle at a time,' she explained to Kiet. 'I just broke it. And I broke the taboo against swearing under the roof of my family shelter.'

Kiet swallowed the last of her broth. She changed the subject before Moireen could have any more accidents.

'Where are your parents?' she asked.

'All the adults are on Innia Loss.' Innia Loss was the name of the largest island. 'Listening to your friends talk about the Residual Alliance.'

Kiet snorted. 'Why wasn't I woken up?'

'They said to let you sleep. You lost a lot of blood yesterday.'

Kiet inspected her arms and legs. The many tiny cuts inflicted by beaks and claws had healed amazingly. She swung herself down onto the sanded floor. She didn't even feel sore.

'Good stuff, that fishy paste of yours,' she remarked.

She walked across to the unwalled side of the shelter and gazed out at the morning.

The sky was a serene blue, with just a few streamers of high white cloud. The waves were large steady swells marching in towards the shore. She could see the spume blowing back from their crests before they broke, throwing up rainbows in the sunlight. The noise of their breaking was a distant boom.

Further away were the gulls. They wheeled and hovered like tiny Vs above the cliffs. They seemed peaceful enough today.

'Do you want me to show you round the islands?' Moireen offered.

Kiet shrugged. 'How? I can't walk across the ropes.'

'I'll teach you to do that first.'

'You think I can learn?'

Moireen grinned. 'If I can, anyone can.'

'Okay, then.'

Moireen turned around to the twins, taking care to rotate in two separate half-circles.

'I'll be back to test you in an hour,' she warned.

8

The trick was to start very fast. Moireen pushed from behind and Kiet sped across the rope with barely a glance at her feet. She spread out her arms for balance. It was exhilarating.

'You're a natural,' Moireen told her, between whoops of laughter.

Kiet practised for half an hour, back and forth, back and forth. A dozen times she nearly fell in – but not quite. She was in no hurry to be shown around the islands.

'Hey, Kiet!' a voice called out.

She completed her crossing before she looked up. It was Ferren. He had come out as far as the next island, with the aid of support ropes and half a dozen adult Sea-folk. Now he goggled at Kiet's new talent.

'Let's go meet him,' suggested Moireen.

The rope to Ferren's island was much longer than the rope on which Kiet had been practising, but she ran across without difficulty. Moireen followed at a walking pace.

'How did you learn to do that?' Ferren demanded.

'You can learn too,' said Kiet.

'You'll *have* to learn,' said Moireen. 'If you're staying for long on our islands.'

Even as they talked, the adult Sea-folk went off, taking the support ropes with them. When Ferren looked round, they were already on their way back towards the larger islands.

'You don't have a choice any more,' laughed Moireen.

She had such an open cheery face that it was imposs-ible not to laugh along with her. Ferren took a deep breath.

'Okay. What do I do?'

Kiet lined him up facing the rope, as Moireen had done with her. Then, without warning, she gave him a mighty push in the back.

'Keep running!' she cried.

Ferren swayed and staggered – but kept running. Almost at the end of the rope, he lost his balance, flung himself forward and just managed to lock his arms over the rock.

Kiet and Moireen cheered. By the time Ferren had pulled himself upright, they had crossed over and stood waiting for him.

'Now, back again,' said Moireen. 'Before you lose your confidence.'

Ferren grimaced. 'What confidence?'

But he tried again and then again, back and forth over the same rope. Gradually, he improved. Kiet ran back and forth behind him, while Moireen watched and shouted advice.

After a while, Moireen had to go back to Fia Mor to test the twins on their learning of rules.

'I'll catch you again later,' she announced. 'Keep practising.'

For the next half hour, Ferren and Kiet kept practising. The difficult thing was to stay balanced at a slower pace. By the end of half an hour, Ferren was as good as Kiet had been – and Kiet was even better.

They also experimented with different ropes. As they became more daring, they progressed to the outlying islands, where the ropes were particularly long and sagging. Still, neither of them had fallen in.

Then they made the fatal mistake of running onto the same rope from opposite ends.

'Go back!' cried Kiet, as they headed for a collision in the middle.

'I can't! You!'

They managed to stop short just before the collision. But now they were motionless. The rope shook and trembled under their feet.

'Don't wobble!' cried Kiet.

But the wobbles became more and more uncontrollable. With outstretched arms, they lurched and adjusted, this way and that. Ferren broke up into laughter.

'I give up!' he yelled.

He fell off backwards with a spectacular splash.

'So do I!'

Kiet fell off with an equal splash in the opposite direction.

They thrashed and kicked and hauled themselves to

dry land. They scrambled out onto Allan Kor, the furthest of all the islands. Unlike the other islands, it didn't have a flat top but rose in a high peaked sugar-loaf. Steps had been carved in its steep sloping side.

Kiet and Ferren squelched up the steps, dripping water. They were still gasping and breathless. The rock was studded with tiny grey limpets and barnacles.

The steps went over the peak and down to a hollow on the other side. The hollow was shaped like a throne and covered with crinkly reddish-brown seaweed. It faced out towards the sun and the open sea.

'Here!' cried Kiet. 'We can dry off here!'

She plumped down onto the seaweed. Bladders of air popped loudly underneath her. She collapsed in laughter all over again.

But Ferren was suddenly serious. He stood on the lip of the hollow, gazing down into the sea.

'Look at this!'

Kiet jumped up and followed the line of his pointing arm. He was pointing through the water to something on the bottom of the sea.

At first she couldn't make out what it was. Colours undulated through the swirl of the waves. Then it came clear.

It was a building, the long tiled roof of a building. The walls were half buried in silt and sand, but the roof was as perfectly preserved as any building in the City of the Dead. In the green depths of the water, its tiles were a beautiful terracotta red.

'Think of the skill!' Ferren said in a whisper. 'The craft of the original human beings!'

There was a yearning intensity in his gaze. Kiet studied him with a secret sideways glance.

'One day we'll be like that again,' he muttered. 'One day we'll bring back the Good Times.'

She raised her eyebrows. 'You really believe that?'

'Yes. Not in our lifetime. But eventually. We *will* do it. I swear we will.'

Kiet might have been inclined to scoff. But the sheer force of his belief overrode her doubts. Truly, every atom of his being was directed towards that dream. She could see it in his eyes, the set of his mouth, the angle of his chin. He wanted so much to have it happen. It was like a fire leaping right out of his body.

She remembered her very first impression of him, when he addressed the Nesters in the Bowl. The same fire, the same energy . . . A strange surge of emotion came over her.

She stood beside him for a while, then sat back down on the seaweed. She closed her eyes and let the sun sink into her, feeling warm all over. This must be *lying-by-the-sea-ish-ness*, she thought with a smile . . .

'Hah! *Here* you are! I never guessed you'd come to Allan Kor!'

It was Moireen, appearing suddenly over the top of the island. She halted on the steps, as if reluctant to descend into the hollow. She stared down at them both curiously.

'We weren't hiding,' said Kiet.

'No?' Moireen seemed to stifle a giggle. 'I suppose you don't still want me to show you round the islands?'

Kiet stood up promptly. 'Why not? I'll come.'

'I think I'll stay,' said Ferren. 'I like it here.'

9

Moireen took Kiet to see the fish-cleaning grounds on Mas Linn, covered in silvery scales. She showed her the lines of drying seaweed on Feth Dan and the basket-pots stacked up on Fain Pellor. Most spectacular of all was the reservoir on Salk Meer, where hundreds of glittering fish teemed in an enclosed pool of seawater.

'The birds once took over Salk Meer,' said Moireen. 'But we won it back again.'

They crossed from island to island on rope after rope. Moireen pointed out the driftnets strung out in channels and the fishing men with poised spears, motionless on the low-lying reefs.

'What's happening over there?' asked Kiet, pointing to one island they hadn't yet visited.

'That's the children gathering for play. The island of Renna Dair. They usually go there this time of day.'

'Can we go see?'

Moireen nodded. 'I often do anyway.'

They crossed over to Renna Dair. On one side of the island was a sheltered basin of small pebbles. The children had congregated in the basin, about fifteen of them, including Jike and Jorika.

They were playing a game with pebbles when Moireen and Kiet arrived. They stopped to congregate around Moireen, who was obviously a great favourite with them. She recited their names to Kiet: Strae, Theal, Hirl, Fiorne, Rythe and many more.

'Go on with your game,' said Kiet. 'Can we watch?'

The game was played on a flat slab of rock. The aim was to toss your pebble as near as possible to a marker stone, while trying to knock other people's pebbles out of the way. It seemed a limited repetitive sort of game to Kiet.

After watching for about fifteen minutes, she made a suggestion.

'I know another pebble game. We used to play it in my tribe. Shall I show you?'

'A *different* game?' The children were interested at once. Apparently, they didn't have many games of their own.

Kiet demonstrated. Her pebble game was much more active and exciting. Everyone had to spin around in a tight cluster. Then one person threw a pebble up in the air, so high it was impossible to guess who'd be hit when it came down. If you were hit, you had to come out of the cluster, and the winner was the last person left in.

The children were enthralled. But then they shook their heads.

'We can't play that,' said the girl called Strae. 'We'd have to break the half-circle rule.'

'And we'd have to do pay-up every time we crossed shadows,' said the boy called Theal.

'What if the pebble landed on our shadows?' added Jorika. 'Think of the bad luck then.'

Kiet pursed her lips. They were all so eager to play, yet so fearful of breaking taboos. Then she had a brainwave.

'Why don't you play at being the people of my tribe?' she suggested. 'If you play at being Nesters, then you can play at *them* playing Nesters' games.'

The children's eyes went wide with this new way of thinking.

'Then it wouldn't be *us* doing it!'

'Only the people we're pretending to be!'

'Skail couldn't blame us for that, could he?'

It didn't take them long to convince themselves. Kiet gave everyone the name of a Nester: Rhinn, Tadge, Flens, Gibby, and so on. Then the game began. Kiet started off as first pebble-thrower.

It was the wildest game ever played on the islands. The pebble could hurt when it hit, especially if it landed on the crown of your head. Half the fun was for those who'd come out of the cluster to frighten those who were still left in. They shrieked 'Look out!' and pointed to the pebble about to land on a particular skull.

They played all through the afternoon, until it was time to go off and help prepare dinner.

'That was the best game ever!' cried Strae. 'Let's play it again tomorrow!'

Kiet grinned. 'I know other different games too,' she told them.

10

Asmodai, Asmodai, Asmodai. Miriael murmured it over and over like an invocation in her mind. When would he come again?

She was too restless for sleep. She rose quietly from her sleeping-shelf and went outside. It was a clear calm night. The moon was a high white crescent shining over the wrinkled sea.

If only she knew of a way to summon him. How had he managed to find her before, in the Nesters' territory? Was it difficult for him to slip away from Heaven without being noticed?

She walked down to the water's edge. Small waves hissed and plashed in the fissures of rock. She sat on the rock and prayed for him to come.

Time passed. Then an oval of light appeared above the horizon. Had her prayers been answered?

Closer and closer the oval came. It was – it was Asmodai! So beautiful! A glittering pathway spread across the sea, stretching from him to her. Her heart pounded painfully in her chest.

His slow approach gave her eyes time to adjust. Around the oval of his globe, rays of sheer white light shot out into the darkness like the points of a star. His sandaled feet hovered above the water, his purple robe billowed like a curtain in a wind.

Finally, he came to a halt in front of her. He wore the same silver circlet on his brow, carried the same tubular wand in his right hand.

'Greetings, Miriael,' he said.

'And to you, Seraph Asmodai.' Her heart pounded painfully in her chest.

'I have returned as I promised. Do you want to hear about the progress of your cause in Heaven?'

'Please.'

'You remember that I was going to talk to other angels and try to win them over? Well, Berial and Meresin are now fully on your side. Berial, the Sixth Angel of Strategy and Meresin, the Fourth Angel of Messages.'

Miriael knew Berial and Meresin only by name. But the mere sound of their names was like music to her ears.

'They also had a suggestion about the next step,' Asmodai went on. 'They suggested an approach to Anaitis.'

'Anaitis? The Archon Anaitis?'

'Yes. I think it's an excellent suggestion.'

'She's very important, isn't she?'

'One of the greatest of Dominions. She doesn't use her power often, but she's highly respected. Even Uriel respects her.'

'Wasn't she the one who pleaded for the return of the Fallen Angels?'

'Yes. When Samael and his followers begged for forgiveness, she spoke up for them in Heaven.'

'So she could do the same for me?'

'Exactly. Berial and Meresin were two of the Fallen Angels she spoke up for. That's why they can sympathise with your case. I went to them deliberately. They know how it feels to lose Heaven's favour.'

'They're back in favour now, though?'

'Yes. Many have even been restored to their old positions. Like Samael himself, who used to be be called Satan. All of the Fallen Angels were allowed to return after the Great Collapse.'

There was a long silence. Miriael gazed and gazed at him, drowning in a dream. His noble face was like a pure pale flame.

'Did you tell Heaven about the importance of the Residuals?' she asked at last. 'About how they're used as raw materials for the Hypers and Plasmatics?'

Asmodai spread his hands in a resigned gesture. 'The information was recorded in the archives for future reference. No change in present strategies.'

'Oh. I don't suppose they'd be interested in my latest news, then.'

'*I* am. Tell me.'

So Miriael told him about the Humen army marching towards the Bankstown Complex. She described the giant Doctor and the mysterious machines and weapons she'd seen. She was gratified to have his attention entirely concentrated upon her.

'It's a whole new threat,' she concluded. 'Heaven ought to act immediately.'

'*Ought* to.' Asmodai nodded slowly. 'I think I should go and take a look for myself.'

Miriael's eyes widened. 'The Bankstown Complex? You can't go there! They'll destroy you!'

'I can observe from nearby. If there are so many machines and as big as you say, I doubt they'll all fit inside the actual Complex.'

He began to glide backwards. Was he leaving her already? Miriael uttered a cry of disappointment.

He stopped and waited for her to speak.

'Don't go yet,' she said. 'Stay and talk to me for a while.'

'What about?'

'About anything. About Heaven. Tell me what work you do in Heaven.'

'My place is with the other nine Angels of Strategy. We take our orders from Anael.'

'Anael, the chief of Principalities?'

'And also a great archistratege. He gives us our orders in the Green Pavilion on the Sixth Altitude.'

'So high! Up there with the Supreme War Council! You must see the topmost branches of the Tree of Life!'

'Yes, the Green Pavilion is shaded by one of the branches. But I'm not there most of the time. More often, I'm journeying through the lower Altitudes, organising supplies and equipment for the Battalions of the South.'

'Do you ever visit the Thirty-first Battalion?'

'Of course.'

'The Fifteenth Company of the Thirty-first Battalion?'

Asmodai smiled. 'Your old company? Yes, I know something about them.'

'What? What's been happening?'

For the next thirty minutes, she bombarded him with question after question. She learned that the Fifteenth Company was currently on sentinel duty, guarding the Gate of the Medallion. The previous commander, Tophiel, had been transferred and promoted, becoming Warden of the Twenty-fourth Heavenly Hall. Now the angel Mendrion was in command. Miriael drank it all in like sweet intoxicating wine.

She could have stayed listening forever. Just to hear him speak of her old comrades brought back glorious memories and associations. But, in the end, he could delay no longer.

'I must return to Heaven before I'm missed,' he said. 'It's already too late for me to take a look at the Bankstown Complex.'

'I'm sorry. I couldn't help . . .'

'I understand. I shall go there another time.'

'And visit me another time too.'

'Yes. Hopefully with good news about Anaitis.'

'You're wonderful. You're doing so much for me.'

'No more than you deserve.'

'I don't deserve anything.'

He gripped his wand in both hands. The tube lit up with a white incandescence.

'Of course you do. You mustn't think like that. What wrong act have you committed? It's mere justice.

Heaven should never have cut you off.'

Miriael felt like crying. She controlled the feeling that threatened to overwhelm her.

He raised his voice. 'If the Fallen Angels can be forgiven, how can you be punished? You haven't rebelled, you haven't shown pride. Heaven doesn't have the right to deny you a reconciliation!'

He seemed very fierce, almost angry, on her behalf. She could see the light rushing and spreading through his limbs. The very veins glowed under his skin.

'I believe in you, and you must believe in me,' he added in a gentler tone. 'Farewell for now, Miriael.'

His departure was a mirror image of his arrival. The oval of his globe moved backwards over the water, dwindling into the distance. The same glittering path stretched almost as far as the horizon.

Only at the very end did he suddenly shoot up in a bright vertical line towards Heaven.

11

'I'm working on something very important.'

'You?'

'Yes, me.'

'What?'

'A new idea. I don't know why you never thought of it yourself.'

Kiet and Ferren were leaning back comfortably in the throne-shaped hollow at the top of Allan Kor. It was another warm day, with hardly a breath of wind. The air was heavy with the tang of ozone.

Kiet explained her idea. 'You know when you were trying to persuade the Guardians? And I organised all the younger members of our tribe to come and hear you speak? And we were the ones who followed you into the City of the Dead? We were the ones who helped change the decision?'

Ferren nodded.

'Well, I'm aiming to do the same with the younger members of this tribe.'

'You want me to speak to them?'

'No. Not yet, anyway. First I want them to overcome their fear of breaking taboos. I've made a start already.'

'How?'

'By getting them to play different games. I realised it yesterday. They're still only learning the system of rules, so their minds are more open and flexible. They're not so completely weighed down as the adults.'

'The adults are weighed down, for sure.' Ferren shrugged. 'But does it matter? They're still willing to join the Residual Alliance.'

'That's not the point. This is much bigger. Don't you see?'

She turned towards him impulsively, impatiently. Bladders of seaweed popped beneath her. Ferren shook his head.

'No, I don't.'

'Look there!' She stabbed a finger in the direction of the drowned building, the red rooftop under the water. 'Isn't that your dream? That one day we can be like the old human beings again?'

'So?'

'So it's not going to come true just because of the Residual Alliance. We can't recover those skills and crafts just by joining tribes together. It needs a total new way of thinking.'

'Mmm.' Now Ferren was beginning to understand. 'And you believe –'

'That only the young can do it! Like you and me and the children! If you want a new kind of society, a new race of human beings – it's only fresh minds that can do it!'

She was carried away with enthusiasm. Ferren sat up straight and gazed down at the rooftop under the water.

'Maybe you're right,' he said.

'Of course I'm right. Think about it. It's *always* the young.'

Ferren thought about it. He remembered his own tribe, the People, when he and Miriael had finally won them over. Yes, it was the young who had been quickest to turn against the Humen, quickest to adopt Miriael's instructions for building a defensive shelter. And in other tribes too, there had been many small occasions . . .

He whistled. 'Why did I never think of that?'

'You're not the only one with ideas.' Kiet's grin spread from ear to ear. 'Who was it drove off the birds by whipping them with seaweed?'

'You saved my life that time,' Ferren admitted.

'A mere nothing.' She blew an imaginary speck of dust from her hand. 'Now I'm going to save the universe.'

12

Kiet continued to work on her idea over the next three days. Every afternoon she met up with the young Sea-folk, usually accompanied by Moireen. Every afternoon, she had another new game for them, which could be played by taking on the names of the Nesters. Little by little, the young Sea-folk were getting used to not thinking about taboos.

Meanwhile, the weather changed. Now the skies were constantly overcast and bitter winds blew in from the sea. The rocks were pounded by towering waves and salt spray cut horizontally through the air. When the island of Renna Dair became too cold and wet, the afternoon gatherings shifted to Fain Pellor. The young Sea-folk rearranged the stacks of basket-pots to create a small sheltered space for themselves.

Kiet had to teach games that could be played without much running around. They played at Bird and Hook, then Turn Over Ten, then King of the Valley. The new games were just as popular as the Pebble Game.

They were playing King of the Valley when two

unwelcome visitors appeared round the side of the basket-pots.

'Well, hello,' said Skail.

Kiet had already heard a great deal about Skail, though she'd never yet met him close up. Though only nineteen, he was said to be incredibly clever. He was an expert on taboos, almost as knowledgeable as the Mothers themselves. His henchman, Lorbie, went with him everywhere.

Now the two of them stepped forward into the middle of the game.

'What are you playing?' asked Skail.

His movements were sharp and birdlike, almost flickering. He had a puckered, tightly drawn kind of face, dominated by the wide smooth curve of his forehead. He looked far older than his age.

By contrast, Lorbie looked far younger than his age. He was big and brawny, with massive biceps, but his face suggested an innocent simplicity. He had small blue eyes and a sagging lower lip.

The children formed up side by side as if for inspection. They were obviously accustomed to Skail's authority.

'We're playing at King of the Valley.'

'We're pretending to be the Nesters.'

'Nesters?' Skail was like an inquisitor. 'What are Nesters?'

'The people of her tribe.' Fiorne pointed to Kiet. 'I'm Rhinn.'

The other children gave their pretend-names too. But they weren't eager to describe the actual game of King of the Valley, in which it was necessary to do the same action repeatedly with the same hand. Kiet wondered if Skail would ask.

He didn't. Instead he swung around to Kiet.

'You're teaching them games from your own tribe, are you?'

Kiet met his gaze without flinching. 'Yes.'

'They're Sea-folk, not Nesters.' He put a scornful emphasis on the word *Nesters*.

'It's only a game,' said Kiet.

There was a long pause. Lorbie looked towards Skail for instructions.

'Good,' said Skail at last. 'Make sure it *is* only a game. Though I'd have thought you were a bit old for playing games with children.' He turned to include Moireen in his comments. 'And you too, you clumsy clodhopper.'

Moireen didn't reply, but a flush spread over her suntanned cheeks. Kiet was about to reply on her behalf, but Moireen signalled *no* with a tiny shake of her head.

Skail observed the signal. His mouth crinkled into a sneer. He redirected the sneer towards Kiet.

'You should stick to playing games with your boy-friend,' he said. 'That's more your sort of game.'

Kiet was momentarily speechless. Then she recovered her voice.

'What do you mean, *boyfriend*?'

'You know.'

'No, I don't.'

'You and that Ferren.' Skail raised his fingers in an obscene gesture. 'Making it on Allan Kor.'

He smiled maliciously. Then he whirled around and marched off. Lorbie followed at his heels like a big dog.

Kiet strode after them with clenched fists. She was ready to explode. But a hand clutched at her shoulder – Moireen's hand.

'Don't! Please don't!'

Kiet allowed herself to be brought to a halt. Moireen's concern was so obviously genuine.

'I'm not scared of him,' Kiet snapped. 'Or his bully henchman.'

'It's not just getting beaten up,' Moireen explained. 'Skail can make trouble in many ways.'

'Bad trouble,' echoed the boy called Hirl.

'You mustn't mess with him,' pleaded Jike.

'Promise you won't,' said Strae.

Kiet hated to back down. But Moireen whispered a warning in her ear.

'The children won't play if you don't promise. They're too afraid of Skail.' She paused for a moment, before adding 'So am I.'

Kiet sucked at her lips. She was making such good progress with the young Sea-folk – she couldn't throw it away.

'Okay, I promise. No messing with Skail. But he's a dirty-minded bastard. Ferren isn't my boyfriend.'

She looked around from face to face. The young Sea-folk were tittering behind their hands.

'It's all right,' said Theal.

'We're happy for you,' said Jorika.

They all think exactly the same as Skail, Kiet realised. She tried to stay calm.

'Why would anyone think that?' she demanded.

'It's why men and women go up on Allan Kor,' said Moireen, with embarrassment.

'*What*?'

'It's where you go for making it.'

'Well, I'm *not* making it with Ferren. Okay? You have to believe me. *Okay*?'

The children nodded willingly enough. But Kiet had the impression they still didn't believe.

13

Making it – what a stupid expression! And Ferren as her *boyfriend* – ridiculous! Kiet kept going over and over it in her mind.

Of course, the Sea-folk couldn't understand, any more than the Nesters. Her relationship with Ferren was something special, something unique. But in what way unique?

She had to admit, things had changed in the last two or three days. Up on Allan Kor, as the weather grew colder, they'd tended to huddle closer and closer together. Not just sitting side by side, but pressing arm against arm. It had seemed the natural way to keep warm, with the wind blustering around them. And yes, she had to admit she'd quite enjoyed it.

But that didn't mean she wanted to mate with him. She had no desire to rub oil into his chest and shoulders. If the ritual of First Intimacies was a necessary stage between a man and a woman . . .

But what if it wasn't? Perhaps there was no such thing as First Intimacies among the Sea-folk? What did they do when they went up on Allan Kor? Perhaps they just lay together in the hollow until – until –

The thought made her go hot and cold. Surely it was only by accident that she and Ferren had gone up there? Wasn't it?

Suddenly, everything appeared in a different light. She thought back over the way the Sea-folk spoke to her, adults as well as children. Half-smiles and significant glances. They all thought she was making it with Ferren!

She hated to have them thinking like that! She would never meet Ferren on Allan Kor again!

Next morning, she stayed in her sleeping-shelf behind the curtain of seaweed. If Ferren was waiting for her up in the hollow, let him wait.

She heard Moireen's parents go off to their daily tasks. Then she heard Moireen practising the twins on yet another set of rules. Finally, Moireen herself went off, leaving the twins to continue their practice.

'*If the word is said as the thing is cooked, that is taboo.*

If things are cooked in fives or sevens, that is taboo.'

The sing-song chant ran on and on. Then stopped when someone came into the shelter. Kiet recognised him instantly by his footsteps.

Jike and Jorika were supposed to say she was in her sleeping-shelf and not to be woken. Instead, they told him she was in her sleeping-shelf – and it was time for her to get up. Kiet could swear she heard a giggle in their voices. They wanted him to find her in bed.

She swung round, parted the curtain and jumped

down to the floor. Ferren halted in surprise, two paces away.

She stared at his familiar black hair and dark eyes. Why did he seem so different today? Of course there was no difference!

'I missed you,' he said. 'I was there in the usual place.'

She was conscious of how close they were standing. Why didn't he back away? Were the twins watching?

'I didn't want to sit in the usual place today.' She stressed the word *sit* for the benefit of the twins.

'No?' Ferren shrugged. 'Okay, here then?'

Before she could reply, he had lowered himself to the floor. Kiet had no choice but to do the same. She made sure there was plenty of clear space between them.

Ferren dropped his voice to a whisper. 'How's your idea with the young Sea-folk going?'

'Don't whisper.'

Ferren looked across at Jike and Jorika. 'You don't mind if they hear?'

'Yes. No. Yes.'

Kiet was in agony. She was monitoring the twins out of the corner of her eye. They had temporarily stopped chanting.

'Get back to your practice!' she snapped.

They smirked and started up the chant again.

'Are you ready for me to speak to them yet?' asked Ferren, again in a whisper.

'No.' She wished he wouldn't lean towards her as he spoke. 'We're still playing games.'

'Hmm. But I could come along anyway, couldn't I? I could join in the games?'

'Why?'

'Why not?'

Kiet knew a very good reason why not. If he was there, the children would be watching what they did together. Watching and thinking things. But that wasn't a reason she could explain to Ferren.

'Let me join in. I'll be just another person playing.'

Kiet struggled to produce an excuse. 'The children won't like it,' she said.

'Yes, we will!' cried Jike and Jorika simultaneously.

Even while chanting, they had managed to overhear. Kiet glowered at them. But Ferren laughed and snapped his fingers.

'There you are!' He appealed to the twins. 'Will anyone mind me coming along?'

'No! No! No-one will mind!'

'So?' Ferren turned back to Kiet with a grin. 'Please?'

Her mind was empty of further excuses. What else could she do?

'Okay,' she said grimly. 'This afternoon. On Fain Pellor.'

14

The game they played was a version of Walk the Melon. Since there were no melons, Kiet made up two round bundles of clothing, tightly bound with strands of seaweed. The players had to pass the bundle from person to person, using only their knees.

It was a comical ungainly business – trying to get a grip on the bundle, shuffling round to face the next person, lodging the bundle between someone else's knees. They had many practices before Kiet decided they were ready to play.

She didn't bother to give out new Nester names for the game. The children kept the same names as in previous games. They'd played so often at being Rhinn, Flens, Bross or whoever, they hardly even thought about it any more.

She divided everyone into two teams. But with Ferren now included, the numbers were uneven.

'I'll stay out and act as judge,' she said.

Immediately there were howls of protest. 'No, no! We want you in!'

'I'm as clumsy as two people on my own,' laughed Moireen. 'The other side needs an extra person to balance.'

So Kiet found herself joining the same team as Ferren. Even worse, she ended up right beside him in the line. The children somehow rearranged themselves and made a space for her before she had time to realise what was happening.

At last the game began. Each team had to pass the bundle all the way down the line and back again. If a team dropped the bundle, they had to start over. There were hoots and cheers and squeals of laughter, there were bumpings and stumblings and knockings of knees. Moireen was almost helpless from laughing so much. With her lack of coordination, the teams were indeed very evenly matched.

Ferren was as wild and excited as anyone. He seized Kiet by the shoulders, holding her steady as their knees met.

'Ready! Now! Now!'

Kiet gritted her teeth. She was sure she could hear a different kind of laughter every time the bundle passed between her and Ferren. Less like squealing and more like tittering . . .

At first it was to be a best-of-three series. Then best-of-three turned into best-of-five, and finally best-of-nine. The contest went all the way though to the ninth game, with both teams level on four victories each.

The cheering and yelling rose to fever pitch. When Kiet had to pass the bundle to Ferren, he wrapped an arm around her waist. She stiffened as he pulled her towards him.

'Okay! Relax! Let go!'

She wanted to shout at him: *Take your arm off me*! But she managed to pass the bundle successfully. She stood breathing heavily as the bundle continued down the line.

Ferren seemed unaware. He cheered for their team, jeered the opposing team. Kiet could feel a bright red flush on her cheeks.

The bundle reached the end of the line and began its return journey. Their team was in the lead. Kiet was rigid with tension.

All around were voices shouting 'Go! Go! Go! Go!'

Ferren swung to her with the bundle gripped between his knees. She couldn't look at him. He took hold of her with both arms around her waist.

'Get ready! Take it now!'

It was like an urgent love-embrace. It was as though they were –

Savagely, she pushed his arms away. She drove at him and broke his hold. He staggered and the bundle fell to the ground.

A whoop of jubilation went up from the opposing team.

'We've won! We've won! We've won!' they cried, as their bundle progressed along to the start of the line. 'Hurrahhhh!' They flung up their arms in triumph.

Kiet hardly noticed. She was glaring at Ferren, who glared right back at her.

'Why did you do that?' he demanded. 'That was your fault!'

'Shut up!' she hissed furiously. 'Stop drawing attention!'

'What's wrong with you?'

While the opposing team continued their victory celebrations, the children in Ferren and Kiet's team clustered around, giggling behind their hands.

'I don't want you touching me!' snapped Kiet.

'This is stupid.'

'*You're* stupid! Get away from me!'

But the children wouldn't let Ferren and Kiet move apart. They clustered closer and closer, all shouting at the same time.

'We'll have another series!'

'Same teams!'

'Don't be angry with each other!'

'Kiss and be friends!'

Kiet drew a deep breath. She was ready to explode. But a cold, quiet voice cut in first.

'Well, well, well. I've got you now, haven't I?'

Everyone whirled and stared. Skail had appeared around the stacks of basket-pots.

He came forward with Lorbie at his heels. The children stood thunderstruck, frozen in position. Skail had a small pinched smile on his lips.

'You've been hiding and spying,' Kiet accused.

Skail paid no attention. He held up the fingers of one hand.

'Let's see. In the last five minutes, what taboos have you broken? First, the half-circle rule. Second, the changing-of-hands rule. Third, the double-contact rule. Fourth, the high-over-low rule.' As he counted each rule, he folded a finger. 'All deliberately broken many times over.'

The children looked down at their feet. But not Kiet. She was still simmering. She transferred her anger from Ferren to Skail.

'What gives you the right to decide?' she demanded.

Skail screwed up his face derisively. 'Stay out of it. This is nothing to do with you. Or your boyfriend.'

On the word *boyfriend*, Kiet exploded.

'You scum! You slime! You dirty little worm!'

She strode towards him in a fury. Her eyes were blazing, her hands were raised to strike.

Skail took one look and skipped back behind the massive figure of Lorbie.

'Come out, worm!'

Lorbie held up his arms to bar her way.

'Lorbie will see to you!' Skail directed his henchman from behind. 'Smack her one, Lorbie!'

But Lorbie only stood with arms extended. Kiet turned on him. She brought her face up very close to his face. Her lips were drawn back from her teeth, her whole body was pumped up with aggression.

'Step aside, Lorbie,' she snarled.

Lorbie blinked his small blue eyes. In size, he towered over Kiet. But she towered over him in ferocity. He lowered his arms and stepped aside.

Skail flicked desperate glances this way and that, looking for help, looking for escape. His face had gone a sickly shade of white.

He tried to backpedal. Kiet came after him. He cringed and lifted an arm in self-defence.

She was about to hit him – but she didn't. He wasn't worth hitting. His cowardice was plain for everyone to see. Instead, she drew back her head and spat full in his face.

He stood there as if transfixed. Strings of spittle ran down over his high wide forehead.

'Wipe it off, worm,' she said.

Skail did as he was told. But there was a vicious look in his eyes. He realised now that she wasn't going to strike.

'You'll pay for this,' he muttered.

Kiet merely curled her lip. Skail pulled on Lorbie's arm until the big simpleton turned to follow him. They retreated out past the stacks of basket-pots.

'You'll pay,' Skail repeated in a louder voice. 'Oh, yes, you'll pay.'

15

Skail launched his revenge on the following day. The Mothers summoned Kiet, Ferren, Miriael and the entire tribe of the Sea-folk to an assembly on Innia Loss.

The wind had dropped overnight, bringing a change in the weather. A soft sea-fog billowed across the islands, covering every surface with a film of moisture. Sounds travelled strangely in the thick heavy air, now loud and close, now faint and faraway. The sun showed through as a small orange ball.

The three Mothers squatted in their usual positions beside the fire. The adult Sea-folk were gathered in a circle around the outspread net. The accused stood to the right of the Mothers: Kiet, Ferren, Miriael and all the young Sea-folk. Skail, the accuser, stood on the left.

Gweir turned to him. 'Begin.'

Skail addressed himself to the young Sea-folk. 'Do you deny that you repeatedly and deliberately broke four major taboos?' He counted off the four taboos on his fingers, just as he had done yesterday.

The children tried to explain.

'It wasn't us,' said Hirl. 'We were being other people.'

'We were playing at Nesters,' said Strae.

'Doing the things that Nesters do,' said Rythe.

'We kept the same names from the day before,' said Jorika.

Skail pounced. 'The day before? How long has this been going on?'

Jorika hung her head. 'Six days.'

'Six days!' Skail swivelled dramatically to face the Mothers. 'Breaking taboos every day for six days!'

'Yes,' said Moireen. 'But it didn't count.'

'Oh, it *counts*.' Skail's tone was absolute and final. 'Who told you it didn't count? She did, didn't she?'

His pointing finger shot out like an arrow. All eyes turned towards Kiet.

'*She* did. And *he* supported her.' The finger swung towards Ferren. 'Our guests. The ones who received our hospitality.'

The Mothers looked troubled.

'Hospitality was the least we owed them,' said Lorne. 'After they fought off the birds for us.'

'Yes, they fought off the birds for us.' Skail smiled, as though he'd been waiting for someone to say this. 'But how did they do it? They did it by breaking the changing of hands rule! We should have suspected them from the beginning!'

'They're not Sea-folk,' objected Krye. 'Their luck doesn't have to have the same taboos as ours.'

'No. But what I want to know is – do they have *any* taboos? Do they have *any* luck?'

Gweir looked very severe. 'Well? Is this true?'

Ferren shrugged. 'Not compared to you, no. My tribe doesn't think in terms of taboos.'

'Nor mine,' said Kiet.

'Nor most of the tribes in the Residual Alliance,' added Miriael. 'Each tribe has its own system of beliefs, but not like yours.'

Skail was almost capering with triumph. 'You see? You see? They came here without their own luck in order to spoil our luck! They've as good as admitted it!'

'We came here to ask you to join the Residual Alliance,' said Ferren firmly.

'Oh yes, your wonderful Residual Alliance.' Skail's lips twisted contemptuously. 'All your tribes that don't have any luck. Why would we want to be allies with you?'

'At least we don't get chased around by *birds*!' snapped Kiet.

There were grunts of disapproval from the adult Sea-folk. Some of them began fingering the objects on their necklaces.

'You have tried to undermine our beliefs!' Skail accused. 'You have tried to corrupt our children!'

'You mean, take them out of *your* control!' Kiet flashed back. 'That's all that matters to you! Taboos give you the power to manipulate people!'

'Disbelievers! Disbelievers!'

She looked at him sharply. 'And you? How much do you really believe?'

A venomous look slid across Skail's eyes. Kiet felt sure that she'd hit home.

'Think about it.' She continued to address Skail,

though she spoke for the whole tribe to hear. 'You say we've been breaking taboos for six days. So why didn't you notice? What effect has it had? Has anything bad happened in the last six days?'

The Sea-folk frowned and scratched their heads. They were obviously trying to think of something bad that had happened. The Mothers whispered among themselves. They seemed to be having a difference of opinion.

Kiet, Ferren and Miriael waited for the verdict. But it was never delivered. Instead, there was a sudden shout from the other end of the island.

'Look!'

Heads turned to face in the opposite direction. The Sea-folk at the other end of the island stared through the fog towards the promontory.

'I see him too!'

'It can't be!'

'He's coming towards us!'

The Mothers raised their eyes. 'Who do you see?'

The answer produced a communal shiver of dread.

'A Selector! It's a Selector!'

16

The Sea-folk eddied this way and that. Some wanted to look for themselves, others wanted to stay as far away as possible. Kiet, Ferren and Miriael exchanged glances.

'We mustn't be seen,' said Miriael. 'Where can we hide?'

Ferren pointed to one of the shelters that were built around the edge of Innia Loss. They hurried across and plunged in through the doorway. In the general confusion, their departure was scarcely noticed. They stood just inside the doorway, peeping out.

They didn't have long to wait. The crowd of Sea-folk parted and fell away as a tall black figure appeared at the other end of the island. His rubbery suit was wet and dripping. Clearly he hadn't walked along the top of the ropes, but had hauled himself through the water. He carried a cone-shaped weapon with a horn-like nozzle.

A hideous face was painted on the black rubber covering his head: white eyebrows around the eyeslits, red lips around the mouthslit. He wore steel-capped boots and a spiked collar like a dog. His chest was decorated with a vertical row of tiny angels – five accredited 'kills'.

He strode towards the Mothers. The Sea-folk were cowed, but their faces were closed and hostile. They muttered as he tramped straight across the outspread net.

'Remember me?' He addressed the Mothers in a harsh jeering voice. 'Cos I remember you.'

The Mothers drew themselves up very stiff and straight.

'We thought you'd stopped coming,' said Lorne. 'You weren't here at the usual time of year.'

The Selector laughed nastily, a dry humorless sound. 'Missed me, did you? Don't worry. The Humen don't abandon their allies.'

'There were always two of you before,' said Krye. 'Why are you on your own?'

'None of your business. Because we're in a hurry. We're preparing a great offensive against Heaven.' He cradled his weapon in one hand, casually, menacingly. 'Enough of these questions. I've come to select three members of your tribe for military service.'

There were shocked gasps all around.

'It's always been one,' protested Gweir.

'Yeah, and now it's three.'

'But we can't – we're not ready.'

'*I* say you're ready. *This* says you're ready.' He patted the barrel of his weapon.

'This isn't an alliance!' A young voice piped up out of the crowd. 'This is bullying!'

The Selector's gleaming eyeslits rotated in the direction

of the voice. But he couldn't locate the speaker.

'What do you know about alliances?' he sneered. 'This is the only alliance you're going to get. There's no other choice for you dummies.'

'Yes, there is!' Another young voice from another direction. 'The Residual Alliance!'

The Selector whirled around in frustration. He zeroed in on Skail, who stood at the front of the crowd.

'You're a smart one, are you?'

Skail gaped. 'Me?'

'That's good. I like smart ones.'

'I didn't say anything. You've got the wrong person.'

The Selector snarled. Suddenly he directed the nozzle of his weapon towards the net on the ground. As he squeezed the trigger, a brief jet of foam shot forth and burst into flame. The ground erupted into licking yellow tongues of fire.

The Sea-folk backed away, covering their eyes. When the fire went out, a metre-wide patch of net had disappeared. Intricate knots and strands were reduced to ash.

The three Mothers cried out in horror.

'What have you done?'

'That's our whole system of luck in that net!'

'You'll bring terrible bad luck onto us!'

The Selector laughed his rasping laugh. 'Yeah, I know. And there's more to come, if you don't shut your traps. Now let's get on with the selection.' He scanned the crowd, zeroed in on Skail again. 'You can be the first of the three. Come here.'

Skail went white. His small pinched mouth opened and closed, opened and closed.

The Selector stepped forward and seized him by the scruff of the neck. Skail flailed with his arms and legs – in vain. The Selector carried him through the air and flung him to the ground.

Skail wriggled around, sat up and pleaded. 'You can't –'

The Selector dealt him a steel-capped kick in the ribs. Skail went sprawling on his face. The Selector rested a boot on the small of his back.

'Can and have.'

Skail struggled to raise his face from the ground. He caught sight of Lorbie, his heavily-built henchman.

'Lorbie! Help me!'

Lorbie looked uncertain. The Selector swung his weapon warningly.

'Anyone makes a move and I'll flame the whole net.'

'Don't listen to him!'

'*Don't listen to him*!' Mockingly, the Selector imitated Skail's appeal. 'I know what this tribe believes. I know how precious your net is. You can soon breed and replace three people selected for military service. But you can't replace your net and you can't replace your luck. Isn't that right? How much bad luck you want?'

Skail was desperate. 'There's no such thing as luck! Lorbie, do something!'

A crease appeared on Lorbie's forehead. 'But I thought –'

'It's all in your minds! Don't worry about the net!'

Lorbie wasn't the only one puzzled. A ripple of amazement ran around the circle of Sea-folk.

'Taboos don't matter!' Skail screamed hysterically.

'Forget about our system! I've never believed in it! Plea–*uggh*!'

His voice was extinguished as the butt of the Selector's weapon came down against the back of his skull. He lapsed into unconsciousness.

'Amazing what cowardice will make people say,' the Selector sneered. 'Now, where were we? Another two for military service.'

Ferren, Kiet and Miriael watched as the Selector continued his selecting. He marched across the net and stood in the middle of the circle. The Sea-folk shrank back as he examined them one by one. They fingered the objects on their necklaces and tried to become invisible.

The Selector seemed to savour their fear. His first choice was a young woman called Koir. He ordered her to go and stand beside Skail.

Ferren turned and whispered to Kiet and Miriael. 'We'll have to do something.'

Kiet nodded. 'How can we take him by surprise?'

'We can't.' Miriael's face was very grim. 'Not before he has time to use his weapon.'

'Wait! Look!' Kiet pointed. 'What are the children doing?'

Ferren and Miriael looked. The children had slipped around the back of the crowd to gather on the far side of the net. Moireen was whispering rapidly into Lorbie's ear.

'They must have a plan!' Ferren exclaimed.

Even as they watched, the Selector selected his final victim – an adult male called Gillen. But before Gillen could move, the children stepped forward instead. All in a line, they stood at the edge of the outspread net.

'I'm Rhinn,' said Strae.

'I'm Tadge,' said Jike.

'I'm Flens,' said Theal.

The Selector stared at them. Metal teeth glittered in his mouthslit.

'What are you playing at?' he snarled.

'We're playing a game called Trap the Enemy,' said Moireen.

'You're in it too,' said Jorika.

'*Play*!' ordered Moireen.

On the word *play,* the children bent and seized hold of the net. The Selector aimed the nozzle of his weapon in their direction. They tugged, he fired.

The nozzle swung upwards as the net snagged his feet. The jet of foam shot high in the sky, flaming harmlessly overhead. Jerked off balance, the Selector went over on his back. His weapon clattered to the ground a metre away.

The children rushed forward with the edge of the net in their hands. Swooping over the Selector, they flung it on top of him. They pulled this way and that until his limbs were completely entangled in the strands. The more he tried to struggle, the more he tied himself up.

Then Lorbie approached, with Moireen at his side. He bore a massive lump of rock in his arms. His cheeks were puffed, his muscles bulging.

'Hard!' urged Moireen. 'Hard as you can!'

Lorbie took up position beside the helpless Selector. He raised the rock on high, then hurled it down with all of his might. It smashed through the Selector's chest with a strange crunching sound.

A cheer of triumph came from the children. After a moment, the adults joined in. So did Ferren, Kiet and Miriael.

'They've done it! They've done it' shouted Kiet.

17

The Sea-folk clustered around the motionless figure on the ground. They were pointing in amazement. Miriael, Ferren and Kiet pushed forward to the front of the crowd.

The Selector lay on his back trussed up in the net. His black rubbery suit had split wide open. The massive lump of rock was implanted in his chest and deep zigzag cracks radiated across his torso. From the cracks leaked thin wisps of a shimmering vapour.

'Is he dead?' Ferren asked Miriael.

She shook her head. 'Not yet, I think. But it's only the net holding him together.'

'What's that stuff coming out of him?' Kiet demanded.

The shimmering vapour expanded in the air and opened out into strange colours and shapes. They were no more than momentary glimpses, flickering in and out of existence. But they looked like a million visual images.

A ring of expectant faces turned to Miriael. The Sea-folk were also waiting for an explanation.

'A Hyper like this is an artificial simulacrum,' she

began. 'Not a real human being, not even a living organism. Hypers are moulded out of inanimate material, the same all the way through. They get their life by injections of psychic deposits from real human beings.'

Kiet gulped. 'Like us?'

Miriael pointed to Ferren. 'Remember what he saw? Remember what he told you?'

Ferren grimaced. 'There's a plug in their foreheads where the psychic deposits are injected. I saw the Doctors doing it in the Humen Camp. And I saw the psychic deposits being extracted from people like us. Stealing our memories and experiences.'

'Stealing your lives so that things like this can be animated.' Miriael pointed towards the leaking vapour. 'What you see here is the volatilising of psychic deposits. Psychic deposits escaping, dispersing, released into images . . .'

She broke off as a long low guttural sound came from the Selector's throat. There was a brightening glow in his eyeslits, an iridescent bubble in his mouthslit.

Miriael took a quick step backwards, drawing Ferren with her.

'We need to interrogate him,' she whispered.

'Why?'

'About this great offensive against Heaven that he mentioned. We need to know the details.'

'Why me?'

'If he sees an angel, he'll clam up. He won't think so much about revealing information to Residuals.'

The Sea-folk had now retreated a little further away

from the Selector. Miriael took another backward step. Ferren nodded and returned to the front of the crowd.

The Selector was staring upwards out of his eyeslits. He seemed unable to turn his head to the side. Ferren leaned forward into his field of vision.

The guttural sound became a growl, the growl became a question. 'Who are you, you stupid sucker?'

'Me? I'm not stupid enough to get rolled up in a net. I'm not the sucker with my chest caved in.'

'You're the suckers we use for fuel.'

'Yeah, and there's your fuel leaking away right now.' Ferren pointed to the wisps of vapour. 'What's this great offensive you were talking about?'

A harsh spitting sound that might have been a laugh. 'As if I'd tell you.'

Ferren changed tack. 'Okay, don't. The Residual Alliance isn't scared of anything you can do.'

'You'll be scared of Doctor Saniette.'

'Him?' Ferren thought fast. 'The big Doctor? I've seen him. He's nothing much.'

'*Everyone* is scared of Doctor Saniette.' The Selector sounded more than a little scared himself. 'He's a superbrain. There's never been a Doctor like him in the history of the Millennial War.'

Ferren sniffed loudly. 'You had ten Doctors before, and they all got wiped out. What's one Doctor going to do?'

'What's he going to do? He's going to become the worldwide Humen leader. He's already in control of this continent.'

The more he boasted, the less Ferren pretended to

believe. 'Big deal. How many Humen are left in Australia since the Bankstown army was destroyed?'

Again the Selector rose to the bait. 'Dummy! Our army now is bigger and better than the old Bankstown army ever was. The Doctor has been working secretly in his laboratories at the North-West Basin. We've got the most advanced warriors and weapons ever developed. Queen-Hypers, Cipherdogs, Septo-sprays. Our attack on Heaven will be the greatest offensive ever launched.'

'Huh! I'll believe it when I see it.'

'You'll see it sooner than you think.'

'When? In a hundred years?'

'Sooner.'

'Yeah? Ten years? A year?'

'Fifteen days, dummy.'

'Fifteen days?' Ferren caught his breath. 'That's impossible!'

The Selector was triumphant. 'See? Didn't know as much as you thought you did!'

'No.' Ferren became very quiet and thoughtful. 'But I do now.'

The Selector realised that he'd said more than he'd intended. He glared at Ferren.

'Who *are* you?' he demanded. 'Why aren't you dressed like the rest of your tribe?'

'Because I belong to a different tribe. Another tribe in the Residual Alliance.'

'There's no such thing.'

Ferren shrugged and turned his back. It was the three Mothers who answered.

'Yes, there is,' said Gweir.

'And we're joining it,' said Lorne.

'We'll never give in to your kind again,' said Krye.

The Selector roared. 'We'll wipe you out! You think you can fight? You'll always give in to us! You hopeless dummies! You can't do anything to anyone!'

There was an equal roar from Lorbie.

'We can do *this* to *you*!'

He charged forward and kicked out furiously with his foot.

Whumffff!

The Selector's body split wide apart. There was a mighty explosion of colours. Everything vanished in a million flickering images. Lorbie was knocked over backwards. The Sea-folk shielded their eyes against the blast.

When the blast finally lifted and cleared, the Selector had been reduced to a dozen scattered chunks of inanimate material. His body was dry porous stuff like grey honeycomb.

Lorbie was sitting on his backside, blinking his small blue eyes. The explosion had singed off his eyebrows and blackened his face and clothes. He grinned a shaky grin.

'I finished him off,' he said.

3

ASMODAI

1

The Sea-folk were no longer worried about joining with other tribes that didn't have taboos. They weren't even worried about not finishing their period of pay-up.

The Mothers would have liked to celebrate the alliance with ceremony and feasting. But Miriael refused. If Doctor Saniette's offensive was a mere two weeks away, there was no time to spare.

She discussed the situation mainly with Ferren, while Kiet sat in and listened.

'I never guessed the new Doctor could be ready so quickly,' she said. 'My fault. This offensive will be under way before we can organise a meeting of all the tribes.'

'But we still have to have the meeting,' said Ferren.

'As soon as possible, yes. The tribes will need a common strategy. And mutual support to resist the Selectors. The Doctor will want more and more Residuals to replenish his raw materials.'

They discussed arrangements for the meeting. Each

tribe would be expected to send one or two represent-atives. Ferren proposed to hold the meeting at the Home Ground, where his own tribe lived. But Miriael shook her head.

'Not central enough. And the People are one of the smallest tribes.'

'What about the Nesters?' Kiet put in. 'Didn't you say we're one of the biggest tribes?'

Miriael considered. 'True. And your territory is fairly central. I can't think of anywhere better.'

So it was agreed that the meeting would take place in the Nesters' territory. As for the time –

'It'll take longer than fifteen days,' said Ferren. 'We'll have to go back and revisit all the tribes. It'll take months.'

Miriael frowned and thought for a moment. 'We'll have to speed it up. We'll split up and divide the tribes between us.'

Ferren wasn't very happy with the idea. 'It'll still take more than fifteen days.'

'Yes, but not more than a month. You and Kiet can go together. We'll call the meeting in a month from now.'

Ferren nodded reluctantly. 'You'll have to draw up a map for me.'

'Of course. And you'll have to make a copy of the map for each tribe you visit. So their representatives can follow a route to the Nesters' territory.'

'I can copy maps,' said Kiet. 'I'm good at drawing.'

'Are you?' Miriael smiled. 'Then let's start now. You can copy a map for the Sea-folk.'

2

It was mid-afternoon by the time they set off. The fog had blown away and the air was warm in the sunshine. Their packs had been refilled, along with a shoulder bag for Kiet. Moireen and the children accompanied them along the beach.

Final farewells were said and final hugs exchanged at the mouth of the gorge. Then Miriael, Ferren and Kiet turned to follow the course of the river. As before, their progress was very slow. For hours they clambered over fallen scree and landslips.

By nightfall, they had almost reached the other end of the gorge. The walls were much lower, the banks much wider. But it was too dark to continue. They decided to spend the night in the shelter of the walls, where a loop of the river enclosed a grassy promontory.

'If Asmodai comes down in the night, please stay absolutely quiet,' said Miriael. 'If you're awake, just look the other way.'

'You can tell him about the great offensive,' said Ferren.

'In two weeks' time,' added Kiet. 'Very important news.'

'Are you expecting a visit tonight?' asked Ferren.

Miriael shook her head. 'I never know when to expect him. I can only hope. It's been six days since I last saw him.'

They stretched out on the grass. Ferren and Kiet were asleep in a matter of minutes. But Miriael couldn't settle.

Every time she closed her eyes, images of Asmodai formed in her mind. She pictured his great lambent eyes, his hair like spun glass, his beautiful beautiful face. Over and again she imagined his oval globe of light approaching through the night.

But when she opened her eyes, he was never there. She ached inside as she scanned the empty sky.

She couldn't deceive herself. She did have important news to tell him. But that wasn't the only need. She wanted *him*, to see *him*. She was addicted to his presence. The feeling had been growing and growing upon her.

What was it about him? Or was it something about her? No proper angel should feel this kind of feeling. It was too personal, too close, too private. Not spiritual love, but person-to-person love. It was an entirely inappropriate feeling between angels.

Again and again she shifted position. But she couldn't get comfortable. The grass was itchy, the ground was lumpy. Restlessness tormented her.

It was the change in her body, of course. Her new physicalised state was the cause of this improper feeling.

Heaven help her – she was no better than a Residual!

Worst of all, the feeling was on her side alone. Asmodai could never feel a similar attraction to her. It was an insult even to think of him that way. He was perfect in virtue, completely out of reach. What he felt for her was only kindness and compassion. The whole thing was crazy, impossible.

And yet – his face was made to be loved. And his strength, his voice, his graceful movements – all made to be loved. Why was he so beautiful if no-one could ever touch him?

She wondered how it would feel to touch him. Pressing her skin against him . . . She remembered the warmth of his golden light, when he bent over her. Yet his white radiance was very pure and cool. She imagined his touch as a kind of tingling, both cold and hot like snow and fire. She shivered pleasurably and rolled over once again.

Oh, it was wrong, wrong, wrong. She ought to be ashamed of herself. But the picture of Asmodai kept forming in her mind. And imaginary sensations . . .

All through the night, she tossed and turned. He was still in her mind when at last she drifted off into an uneasy drowse. Her dreams continued on where her waking thoughts left off.

3

Next day, they emerged from the gorge and trudged along parallel to the river. They were due to separate after an hour or so's walking. For Ferren and Kiet, the first stop was the territory of the Nesters. Miriael would take a more westerly route towards one of the other tribes.

Ferren was puzzled about Kiet. He'd never understood her outburst during the game of Walk the Melon. Now she seemed friendly again – but very mysterious. Over breakfast, she'd whispered that she had something to tell him. But she refused to speak while Miriael was around.

Finally came the parting of the ways. Far ahead in the distance was the straight black line of the overbridge. Ferren and Kiet continued on towards it. Kiet was almost hopping with excitement. Yet still she wouldn't speak until Miriael was completely out of sight.

'Come on,' Ferren insisted. 'What is it?'

Kiet snapped her fingers. 'You remember what you told me about Miriael becoming more secretive? As if she wanted to keep this Asmodai to herself?'

'Mmm.'

'Well, I've discovered the reason why.'

'Oh?' Ferren frowned. 'Did he come down to visit Miriael last night?'

'No. But she wanted him to.'

'What do you mean?'

'She was calling out for him in her sleep. So loud she woke me up. Moaning his name over and over.'

'Why?'

'Can't you guess?' She imitated a drawn-out moaning sound. '*As-mo-dai*! *As-mo-dai*!'

Ferren came to an abrupt halt. Kiet halted too, facing him.

'I think Miriael wants to *mate* with him,' she said.

The blood drained from Ferren's face. 'Don't be ridiculous.'

'What's ridiculous? She's a female angel. He's a male angel.'

'Angels don't mate. It doesn't matter which sex they are. They just take on a masculine form or a feminine form.'

'Huh! You know all about angels then?'

'I know about Miriael. She could never want to . . . I mean, she doesn't . . . She's . . .'

He stumbled over his words, his thoughts. Kiet tossed her dark red hair.

'Ah, but you haven't seen Asmodai. *I* have. He's incredibly beautiful. So handsome, so charismatic. I'd go for him too, if I was an angel.'

Ferren had no reply. Kiet grinned.

'She wants to mate with him,' she repeated. 'She's not

so pure and holy as you thought. *As-mo-dai*! *As-mo-dai*! *As-mo-dai*!'

Ferren shook his head as though trying to shake away the mere idea.

'It's not such a big thing,' said Kiet. 'Why shouldn't she be attracted to him? She's not so far above us after all. I think –'

But Ferren had already turned and walked on. He set a blistering pace, covering the ground in huge strides. Kiet almost had to jog to keep up.

4

Kiet was puzzled about Ferren. He remained strange and withdrawn all day. He spoke impersonally when he spoke at all, as though his mind was elsewhere.

The sun had set by the time they arrived at the Nesters' territory. They made their way towards the central area of nests. It was the twilight hour after family dinner. The adult Nesters were in their homes and only the young Nesters still roamed the green tunnels.

The first person they met was Rhinn. Her jaw dropped at the sight of them.

'You're back! Where've you been?'

The question was addressed to Kiet – the returned runaway. Kiet laughed and pointed to Ferren.

'I was with him. And Miriael.'

'We thought so.' Rhinn's momentary severity dissolved into a smile. She held out her arms. 'It's good to see you again.'

They walked on together. The news spread as if by magic and half a dozen other young Nesters came running up to join them. Tadge, Flens, Gibby, Ethamy . . .

Everyone was trying to talk over the top of everyone else.

'I've seen amazing things!' Kiet told them. 'An army of Humen! A Selector! We killed him! You wouldn't believe! There's a whole new danger from the Humen!'

The young Nesters whooped and cheered at the prospect. The new danger from the Humen didn't frighten them.

More and more Nesters came up, now adults as well as children. Soon there were so many people that the tunnel was blocked. Forward progress was impossible.

Kiet continued to tell her adventures. She was the centre of attention. At the same time, the young Nesters tried to explain developments to her.

'It's different to when you left –'

'We don't worry about Stocks so much –'

'Anyone can offer suggestions to the Guardians –'

'We don't always follow the old duties –'

Flens managed to squeeze in a comment. 'Just like you wanted, Kiet. Remember how you wanted everything to change?'

Ferren didn't have much to say. He was so quiet that Kiet didn't even notice when he slipped off. It was a while before she realised.

'Where's he gone?'

'He said he was going to talk to the Guardians,' Ethamy answered.

'Oh. Then I ought to –'

'Come and see mother!' cried Tadge. 'Come on!' He pulled at her arm. 'She's been worrying about you.'

Kiet shrugged. Okay, let Ferren talk to the Guardians and make arrangements for the meeting. He could persuade them without her help.

The crowd accompanied Kiet and Tadge as far as their family nest. Tadge crawled in first through the entrance-hole.

'Kiet's back!' he announced.

When Kiet crawled in, Nettish almost flung herself upon her. Her motherly affection showed itself in a frenzy of fussing and flustering.

'You're back, you're back, you're back, you're back!' was all she could say for several minutes.

Then, recovering her breath, she went on to 'I've been so worried! So worried! I don't know how worried!'

Kiet gently disengaged herself. Nettish spun away across the nest. She snatched up baby Twy and dandled her in midair.

'Your little sister's been missing you too! Haven't you, Twy?'

'Waaaaaaah!' bawled baby Twy.

'You see? You see how much she's been missing you?'

'Waaaaaaah!'

'Enough! Shush! Kiet's back now! Look! Back now!'

As Twy continued to bawl, Nettish rocked and patted the baby furiously. For a while, the nest was pandemonium. Kiet waited for a quieter moment.

'It's good to be back,' she said at last. 'But I can't stay long.'

Nettish rattled on as though she hadn't heard. 'They all said you'd lost your chance with Bross. But you're still in time. We'll invent reasons. We can still arrange

Second Intimacies. They can't back out now. I won't let them. Not with my favourite daughter.'

'I can't stay long,' Kiet repeated. 'I'm only here for a day or so.'

A succession of expressions flitted across Nettish's face. She smiled uncertainly, shook her head, looked hurt. Kiet sucked at her lips and felt bad.

The tension was broken by the sound of someone coming in through the entrance-hole. It was Grandfather Niot. He gazed at Kiet, beaming with satisfaction.

'You're looking well, granddaughter,' he said. 'Give me a hug.'

Hugging Grandfather Niot was like burrowing into a tufty brush of beard. Kiet made it last as long as possible. But her mother was still waiting, still fretful.

'She wants to go away again,' she lamented. 'How can she mate with Bross if she goes away?'

Grandfather Niot sat back on his haunches. 'I don't know. How can she?' He looked from Kiet to Nettish and back again. 'Why do you want to go away?'

'I have to go with Ferren and visit fifteen other tribes in the Residual Alliance. It's urgent.'

Nettish flapped her arms in despair. 'What's urgent is settling down with Bross. After all my hard work! What have I done to deserve this?' She appealed to Grandfather Niot. 'Tell her she mustn't go away.'

The tiny wrinkles on Grandfather Niot's face seemed to deepen. He looked very solemn.

'It's not for me to tell her.'

Nettish gasped. 'But this is important! You *know* how important!'

'Yes, I know how important a good mating is. But I don't know how important visiting other tribes is. Perhaps the Residual Alliance is even more important than a good mating. I think she can decide better than you or me.'

'But we ought to decide! We've always decided!'

'There's a new way of thinking, Nettish. We can't be sure of things any more. I don't understand it, but the young people do. It doesn't bother them, not knowing what differences tomorrow will bring.'

'I *like* not knowing!' said Tadge, speaking up suddenly. 'It doesn't bother me.'

'Ah.' Grandfather Niot smiled. 'Exactly. Whereas what I like is what I know. The smell of a stew cooking over the Firepit, for example. That's always enough to put me in a good mood. Or sitting in the sunshine with the insects buzzing in the flowers. Fresh pears and peaches to eat in summertime. And singing the old songs with Uncle Abnel. Those are the things that matter to me. Always the same, always the way I like them.'

Moved by an irresistible impulse, Kiet leaned forward to give him another hug.

'Don't ever change, Grandfather Niot! Always stay the way you are!'

Nettish sniffed. She looked unhappy at being left out. Kiet moved across to give her a hug too.

'Everything will turn out all right, Mother. Don't worry about me. You'll see.'

5

They continued to chat for another half hour, until it was completely dark. Then Grandfather Niot took himself off and Nettish settled Twy down in her blankets of rabbit fur. It was time for bed.

But Kiet wasn't yet ready to sleep. She wanted to talk to Ferren. He'd surely have finished his conference with the Guardians by now. So where would he be?

She slipped out of the family nest and headed towards the nest where Ferren and Miriael had stayed before. Her guess proved correct. Ferren was sitting in the middle of the floor, a motionless shape in the dark.

Kiet sat down facing him.

'Hi! How did it go with the Guardians?'

'Yes, they're pleased to have the meeting of the alliance take place here.' He answered in a monotone. 'They see it as an honour.'

'Which it is!'

'They're determined to resist any Selector who turns up in the meanwhile.'

'Must be the quickest they've ever decided anything.'

'They seem less narrow-minded than they used to be.'
Still the same flat monotone.

'So it went well?'

'Couldn't have gone better.'

'Then why are you so gloomy?'

There was a long pause.

'Am I?'

'Oh, come on. You've been gloomy all day. What's wrong?'

'Not gloomy.'

'What then?'

'I don't want to talk about it.'

'You can tell me. Don't be distant. We trust each other, don't we? I'd share things with you I'd never share with anyone else.' Still Ferren remained silent. 'Why can't you share it? Is it something to do with me?'

'No. It's something to do with Miriael.'

'That's all right then. Are you worried because she's being secretive about Asmodai?'

'No . . . not exactly.'

'Hah! But I'm getting close, right?'

'It's me and Miriael.'

'Go on.'

'I think . . . I think I'm in love with her.'

Kiet froze. She felt as though she'd been struck a terrible blow under the heart. She didn't know what or why.

'*In love?*' she demanded. 'What does that mean, to say you're in love?'

'It means she's the one special person in the world for me. It means this feeling when I'd do anything for her.

When I think how beautiful she is, I go almost dizzy. I can't be happy without her.'

'Ah.'

'All day today, every single minute, she's been in my mind. Even when I was talking to the Guardians. I can't stop thinking about her.'

'Thinking about someone a lot.' Kiet spoke numbly, bitterly. 'So that's what you call being in love?'

Ferren didn't seem to hear. Now he'd launched into his confession, he couldn't hold back.

'I've been keeping it in all day. You won't make fun of me, will you? I couldn't say it if I thought you'd make fun of me.'

'I'm a friend, aren't I?' Kiet had to force the words out.

'A best friend. The best friend I've ever had. That's why I know you'll understand my deepest feelings.'

'Your deepest feelings for Miriael.'

'Yes. I never realised how deep until this morning. I always admired her. Adored her, idolised her. But I didn't realise it was love. Until you said that about her and Asmodai.'

He had become very intense, leaning forward and gesticulating. Kiet had turned into a block of wood. She just wished she could put her hands over her ears.

'It hurt so much,' he went on. 'It was like hot knives cutting and twisting in my chest. You couldn't imagine how much it hurt.'

'Ah, that.' Kiet nodded. 'Hurt.'

'Because I was jealous. I couldn't bear to think of her caring for him as much as she cared for me. And then I realised. I was in love.'

Don't move a muscle, she told herself. It'll pass. Everything is still the same. The close darkness. The clay smell of the walls. The beaten earth of the floor. Nothing changed. And yet . . .

'It was so obvious. I'd been so blind. I thought back, and the feeling had always been there. Ever since the very first time I saw her. Did I ever tell you about the first time I saw her?'

He waited a moment, then answered his own question.

'No, of course not. It was after the Humen had shot her out of the sky. Her globe was shattered and she was lying there in the grass. I came up to look and she was like a miracle. Her incredible golden hair. Her clear blue eyes and perfect face. The sight of her took my breath away. I couldn't . . . are you okay?'

Kiet felt as though her own breath had been taken away. Perhaps she'd forgotten to breathe. She made a gulping noise that Ferren interpreted as an *okay*.

'I want to tell you the whole story,' he went on. 'I'm glad you made me let it out. I feel better for being able to talk about it.'

Kiet gripped at her stomach with both hands. 'I'm not well.'

'What's wrong?'

She gripped harder. Her insides were churning and cramping. She wanted to vomit, scream, explode. Something, anything.

'Got to go,' she mumbled, turning away.

'But –'

Desperately she scrambled for the entrance-hole. She burst out into the open and ran, ran, ran.

6

He was toweringly beautiful. His light cast silver on the trunks of the trees, making them leap forward suddenly out of the darkness. The leaves seemed to be bending in reverence towards him. Moths flew round and round, batting against the glass of his globe.

Miriael had been asleep on a flat slab of mossy rock. Now she sat upright and exchanged greetings with him.

She was as if spellbound. When she gazed at Asmodai, she seemed to look straight through into Heaven. He was like a small piece of the celestial realm brought down to her on the Earth.

Then she remembered her news: the Selector's revelations and the great offensive now only thirteen days away. Asmodai's brow darkened as she told him the details.

'This is very serious,' he said grimly. 'This could be the most threatening development since the time of the Great Collapse.'

But nothing seemed too serious or threatening to Miriael, not in that moment. She felt his light pouring down upon her, seeping into her bones. Hot and cold like fire and snow, she thought. Again she wondered what it would be like to touch him. Of course, it was impossible. But she couldn't help wondering . . .

He talked on: about passing the information to his superiors, about their hidebound habits, about their reluctance ever to make a preemptive attack. As if from a distance, Miriael heard his voice and her own voice answering. She came out of her trance only when he began to talk about her.

'They should consider themselves in your debt, Miriael. With information like this . . . no-one could have done more to help Heaven's cause. They'll have to admit it in the end.'

Miriael smiled. 'Has anything happened with the Archon Anaitis?'

'Indeed it has.'

His globe descended lower and lower until it was hovering beside the mossy rock. His enormous gentle eyes rested steadily upon her.

'I can show you, if you like,' he said.

'Show me?' Miriael didn't understand.

'I can transfer a memory across to you. My own memory of what happened.'

Now Miriael understood – but she didn't believe. 'How?'

Asmodai lifted the silver circlet from his brow and held it in his hand. Then he knelt and pressed his forehead to the glass surface of the globe.

'Stand up. Touch the other side of the glass with your forehead.'

Miriael goggled. 'Against yours?'

'Yes, against mine.'

'But how does it – I mean –'

'Touch with your forehead,' he repeated patiently, insistently.

Miriael stood up on the slab of rock. She took a pace forward to the edge. She hoped he wouldn't notice how she was trembling.

So close, so close! His soft-spun hair billowed in waves, his wings stirred above his shoulders. She could see the tiny tip of gold on every feather. She stared at the place where his pale forehead made contact with the glass.

She couldn't do it! Not face to face!

But the blood was mounting to her cheeks. She couldn't bear for him to see the blush.

She did it. She shut her eyes and bent quickly towards the glass.

Cold glass. Warm light. A tingling sensation, like a tiny ringing vibration above her brows.

A strange impression drifted into her mind. She imagined that her head was being gripped between two hands, that her attention was being guided towards a dark space in front of her. Soon it was as though her forehead had melted away. The dark space was like a vacuum drawing her out, drawing her forward.

Then far off and floating in the vacuum, she saw something like a glowing bead. She focussed on it. It was a tiny sphere shimmering with pictures. She had the idea that the pictures were infinitely compressed and concentrated.

The act of focussing seemed to bring her closer, much closer. She reached out with her mind and the pictures began to unfold.

It's the memory, she told herself, Asmodai's memory is being transferred across to me. She gasped as it opened out, wider and wider. Now she could look right into it, step inside.

Suddenly, she was standing in the clear early morning light of Heaven. With a flash of realisation, she knew she was on the Fourth Altitude, in the Terraces of Shereth. The memory contained understandings as well as images. She waited for the scene to resolve itself.

But it wasn't a single scene. The memory was a point of experience, and the experience incorporated many previous moments. Glimpse by glimpse it opened out in all directions, both in time and space.

She was standing by a pool in the centre of a rose-garden. The surface of the pool was like a mirror. Four kneeling female angels dipped their fingers into the pool and drew out threads of sheer reflective glitter. They shuttled the threads from hand to hand in a kind of weaving.

The ground underfoot felt soft as velvet. The rose-bushes were low hedges arranged in concentric circles. Springs of crystal water bubbled out of the ground and trickled down into the pool. Around the perimeter of the garden stood eight tall urns of stone.

Glimpse by glimpse, wider and wider ... Now Miriael took in the green curving sweep of the Terraces themselves. She saw the blue roofs and yellow columns of the long open corridors running above the ground.

She saw the twelve Trees of Wisdom with their cande-
labra branches and the heavy golden orbs of their fruit.
And far off in the distance, she saw phoenixes strut and
display their flame-bright bodies, their tails like showers
of sparks.

The shifting multi-angled perspective made her dizzy.
But now she had her bearings. She came back to the
pool in the rose-garden.

A conversation was going on. One of the four female
angels had stood up to talk. She wore only the simple
maroon robe of the Order of Dominions, with no
obvious symbol of her rank. Her fair complexion was as
smooth as pearl, her eyes were warm and grey.

It's Anaitis, Miriael realised. She's talking with
Asmodai. And not only with Asmodai. Two other
angels stood to the left and right: one in the white robe
of the Order of Principalities, the other in the orange
robe of the Order of Thrones. By the thoughts in
Asmodai's memory, she knew that the white-robed
angel was Berial and the orange-robed angel was
Meresin.

In the same way, she understood that Asmodai, Berial
and Meresin had been pleading her case. She heard no
actual words spoken, but somehow she knew what had
been said. About her own unfortunate state . . . the way
she was still assisting Heaven . . . the comparison with
the Fallen Angels of the past . . .

And what was Anaitis's answer? Had she already
answered? There was no movement of time within the
memory. Every part of the conversation was simultan-
eous, wrapped up together.

But then she worked it out. Of course – Asmodai would have transferred the very moment of Anaitis's answer. Therefore, the answer must be at the core of the memory. All she had to do was to keep letting it unfold.

Deeper and deeper towards the core. Anaitis requesting further details ... Asmodai, Berial and Meresin suggesting an appeal to Uriel ... Anaitis smiling ...

And finally, there it was! At the very core, the answer! This time Miriael heard the actual words spoken.

Yes, she deserves my help. I'll do what I can for her.

Her heart leaped. *Yes, she deserves my help.* The words seemed to hang in air, timeless and echoing. *I'll do what I can for her.*

It was a moment of complete happiness. The clear light of Heaven, the fragrant air. The tranquillity of the roses in the rose-garden. The crystal water, the reflecting pool, the faces of angels weaving and smiling. She wished it could last forever.

But the memory had come to an end. Already the scene was starting to blur. She had a sense of something interposed.

She struggled to maintain contact. She couldn't bear to lose the vision. It was as though a screen of glass had come up in front of her.

She tried to look through but her focus had changed. She couldn't ignore the glass. A nearer reality had blocked off the reality of Heaven. She opened her eyes.

The nearer reality was the surface of Asmodai's globe. Useless to press with her forehead, useless to clasp at it with her hands. Asmodai's forehead was no longer making contact on the other side of the glass.

She lifted her own forehead away. Tears were running down her cheeks. Asmodai stood tall and radiant inside his globe.

'Was that better than hearing me tell you what happened?' he asked.

'It was wonderful.'

'Why are you crying?'

'With happiness.'

'Ah. Tears of happiness.'

'How long did it last?'

'Only a few seconds in Earthly time.'

She rubbed at the wetness around her eyes. 'How did you do it?'

'Transferring a memory? It's a simple application of spiritual powers. A technique I've learned.'

'Another of your new techniques?'

He nodded. 'Every angel could do it. If they wanted to learn.'

'But they wouldn't.'

'No. Because it's not traditional.'

She looked up at him through eyes still bleared with tears. 'You're amazing. You're very very special.'

For a moment she feared she'd gone too far. But her fears turned to joy when he replied.

'You're very special to me too, Miriael.'

She swallowed the huge hot lump in her throat and looked away, unable to meet his eyes.

His globe rocked and rose higher off the ground. He lifted his eyes to the night sky. Miriael realised he was about to depart.

She couldn't even ask him to stay a little longer. Her heart was too full of happiness.

I shared your memories, she thought to herself. You let me into your mind. Your beautiful heavenly mind. You considered me worthy . . .

'Goodbye, Miriael,' he said. 'The next time I visit, I shall bring an answer for you from Uriel.'

There was a sudden loud *whoosh*! and a rush of white light shot up like a geyser. Miriael couldn't see for the dazzle. She could only feel the flapping of her robe and the blast of wind on her face.

When she recovered her sight, the trees looked darker than ever. The branches were still swaying, the leaves still rustling in the afterdraught. The air seemed chill without his glorious light.

But she was glowing inside. It was almost more than she could bear, the glowing inside!

7

Kiet had disappeared. No-one had seen her all morning. Ferren asked at her family nest, but Nettish and Tadge hadn't seen her since the previous evening.

Then he had an inspiration. He followed the route to the rhododendron bush, turning off the path, passing between the two closely growing tree-trunks. There she was, half-hidden under the leaves and flowers.

She was sitting on the usual log, elbows on knees and chin in her hands. She looked as though she'd been in the same position for a very long time. Her hair was bedraggled and there were dark circles under her eyes.

Ferren came in under the canopy. She scowled at him, then stared pointedly in another direction. Her eyebrows were set in a straight black line. He remained standing, awkwardly stooped.

'Have you been here all night?'

'What do you think?'

'Are you angry with me?'

Kiet shrugged and said nothing.

'I don't understand this. Aren't we friends?'

She threw him a sharply penetrating look. 'If you say so.'

The conversation was starting badly. Ferren wondered whether to bring up what had happened last night. But he wasn't sure what *had* happened last night. He didn't know how to talk about it.

'We need to move on to the next tribe,' he said. 'We need to make plans.'

'You make plans.'

'Why not you?'

'I'm not coming.'

'Uh?'

'I've decided to stay here. My family needs me.'

'So do I.'

'No, you don't. You can talk to the tribes just as well on your own.'

'But I . . .'

It was true, he could talk to the tribes on his own. But his heart sank at the idea of continuing on alone. He needed Kiet for company. Only he couldn't bring himself to say it.

There was a long silence. Kiet stared at the ground, twisting her fingers in her hair. Ferren sensed a dangerous inward smouldering. *Handle with care,* he thought to himself.

He decided to sit down. Beside her on the log, but not too close. He contemplated an indirect approach.

'Do you remember the first time you brought me here?' he asked. 'You pulled on the branches and drowned me in rainwater.'

'Yes.' Kiet's smile was humorless, showing her strong

white teeth. 'And I remember another time, when I told you about Asmodai visiting Miriael in the night. Your Miriael, with a beautiful male angel hovering over her.'

She turned towards him. The smile sharpened at the corners of her mouth.

'So tall and powerful. So incredibly good-looking. No wonder Miriael wants to mate with him.'

Ferren knew she was trying to hurt. But he couldn't help rising to the bait.

'Don't be ridiculous! He's shut up in his glass globe. He couldn't –'

'And you could?' Her words cut across him like the crack of a whip. 'You really imagine that Miriael is attracted to you?'

'I never said that.'

'You really imagine that an angel could be *in love* with you?'

'I never said that!' he repeated hotly.

'Who do you think you are? You're out of your class. What would she see in you? Compared to her, you're nothing. Compared to *him,* you're nothing. You don't have a chance.'

'I never said I expected her to be in love with me!'

She confronted him face to face. 'What then? What do you expect?'

'I don't expect anything! I don't expect her to have the same feelings for me!'

Kiet was incredulous. 'You're going to be in love all on your own?'

'I may never tell her. She'll probably never know about my feelings.'

'You're going to follow her around and yearn from a distance?'

'Yes.'

'Phuh! You don't live in the real world.'

'You wouldn't understand.'

'There's nothing to understand. It's all a dream in your head.'

'Every man needs a dream.'

'Why?'

'A dream of something higher and nobler. An ambition, a goal. Even if it's impossible.'

'That's what it is. Impossible.'

'Okay. My dream is impossible. But I still have to believe in it.'

'You're an idiot then.'

Ferren shook his head. 'I said you wouldn't understand.'

He turned away, looking sad and pained. Something about his look seemed to infuriate Kiet beyond measure.

'Idiot! Idiot! Idiot!' She jumped to her feet, she danced with rage in front of him. 'You only want what you can't have! You only want it because you can't have it! That's not a man, that's a little boy! You want to play at being heroic! You want to suffer in secret! It's the stupidest thing I ever heard in my life! Why don't you just drop dead with love and get it over with? You're a joke! You're a waste of space! You're – you're – you're –'

Ferren was stunned by the violence of the attack. As she ran out of words, she drew back her hand to hit him.

'Don't do it!' he threatened, jumping to his feet.

Her temper was at white heat. His threat meant nothing to her. But suddenly her face changed. She lowered her hands and took a backward step.

'Dreams!' she spat out with infinite scorn. 'I've had enough of your dreams! I'll never believe in you ever again!'

She spun on her heel and left him standing there, completely bewildered.

8

All around were massive pillars rising in red and gold, radiating out into arches overhead. The vault itself was invisible: only the crisscross of arches one above the other, as high as the eye could see. Beams of light passed among the arches, and the white dove-like shapes of Blessed Souls. There were soft flurries and beatings of wings . . .

Miriael was experiencing what Asmodai had experienced. Unfolding in her mind was the deputation to Uriel in the Hall of a Thousand Steps. Uriel's decision lay at the core of the memory.

Step by step they mounted: Anaitis, Berial, Meresin and Asmodai. She could see the others, but she looked out through Asmodai's eyes. They were accompanied by the Warden of the Hall, who wore a breastplate of polished bronze.

At the top of the steps was a wide floor tiled in green and blue. A dozen high-backed thrones were arranged in a line. Uriel's was in the centre, moulded in antique gold with armrests like the paws of a lion. In three of the thrones sat a trio of angelic musicians, playing on lutes and citherns. Lingering string music floated in the air and echoed among the pillars. Uriel's throne was empty.

Glimpse by glimpse, unfolding . . . Now they had moved on to where a group of angels were talking in low voices. Some held compasses and rulers, others knelt on the floor with scrolls of paper. In the centre of the group was a gigantic globe, a representation of the Earth with green-painted land and blue-painted seas. Uriel stood beside the globe, frowning.

He was much as Miriael remembered: the same long flowing hair, the same clearcut aquiline face. The snowy brightness of his aura was even more intense without an enclosing globe. The mighty Sword of Judgement hung down from a strap at his waist.

Miriael skimmed over the discussion that followed. Anaitis pointed out the parallel to the case of the Fallen Angels. Berial and Meresin pointed out that Miriael had never even rebelled. Asmodai pointed out that she was still helping Heaven in many ways, especially with the Residual Alliance.

Miriael was aware of all the arguments without exactly hearing them. Uriel paced up and down while the deputation remained on their knees before him. He gripped the pommel of the Sword of Judgement and the edges of the blade pulsed with an ice-cold brilliance.

What was his decision? It seemed to take forever to arrive. Surely the arguments of the deputation were good? But the ice-cold brilliance of the Sword of Judgement unnerved her.

At last she penetrated to the very core of the memory. As with the memory in the rose-garden, she heard the actual words spoken. But these words shattered all her hopes.

No, she has chosen her own course, he said. *Reconciliation would not be appropriate at the present time.*

His face was stern, his tone unyielding. The distant music of the angels seemed like a mockery. She could hardly believe it. He had said *No*!

There were no further arguments, no further unfoldings of the memory. She had had her answer. She was thankful when the vision started to blur, when the scene was screened off.

'I'm sorry, Miriael.'

She lifted her forehead from the cold glass surface. But she still didn't want to open her eyes. She felt numb.

Again Asmodai spoke to her. 'It's an unexpected setback. But it isn't the end.'

She opened her eyes and blinked away the tears. 'It sounded like the end to me.'

'The answer was, *not appropriate at the present time.*'

'What does that mean? What would be an appropriate time?'

'I can't say. But circumstances may change.'

'How?'

'Well, circumstances changed for Satan and the Fallen Angels. They were waiting for centuries. Repentant, pleading to be forgiven. Anaitis didn't give up on them. And she won't give up on you.'

225

Miriael brightened a fraction. 'What changed for them?'

'The strategic situation after the Great Collapse.'

'I don't understand.'

'The War Council took over after the Great Collapse. Their first priority was to build up Heaven's armies against the armies of the Earth. The return of the Fallen Angels increased our numbers by a third.'

'So it wasn't an ethical decision at all!'

'It wasn't *only* an ethical decision.'

Miriael was indignant. 'That's so cynical! There was a benefit in forgiving the Fallen Angels because there were tens of thousands of them. But there's no benefit in forgiving me because I'm only a single angel.'

Asmodai shook his head sadly. 'That's why I mentioned the Residual Alliance. You're getting the tribes to fight against the Humen, so you're adding forces on Heaven's side. Unfortunately, Heaven doesn't much want Residuals on its side.'

'Why not? That's stupid.'

'I'm only explaining the attitude. Residuals are physical creatures and Heaven disapproves of the physical.'

'Whereas the Fallen Angels are acceptable because they're spiritual.'

'Yes.'

Miriael thought for a moment. 'What about the Morphs?'

'Morphs? What about them?'

'They're spiritual beings. They'd become Blessed Souls if they were allowed into Heaven.'

'Mmm. Yes.' Asmodai obviously wasn't in the habit of thinking about the Morphs.

'What if they joined in on Heaven's side? The Blessed Souls fight for Heaven.'

'But the Morphs have no military value. They're just lost and scattered and hopeless.'

'Not so scattered. There are hundreds and hundreds of them living together in colonies.'

'Colonies? Is that so?' Asmodai was surprised. 'But still, they could never be welded into a fighting unit. They're too passive, surely?'

Miriael shook her head. 'Only because they're shut out of Heaven with nothing to hope for. They could act purposefully if they had a purpose. And they definitely don't like the Humen.'

'How do you know?'

'I've talked with them. Several colonies of them.'

'Talked? You've been able to talk with them?'

'A singing sort of talking. I discovered how to do it.' She smiled. 'A new technique of my own.'

'Could I do it?'

'I could show you.'

There was now a definite gleam of interest in Asmodai's eye. 'Where's the nearest colony?'

Miriael didn't have to think long. 'The nearest would be a place called the City of the Dead. A day's walk from here.'

'I'd like to see. Will you show me?'

Miriael pursed her lips. 'I'd have to make a detour. I'm supposed to be visiting tribes in the Residual Alliance.'

'It won't take long if you start right now.'

'Start walking there now? In the middle of the night?'

'This could be very very important.'

'You think so?'

'For you *and* for Heaven.'

He turned his eyes full upon her. Miriael's resistance melted.

'All right, I'll start there now.'

'Thank you, Miriael. I'll meet up with you again in, say, eight or nine hours' time.'

'You won't be coming with me?'

'Impossible. My absence would be noticed in Heaven. Also, I need to do some research on Morphs. Eight or nine hours time.'

9

True to his word, Asmodai rejoined her nine hours later, just as she arrived at the Nesters' territory. Entering the jungle of lantana bush from an unfamiliar direction, she planned to make her way directly to the City of the Dead. She didn't want anyone to know about her detour, so she didn't intend to visit the Nesters.

She might have had trouble locating the City on her own. But Asmodai in his globe rose up above the vegetation and picked out a route according to her directions. It was midday when she came to the valley and walked upstream among the rivulets. Ahead were the walls of the City of the Dead.

The last part of the route was more familiar. She climbed to the concrete platform, then passed through the lane under the tangle of bushes. When she came out into the street, Asmodai descended to hover beside her.

He hardly gave a glance to the buildings of the Old Ones. He was more interested in communicating with the Morphs.

'Tell me about this singing technique,' he said.

'Have you ever seen a Morph close up?'

'Never. Only illustrations in books.'

'They're very different in real life. You can't help feeling sorry for them. They take fright so easily.'

'But they don't take fright when you sing to them?'

'That's right. They like music. So everything you say has to be turned into a song. A gentle soothing melody.'

She gave a demonstration. Asmodai nodded.

'I think I could do that.'

Miriael smiled. 'Then let's sing a first song to them together.'

They worked out words and tune as they proceeded along the street. When they came to the square, Miriael put a finger to her lips. They advanced very quietly around the final corner.

To angelic eyes, the Morphs were sheer diaphanous structures, like geometrical diagrams drawn in white glimmering lines. They had the shape of stars, with four, five or six branching points. They congregated most thickly in the places where there was most grass and fallen rubble.

'Amazing,' murmured Asmodai.

'Aren't they wonderful?'

They walked out across the square. As yet the Morphs had made no sound. But they were trembling nervously in the sunlight.

Miriael led the way to a place where the grass rose half a metre high in the cracks between the flagstones. She chose a group of three Morphs out of the multitudes all around. They were arranged one above the other, with their points attached to the same stalks of grass. They were delicate as crystal, frail as snowflakes.

Miriael knelt before them. Asmodai in his globe knelt right behind her.

'Ready?' she whispered.

They sang together in perfect harmony.

'We want to be your friends
Coming to talk to you.
One of us you've met before,
The other one is new.'

A kind of twittering spread across the square. Evidently all the Morphs were listening. But it was the nearest Morph who replied.

'We remember you. But why does the other one come in his globe? He should be up in Heaven.'

The tiny piping voice sounded half peevish and half fearful. Miriael sang an answer on her own.

'He is a good kind angel
And worthy of your trust.
He does not scorn the things of Earth
But will give help to us.'

'Let me try too,' said Asmodai.

Miriael backed away to make space as his globe floated forward. Hovering mere inches above the ground, he created a fresh tune for his words.

'I only want to help you,
I see your grief and woe.
Tell Asmodai your sufferings
So I can share and know.'

The sweetness of his singing brought tears to Miriael's eyes. Even in musical ability, he was so far above her. She listened in awe as he developed yet another tune.

'I think I understand the cause.
Heaven is your natural home,
But you have been shut out from there,
Abandoned and alone.'

The Morphs were equally affected. Their diaphanous structures swayed to the rhythm of his singing. They were no longer fearful or suspicious, only very very sad.

'Yes, yes, alone, alo-o-o-o-ne!' they chorused. 'We're shut our from our ho-o-o-o-o-ome!'

Already he had won them over. Truly, he was no ordinary angel. Miriael could see the light spilling out from the radiant centre of his heart. Surely he ought to be more than a mere Tenth Angel of Strategy! He ought to be a great Hierarch in Heaven!

Still he sang on to the Morphs, soothing away their sadness. One by one, they stopped wailing.

'You do not merit such a fate.
I know just how you feel,
Shut out from the celestial realm
With no hope of appeal.'

Miriael said nothing. But a sudden thought occurred to her. She stayed in the background as Asmodai went on to question the Morphs about their past lives and present existence. But now she had a question to ask *him*.

10

They walked back along the street from the square. Asmodai had conversed with the Morphs for nearly half an hour. He was full of enthusiasm.

'I didn't tell them about their military value,' he said. 'I didn't want to unsettle them. They have no idea of their own potential. They could be an entirely new kind of force.'

Miriael couldn't think how to ask her question. She didn't want to turn him against her. If she was wrong, he might be deeply offended.

'No need for them to go up to Heaven,' he continued. 'They could play a crucial role down here below. According to my research, there may be as many as twenty thousand Morphs on this continent alone. And their numbers are increasing all the time.'

He talked on until they arrived at the lane, where Miriael would have to creep through under the bushes. Then he halted.

'Now I must return to Heaven,' he said. 'I shall examine the archives for further information on Morphs.'

Miriael nodded. 'Asmodai,' she began.

It was now or never. If she couldn't ask her question tactfully, she'd just have to ask it anyway. She looked him firmly in the eye.

'Asmodai, were you once a Fallen Angel?'

A sudden vulnerability showed on his beautiful face. He didn't deny it.

'Why do you ask me that?'

'Because of what you sang to the Morphs. *I know just how you feel, shut out from the celestial realm with no hope of appeal.* Were you shut out yourself?'

He hung his head with an expression of pain. His aura shrank and dimmed.

'Yes,' he answered in a whisper.

'You were expelled from Heaven? Then you repented, like Berial and Meresin? You were allowed back in only after the Great Collapse?'

'Yes.'

The word was almost a sob. Her heart melted for him.

'Look at me,' she said.

Slowly he raised his eyes. Large as ever, mild as ever – but the glow within was muted. No light streamed out of him now. Miriael frowned.

'Why didn't you tell me?'

'I was ashamed.'

'In front of *me*? At least your fall was in the past.'

'It doesn't seem in the past to me. Not in Heaven. I'm always afraid that someone will speak of it. I'm always aware that I'm seen as different. I can never be as good as an unfallen angel.'

Miriael remembered how other angels had once stared at her own changed body. She remembered the looks on the faces of Chrymos and Neriah, Bethor and Cedrion, Gethel and Asiel. She too knew how it felt to be seen as different.

'They treat me as fairly as they can,' he continued. 'It's not that they're not merciful. I have their forgiveness. But I wish they could forget as well as forgive.'

'Angels don't have the power to forget,' said Miriael.

The glow rekindled a little in his eyes, as he realised she wasn't condemning him.

'Even if they could forget, could I ever forget myself? My own conscience keeps reminding me. Past folly, past error, past stupidity.'

'But you could forget when you were talking to me?' Miriael suggested shrewdly.

'Yes, because you're outside of Heaven. You're cut off and isolated. Also because you're different in yourself. I don't know how to explain, but . . .' He hesitated over his words. 'I was so happy to have you believe in me. To be able to do someone a kindness for the sake of kindness, and not have it thought I was only trying to compensate for the past. I can't tell you how wonderful it felt.' His voice sank suddenly. 'And now you've found out anyway.'

'I have.'

'So I've come down even lower in your opinion.'

'No, you haven't.'

'But I lied to you.'

'You held back the truth. It wasn't a bad lie.'

'It wasn't?'

Miriael smiled. 'I always thought you were too perfect to be true.'

'Oh! You suspected?'

'Not exactly. But I always thought there was something else about you.'

'Now you know.'

'Now I know. And it isn't so important after all.'

'Being a Fallen Angel? You don't think that's important?'

'Not as important as what you said a moment ago.'

Asmodai looked puzzled. Miriael explained.

'You said how happy you felt to do someone a kindness for the sake of kindness.'

'Yes.'

'Well, that's *real* goodness. Deep-down goodness. And I'm sure it was always there. Even when you were a Fallen Angel.'

Asmodai stood taller and straighter in his globe. Now the light was streaming out of him again. Light like a wind, billowing his robe, stirring the fine spun-glass of his hair.

'Miriael, Miriael! If you believe in me, that's all I need!'

'Perhaps my belief will help you to leave the past behind.'

He laughed outright. 'Not yet! Not until I've completed my act of kindness! I won't forget my past until you're also redeemed and reconciled with Heaven!'

'You shouldn't –'

'I shall *make* them value you! With what you've discovered about Morphs! I'll confront even Uriel himself!

I won't reveal your singing technique, I won't say a thing about it! I'll tell them that only *you* can show them! Then they'll *have* to come down!'

His smile was so radiant, Miriael could hardly keep looking at him. She wanted to say, *Don't risk your own position in Heaven for me.* She wanted to say, *Don't risk them forbidding you to come down, because your visits matter most of all.*

But the words never left her mouth. Asmodai cried out at the top of his voice.

'They'll never ignore you again, Miriael!'

His globe bobbed and rocked like a bubble in the air. Then, with a mighty blast of light, he soared upwards into the sky.

11

Miriael retraced her tracks as far as the edge of the Nesters' territory. Then she examined her map for the first tribe on her list. She calculated the shortest possible route and set off in a fresh direction. She would have to try and make up the time she'd lost by her detour.

Hour after hour she strode along at a constant pace. She scarcely noticed the varying landscapes through which she passed. She was daydreaming about Asmodai.

Things had changed between them, she was sure. After this morning's revelation, they were more on a level. He too was less than perfect, he too had known weaknesses. She was delighted by the idea.

Just thinking about it, she felt a new kind of closeness to him. No longer would she be frozen by awe in his presence. She would respect him for what he really was – for his kindness, his beauty, his loving nature . . .

By late afternoon, she had come to a flood-plain of gravel and weeds. The puffball tops of dandelions balanced on delicate stems, motionless in the still air. Long grey bands of cloud lay across the face of the sun. Beyond the plain was an array of strange mounds covered in bright green grass. They looked too round and regular to be natural.

Then she saw him. Asmodai!

He stood in front of one of the mounds. Even at a distance, she could tell he was looking in her direction. He must be waiting for her. The light within his oval globe seemed almost milky.

She altered course to head towards him. Why was he waiting there? What did it mean?

She redoubled her pace. The clouds cast purple shadows over the plain, patches of shadow alternating with patches of sunlight.

Still he waited in front of the mounds, making no move towards her. She could see that he was smiling as she approached. Perhaps he had good news? Her heart beat faster in hopeful anticipation.

Then suddenly he raised his wand and the tube lit up with a white incandescence. It had to be good news!

She broke into a run over the last stretch of ground.

'What happened?' she cried as she came up to him. 'Are they going to come down?'

'I have a surprise for you.'

'What? Show me! Transfer the memory!'

She was bursting with excitement. Asmodai was clearly excited too.

'No. No need. We can do better than that.'

He pointed his wand towards the mounds, towards a channel between the two nearest mounds.

'Through there?' She was momentarily mystified.

'Not far.'

'Ah!' She clapped her hands. 'A visitor? Already?'

Asmodai refused to answer. But his smile gave the game away. There was no grand manner now, no standing on dignity. He was as pleased for her as she was for herself.

He turned and led the way between the mounds. The grass was spotted here and there with crimson flowers.

'Who is it?' Miriael insisted. 'Is it an angel? Tell me!'

Asmodai laughed and shook his head. His lips were sealed. They passed along the channel between the first two mounds, then right and left between further mounds.

Every mound was similar in shape and size. But the flowers grew more thickly as they penetrated deeper. All around, the smooth green slopes were splashed with glorious crimson. A sweet floral perfume filled the air.

Miriael scarcely noticed. An even more staggering thought had just occurred to her.

'It's not *Uriel*, is it?'

'Wait and see!' said Asmodai. 'You'll be amazed!'

He seemed hardly able to contain the secret himself. He hurried on, beckoning for her to follow. They went round another mound and came to an intersection of several channels.

Here the flowers grew side by side in a sea of bright red. Huge wide petals nestled in soft green leaves. Where the sunlight fell on them, the rich glowing colour was even more intense.

'When? When? When?' Miriael pleaded.

Asmodai took a step to one side. '*Now*!'

His tone had changed. At the single crisp word of command, six black-suited Hypers leaped from behind the surrounding mounds. An evil gleam shone in their eyeslits and mouthslits. Snarling and snapping their metal teeth, they came hurtling towards her.

12

She was easily overpowered. She couldn't think, couldn't act, couldn't believe. The Hypers knocked her down, kicking her legs from under her. All she knew was the sick, sick feeling in the pit of her stomach.

Spiked boots pinned her to the ground. Two Hypers had their clammy rubber-covered hands around her wrists and ankles. But still she turned her eyes towards Asmodai. He was watching from five metres away.

'Help! Help me!' she cried.

She understood – and yet she didn't want to understand. A part of her still couldn't accept that such treachery was possible.

Asmodai continued to watch. He raised his eyebrows as her eyes met his.

The Hypers were equipped with spools of silvery plastic tape. They rolled her over, this way and that, and bound her from head to foot. They bent her arms so that her hands were behind her neck, elbows pointing outwards. Then they taped her wings to her arms.

It was all over in a matter of minutes. She was completely immobilised in a cocoon of silvery plastic. The tape was tough and sticky and very very tight. Only her face was left exposed.

Then Asmodai came forward in his globe. He halted beside the six Hypers and looked down at her. Side by side, the white radiance of the angel and the black menace of the Hypers.

'Very good,' he said. 'Now for your side of the bargain. I'll keep a watch on our captive.'

The Hypers marched off, disappearing behind a nearby mound. Miriael glared at Asmodai. She could no longer deny the truth.

'You traitor!' she spat at him. 'You fake! You Humen-lover!'

Asmodai's smile sharpened, but he said nothing. Even his radiance seemed somehow stained and dirty. Miriael struggled uselessly against her bonds.

A minute later there was a chugging rumbling sound and the Hypers returned with a transport machine. It was a Plasmatic-powered trolley with a dozen iron wheels. It was piled high with what looked like wire mesh screens.

It halted in front of Asmodai, who stepped forward to inspect. The wire was very fine, the frames of the screens very light.

'Specially constructed to your requirements,' rasped one of the Hypers. 'For whatever purpose.'

Obviously he didn't understand the purpose – and Asmodai didn't intend to tell him.

'Doctor Saniette is as good as his word,' said the

angel. He pointed to a flat space of grass not far away. 'Set it out over there.'

One of the Hypers uttered a mathematical command and the transport machine trundled off in the direction indicated. The Hypers marched along behind. Another mathematical command brought the machine to a stop.

The Hypers began unloading the screens, laying them out flat on the ground. They clipped them together to produce a single larger structure.

Asmodai turned to Miriael.

'Well, Miriael. Didn't I say you'd be surprised?'

She didn't want to speak with him. But she had to know. 'Why?'

He laughed. 'Why not? You're so narrow-minded. However, I'm not a Humen-lover. I could have been loyal to Heaven if they'd wanted to listen to me. All they had to do was let me put my strategies into practice. I could have won the Millennial War for them.'

'And ended up in supreme command.'

'Naturally. As my talents deserve. They have only their own folly to blame.'

Miriael scowled. 'They were right all along about you.'

'Oh, no. That was merely a matter of prejudice. No Celestial ever penetrated my disguise.'

'What about my information? Did you pass any of it on?'

'About the importance of Residuals? Or the arrival of the new army? Or the date of Doctor Saniette's offensive?'

'Everything,' she snapped. She could see he was toying with her.

'I'm afraid that Heaven remains in a state of beautiful innocence about all of those developments.'

'And you never spoke to anyone about me?'

'Of course not. Now you're beginning to understand.'

'Those transferred memories –'

'Were artificial constructs. Real images of Heaven, but reshaped and combined with imaginary words and thoughts. Quite clever, wouldn't you agree? Not exactly the new technique I described to you, but equally remarkable in a different way.'

Miriael gritted her teeth. 'You've been planning this treachery for years, haven't you?'

Asmodai shrugged. 'Centuries.'

'You never stopped being a Fallen Angel, even when you were allowed back into Heaven. You never repented at all.'

'Repent? No, no. But I did learn. I examined the conduct of the Satanic rebellion and saw the mistakes to avoid. In particular, premature confrontation with superior forces. Unfortunately, our leader was too proud to work in secret. Whereas I've been able to bide my time. And now I have the means to win.'

A chill realisation clutched at Miriael's heart. 'The means to win?'

'Which you discovered for me.'

'The Morphs?' Miriael's voice was barely a whisper.

'Exactly. A new kind of force. *My* force. Thanks to my research, I know how to weld them into a fighting unit under my command. With their assistance, I shall be able to control the skies between Heaven and Earth.'

He was gloating in his own cleverness, Miriael could see. He might have learned to work in secret, but he hadn't learned to shed his pride. He couldn't resist the opportunity to boast.

'You've been visiting the City of the Dead on your own,' she said flatly. It wasn't even a question.

'Yes. I went back not long after our visit together. Sang to them sweetly for an hour or two. I'm glad to say they now trust me completely. As you did yourself, until a very short time ago.' He smiled. 'I seem to have a talent for building up trust. Even Doctor Saniette trusts me.'

'Until you're ready to betray him too?'

'Oh, our interests coincide for a while. He'll trust me even more now that I've handed you over. Ah – here's your escort coming to collect you.'

The Hypers had finished setting out the screens, which composed a huge delta triangle on the ground. They followed in the wake of the transport machine as it chug-chugged back towards Asmodai and Miriael.

Asmodai smiled lightly. 'Have a pleasant time in the Humen Camp, Miriael. I expect they'll be taking you to their surgeries.'

He turned to the Hypers. 'And farewell to you too. Give my regards to Doctor Saniette.'

He glided away towards the screens. The Hypers gathered around Miriael's plastic-shrouded body. They seized hold of her, lifted and dumped her on top of the transport machine.

13

Gibby bent down and called softly into the entrance-hole.

'Bross. Bross. *Bross.*'

'Shh, not too loud,' whispered Rhinn. 'You'll wake the whole family.'

They waited and listened outside Bross's family nest. Rhinn crouched behind Gibby, Tadge and Ethamy stood behind Rhinn. The moon had gone down and the night was very dark.

'Who's calling?' came a sleep-slurred voice from within. Bross's voice.

'Come outside,' whispered Gibby. 'We want to talk to you.'

A few moments later, Bross crawled out to join them. They sat in a circle, a short distance away from the nest. Bross was yawning and rubbing his eyes.

'What's going on?' he demanded. 'What time is it?'

'Middle of the night,' said Rhinn.

'What are you doing out in the middle of the night?'

'We've been talking,' answered Rhinn. 'We're worried about Kiet.'

'First she's travelling on with Ferren,' said Ethamy. 'Then she isn't. Now she won't say what she's doing.'

'They should have left yesterday.' Rhinn spread her arms in despair. 'She won't make up her mind. Nor will he.'

'We thought you might know something,' said Tadge.

'Are you still going to be mated with her?' asked Ethamy.

Bross scratched his head. 'I'm not sure.'

'What about Second Intimacies?' asked Rhinn. 'When was that supposed to happen?'

There were stifled giggles from Gibby and Tadge. In Second Intimacies, the male and female washed each other in spice-scented water, wearing special garments with cut-out holes. Rhinn quelled the giggles with a frown.

'We didn't do Second Intimacies.' Bross sounded vaguely bemused. 'It was supposed to be this afternoon, but it got called off before it began. Kiet got into an argument and shouted at Clemmart.'

'She lost her temper with a Guardian?'

'Yes. Shouting and yelling. My parents say she's gone back to her old ways. They want to cancel the mating.'

'Oh.' Rhinn clicked her tongue. 'What do you want?'

'Me?' Bross stretched his limbs and thought for a moment. 'I never cared much about mating. If it has to be anyone, I don't mind Kiet. But I –'

'What's that?' Tadge sat up, suddenly very straight. 'What?'

'The smell.'

Everyone sniffed the air.

'Smoke!'

'A fire!'

Gibby and Tadge were the first on their feet, followed by Rhinn and Ethamy. They hurried to an open space where they could see the sky. On one side of the sky was an ominous red glow.

'It's a bushfire!' cried Tadge.

Rhinn studied the direction and distance. 'It's somewhere near the City of the Dead,' she said grimly.

14

Daylight revealed a scene of devastation. The bushfire had halted on the other side of the valley, unable to jump the network of rivulets. But the vegetation around the ruins had been burnt to the ground. Bare soot-blackened walls rose up against a pale dawn sky.

The Nesters gazed in awe across the valley. They had gathered gradually during the night, lining up along the rocky outcrop as though for a Summoning. No-one spoke, but the same question was in every mind. Had the Morphs survived?

Kiet stood with her own Heartstock. Ferren was at the front of the outcrop, ten metres to her right. She saw him, but looked quickly away. She noticed that he didn't look at her either.

The Guardians waited until the sun was fully risen. Only then did they decide it was safe to enter the ruins. Columns of smoke spiralled up in the air, but there were no visible flames. The Guardians and young Nesters led the way across the valley.

The Guardians carried the carved instruments of

wood and animal skin that they used for a Summoning. They attempted a Summoning on the platform outside the walls. The concrete was hot underfoot.

There was no response. In vain the Guardians banged on their instruments and yelled at the tops of their voices. When the noise ceased, the City of the Dead remained silent.

Then the young Nesters took over the lead and entered the narrow lane. The bushes in the lane were now mere charcoal skeletons of themselves. There was no need to crawl underneath: a touch was enough to shatter them.

The street beyond was equally transformed. Not one tree remained standing. All that was left were charred and broken sections of log, lying this way and that across the roadway. In some places, the wood still smouldered with a dull red glow.

The stale dry smell of smoke caught in their throats and made them cough. They wove a route around and between the logs. Dead cinders crunched under their feet. Their eyes watered as the air grew smokier.

Finally they arrived at the square. Kiet gazed around in dismay. This time she had no sense of invisible presences.

The entire square was carpeted in grey ash. Ash in the cracks between the flagstones, ash piled up in the corners, ash forming tiny drifts in the lee of the rubble. The blades of grass had vanished completely.

The Nesters stopped in the entrance to the square and the Guardians again attempted a Summoning. Clouds of powdery ash flew up around their feet as they danced and banged and yelled. The silence afterwards was more absolute than ever.

Then everyone spread out across the square. Dislodging the Morphs was no longer a consideration. They swept this way and that with outstretched arms. They moved through the rubble where Miriael had once knelt to sing. If only a Morph would wail in protest . . .

But there were no wails of protest.

'Gone,' sniffed Dunkery miserably. 'Our Morphs have gone.'

'I can't believe an ordinary fire would've done this,' said Ferren.

Everyone stood around looking hopeless.

Then Ethamy gave a sudden shout. She was staring into a gap between the buildings, where a passageway opened off from the square.

'I think I can hear one!' she cried.

15

'Where are you hiding?
   There is no need to fear.
   Say something back to me,
   Let me know you hear.'

Ferren couldn't compose tunes like Miriael, but he did his best. He stood at the front of the Nesters, halfway up the steps. The Morph responded with a long trembling wail.

The steps ran up between the walls of the passageway. One of the steps had caved in, revealing a dark hole underneath. The Morph had lodged somewhere inside the hole.

Again and again, Ferren repeated his chant. He crouched over the hole and tried to make his voice sound soothing. With each repetition, the Morph became a little calmer. Finally, it was able to answer in words.

'Only me! Only me! Only me-e-e-ee!'

The Nesters were pressing against Ferren's shoulders from behind. He held up his arms to dam them back.

'Where are the other Morphs?
Where have they gone?
Did the fire burn them?
Please answer my song.'

'It wasn't the fire!' the Morph piped out from the hole. 'It was Asmodai!'

Ferren frowned. Kiet whistled. The other Nesters looked puzzled. The name meant nothing to them.

Ferren sang out another chant, requesting more information. The Morph had become agitated again, and answered at first in fits and snatches. But gradually the whole story emerged.

'He sang so beautifully to us. He came with the angel Miriael and she introduced him as a friend. She told us to trust him and we did.

'Then he came back later on his own. He said it was unfair we were shut out of Heaven; we had to demand entry. We had to appear ourselves at the gates of Heaven. He wanted us to link up and fly together. He could show us how to do it, he said. But some of us weren't so sure. We didn't want to let go of our lodging-places, not until we were sure.

'He smiled and said to take our time. Then last night the fire began. We could smell the smoke and see the glow. It started on the edge of the City of the Dead. But the breeze was carrying it in our direction.

'It was terrible. We were afraid to lose our lodging-places. We knew we'd be scattered and lost for years and years. There were sparks in the air floating down. Then Asmodai appeared.

'He rose up over the buildings against the sky. His

globe was like a big bright eye in the middle of a huge flying triangle. It was a delta wing made out of wire. He called to us: *I'll carry you to safety!*

'He sailed down lower and lower. The wing stretched halfway across the square. He told us to let go of our bits of grass and stone, and catch onto the wire. He said he'd tow us clear.

'We were shaking and wailing. We could see the glow of the flames getting nearer, sparks raining down on us. But we didn't want to lose our lodging-places.

'Then the wire began to jingle. It was like music, little notes of music. The first Morph jumped across, then more and more. They reattached themselves to the patterns of the wire. But I couldn't make up my mind. Even when I was the last one left, I couldn't make up my mind.

'Asmodai thought everyone had made the jump. Suddenly the wing lifted away from the ground. He cried out in a tremendous voice: *Now! Be fixed!*

'And something ran through the wires like a force. It spread out around his globe, crackling with energy. The Morphs screamed. But it was too late. They were fixed rigid, locked into position on the wire.

'Then he laughed out loud. *Welcome to my flying wing! Congratulations! You are the first colony of Morphs to come under my command!*

'He was mocking them. And all the time the fire was getting worse. The grass in the square started to catch alight. But he didn't fly off. He deliberately came down low again, so low that the Morphs were right against the flames.

'*This is your first training,* he told them. *I don't want cowards in my wing. You'll experience fear until you can't be fearful any more. Until you become the perfect extensions of my will.*

'He kept talking and talking, boasting and boasting. He didn't care about their screams. He had to tell them everything he'd done, how clever and wonderful he was.

'I was terrified he'd see me. And I was terrified the fire would get to me. Flames were jumping from stalk to stalk, coming towards my corner of the square.

'Still he kept boasting. One of my stalks started to burn. If I let go, he'd be sure to see me. But I couldn't bear the heat. It was dreadful, dreadful, dreadful!'

The tiny fluting voice broke down in a drawn-out wail. Ferren and the Nesters waited patiently. It was several minutes before the Morph was able to finish the story.

'I let go just at the moment when he took off. He never saw me. The wing went soaring high in the sky and I was blown away on a gust of hot air. I ought to have been burnt up, but I wasn't. I was blown into this dark hole. I've been here ever since.'

Ferren knit his brows. He was troubled about the fate of the other Morphs and troubled about the treachery of Asmodai. But most of all he was troubled about something the Morph had said at the start.

He struggled to turn his question into a song.

'You said the angel Miriael
Came back with Asmodai.
How many days ago was that?

256

And can you tell me why?'

'It was yesterday,' answered the tiny voice. 'She came back with him, then he came by himself, then he came with his flying wing. She brought him so that he could talk to us.'

'But she couldn't have been involved in his plot!'

He had forgotten to speak in a song. The Morph uttered a peep of protest, then answered nonetheless.

'No, not in his plot. He betrayed her too. He boasted about it. He said he'd handed her over to the Humen, and they were taking her off to their surgeries.'

Ferren staggered as the words sank home. He couldn't speak. He pressed a fist against his forehead and turned away from the hole. He needed time to think.

The Nesters pressed forward. Even though the Morph was invisible to them, they were curious to look into the hole. They discussed the situation in whispers among themselves.

Then Grandfather Niot and Uncle Abnel came up to the front of the crowd. They knelt on the step beside the hole. Grandfather Niot counted to three. On the count of three they began to sing.

'O take heart, O be strong, O be brave!
We'll sing you a song in your cave!
You won't be alone, never fear!
The Nesters will care for you here!'

It was an old song with new words. Grandfather Niot's bass mingled with Uncle Abnel's baritone. They sang it very softly, very soothingly.

16

The young Nesters had gathered around Ferren in the square. The adult Nesters and Guardians remained in the passageway, entranced by the singing of Grandfather Niot and Uncle Abnel. Kiet joined in at the back of the crowd in the square.

'I need to ask an urgent favour,' Ferren was saying. 'I can't continue with my mission to the Residual tribes. I need volunteers to take over from me. I'll tell you where to go and what to say.'

Someone asked the obvious question. 'Why can't you continue?'

'Because I have to try and rescue Miriael.'

There was a moment of stunned silence. Kiet noted the jut of his jaw and the look in his eyes. He's absolutely determined, she thought to herself. It's what he said, about being in love. He'd do anything for her.

The young Nesters began to recover their voices.

'Rescue her from the Humen Camp?'

'That's impossible!'

'It's suicide!'

'No, it isn't.' Ferren shook his head. 'I've been inside the Humen Camp before, remember? I told you. Anyway, I'm going to do it.'

Flens stepped forward. 'I'll do it with you,' he announced.

Ferren seemed completely taken aback. Flens grinned his daredevil grin.

'Other people can volunteer for the mission to the tribes,' he said. 'I volunteer for the rescue party.'

A reluctant smile broke out on Ferren's face. 'I'd be glad to have you along,' he confessed.

'Me too!' cried Gibby, also stepping forward. 'I volunteer for the rescue party!'

Then everyone started calling out and stepping forward. For a while, there was complete chaos. Finally the volunteers sorted themselves into separate groups. The volunteers for the rescue party congregated on the right, the volunteers for the mission to the tribes on the left.

Kiet remained with the rapidly dwindling group in the middle. She was in a quandary. On the one hand, she was the only young Nester who had experience of visiting another tribe. So that was a very good reason for joining the mission to the tribes.

On the other hand, she felt a kind of personal responsibility towards Miriael. She remembered the time they'd fought side by side against the seagulls, and the time they'd hidden together in the overbridge while the Humen army went by on top. If people who hardly knew Miriael were willing to risk their lives . . .

'Kiet!' It was Rhinn turning around to address her in

a loud whisper. 'What will you do? I'll do the same as you!'

Still she couldn't decide. She glanced away – and caught Ferren's eye upon her.

What was his expression? Curiosity? Concern? He was probably hoping that she'd join the mission to the Residual tribes.

'I'll go with the rescue party,' she said.

4

DOCTOR SANIETTE

1

The smell of hospital anaesthetic. Clean white surfaces of glossy plastic and enamel. Cold white glare of light-panels on the ceiling. Immobilised in her cocoon of tape, Miriael shuddered.

It was what she'd always dreaded. Long ago, when first captured by the Humen, she'd nearly been taken to their surgeries in the Bankstown Complex. Then she'd escaped, miraculously. She could hardly believe she'd fallen into their hands again.

She rotated her eyes towards the machine that awaited her. The machine that would extract her memory slice by slice.

It was a huge hollow cylinder in telescopic sections, closed off by fan shutters at either end. Attached all around were Plasmatics in transparent chambers. Flexible nerve-tubes carried signals to the Plasmatics from a branching pipe overhead. The pipe itself emerged from a frosted glass window occupying one whole side of the room.

'Looking forward to it, are yer, sweetypants?'

She shifted her gaze to the two medical assistants. She didn't know which of the two had spoken. They were clad in the usual close-fitting suits of black rubber, with the addition of gauze masks over their mouthslits. One carried a holster-like pouch strapped to his thigh and a stethoscope round his neck. The other wore a message-screen on his chest.

'What's the point of this?' Miriael appealed. 'I'm not in communication with Heaven any more. I don't have any secrets to reveal. You might as well kill me now.'

The Hyper with the message-screen only jeered. 'What, and miss out on seeing you suffer? You wouldn't want to take away our fun, would yer?'

The other Hyper opened his pouch and produced a sharp-pointed pair of scissors. He snipped at the plastic tape covering the top of Miriael's head. When he pulled the lengths away, the adhesive almost ripped out her hair at the roots.

She clamped down on the cry that threatened to escape from her lips. She had the satisfaction of hearing a small grunt of disappointment.

A ping-pinging sound announced that a message had come in for the Hyper with the message-screen. He glanced down at his chest and read off the luminous blue symbols.

'Time to begin,' he said.

They swivelled the hospital trolley on which Miriael lay. Suddenly brusque and business-like, they lined her up with her head towards the lower end of the cylinder.

At the same time, the Plasmatics stirred in their chambers. Pink tissue dilated, grey-blue muscle heaved.

The fan shutters rolled away to open the ends of the cylinder. Adjusting for length, the sections of the cylinders telescoped a few centimetres outwards.

Then the trolley began to move forward. Miriael could see all the way through to the other end of the cylinder. No use struggling – the cocoon had defeated her best efforts ever since she'd been captured. She took a deep breath and waited for the agony to begin.

With a smooth low hum, the electronics switched on. The tips of a dozen valves glowed green and red. Brighter and brighter and brighter they glowed. One of the medical assistants gave a cry of alarm.

There was a sudden fizz of dazzling light. A violent *pop*! Then all the lights went off.

The breath rushed out of Miriael in a gasp. The electronics had blown up! The machine had malfunctioned!

Saved!

She couldn't see a thing in the dark. The Plasmatics made squishy gurgling sounds. A smell of scorched plastic drifted in the air. She heard the Hypers swearing, felt a bump as they knocked against the trolly.

'Must've been the power supply.'

'Some kind of overload.'

'I bet it's another bloody sabotage.'

A dim half-light returned. It came from a room on the other side of the frosted glass window. Miriael could see a silhouetted figure behind the glass.

Then the figure moved away. A moment later a door opened, beyond the range of her vision.

'The control system's fused,' rasped a harsh voice. 'Half the equipment wrecked.'

It was the typical voice of a Hyper – yet also somehow different. For one thing, it was unmistakably female.

'Another bloody sabotage,' said the Hyper with the stethoscope.

'What?' There was latent ferocity in the tone. 'What do you mean, *Another bloody sabotage*?'

'It's happened before,' stammered the Hyper with the message-screen.

'When?'

'When the old Doctors were in charge. Before you came. Every week or so, something would go wrong somewhere in the Camp.'

'Like what?'

'Like sudden electricity surges. Engines tampered with. Taps on tanks left leaking. Only small things.'

'Small? Small? You call this *small*?'

As the medical assistants backed away, the female Hyper came into view. She was taller than any ordinary Hyper and moved with a menacing feline grace. Her black rubber suit was half hidden by external attachments: a domed white blister between her shoulder-blades, tubes running down her arms and legs, a maze of copper circuitry on her neck and cheeks. Unlike the metal ornaments beloved by all Hypers, these attachments were clearly parts of her own body.

Miriael remembered similar augmented Hypers that she'd seen leaping in great strides along the overbridge. She also remembered the Selector's phrase: *Queen-Hypers*. This must be one of Doctor Saniette's new warriors.

The two medical assistants were clearly in awe of her. They stumbled over one another in their eagerness to explain about the sabotage.

'It was suspected someone had gone off the rails.'

'Some disaffected Hyper.'

'Wanting revenge.'

'The old Doctors never found out who.'

'You ought to inform Doctor Saniette.'

The Queen-Hyper shut them up with a snarl. 'I don't need to inform him. He already knows.'

The Hyper with the stethoscope looked puzzled. 'But *you* didn't know. Why should he –'

'Doctor Saniette knows everything. He's the supreme intelligence. He's the most conscious being that ever existed.'

'Why doesn't he catch who's doing it then?'

A sudden animalistic rictus took possession of the Queen-Hyper's face. Mouthslit stretched wide, metal teeth quivered.

'Fool! You want to be at the front of the first battalion in the great offensive?'

The medical assistant shook his head desperately. 'I didn't mean –'

She sprang forward and caught hold of the middle finger of his left hand. With a sharp wrench, she snapped it clean off.

There was a small release of multi-coloured vapour. The medical assistant moaned and gripped the stump in his other hand, staunching the leak. The Queen-Hyper tossed the broken digit indifferently on the floor.

Ping-ping!

The Hyper with the message-screen looked down at the new message coming in. The symbols this time were in luminous red. The Queen-Hyper bent to read it too.

'Didn't I say he knows everything?' She pointed to the message. 'He's already aware of what happened here. He orders me to report to him immediately.'

She whirled around and moved towards the door. She covered half the distance in a single stride.

'Er, what about her?' asked the Hyper with the message-screen.

The Queen-Hyper halted, glanced back at Miriael on the trolley.

'Keep her exactly as she is. This is only a postponement.' She uttered a sound that might have been a laugh. 'Who knows, maybe Doctor Saniette will perform the operation himself. I've seen him do it. It hurts much more than any machine when *he* does it.'

Another long bounding stride took her out of the room.

2

The Humen Camp was very different to the way Ferren remembered. The changes had been obvious even last night, when the rescue party had arrived on the outskirts. Walking in under an overbridge, they had goggled at the huge pyramid-like shapes looming all around in the dark. Machines and constructions of many kinds extended far beyond the Camp's original boundaries.

The machines and constructions seemed to offer more cover than the overbridge itself. The rescue party had taken refuge in a towering frame of tubular steel, sheltering behind panels of sheet metal. It was like being in an iron tent. A distant mechanical rumble troubled their sleep all night.

Now, in the morning light, they were able to take a better look. Peering out from their refuge, they studied the Camp in front of them.

As on Ferren's previous visit, it was shielded against Heavenly attack by vast rotating overhead canopies. But it was no longer so strongly guarded at ground

269

level. Now there were dozens of makeshift bridges spanning the moat, crossing over the embankment. It seemed that the preparations for Doctor Saniette's offensive required not only an extension beyond the original boundaries but also easier access into the Camp itself.

Ferren called everyone together after breakfast. He told them that Doctor Saniette would be launching his offensive very soon.

'It may help us if everything's more chaotic than usual,' he said. 'But the offensive isn't our business. We go in to rescue Miriael.'

The young Nesters listened with serious faces. Ferren paused and looked around. Were they all equally committed to the rescue of Miriael?

'However, we can't all go in,' he continued. 'We'd be sure to be noticed. I want a team of eight – me and seven others. The rest to wait out here as a back-up party.'

Groans of protest arose. 'We all volunteered,' they complained.

But Ferren stood firm. He turned to Flens. He had no doubts about Flens's fearlessness.

'You were the first to volunteer,' he said. 'You know everyone here better than I do. You choose another six for the team.'

Flens scratched his big ugly nose and looked sheepish. He scanned the group of young Nesters. He nodded with relief when his gaze fell upon Kiet.

'Kiet for one,' he said.

She seemed pleased enough. She came out to stand

beside Flens. The two of them put their heads together, and the remainder of the team was chosen by whispered consultation. First Rhinn, then Tadge, then Gibby, then Ethamy. There was a longer consultation before Flens announced the final team member.

'Bross,' he said.

Bross looked delighted. It was obvious he hadn't expected to be picked. Yet his physical strength and athletic ability made him a natural choice.

Ferren nodded. 'Okay, that's eight of us. We'll aim to break in under cover of night. For the rest of you, your task is to turn this place into a proper base. Better protection, better camouflage. Mount a lookout at all times.'

Then he took the team aside to talk separately. He wanted them to understand the risks of the rescue.

'Our only advantage is, we're small enough to get in under the Humen defences. That's how I survived in the Camp before. They won't dream that anyone would just walk right in. Least of all a bunch of Residuals. But even when we're in, we've still got one huge problem – I don't know where to find the surgeries. I don't even know what they look like. I tried once before and couldn't find them.'

'Perhaps we should capture one of the Hypers,' suggested Flens. 'Force him to tell us.'

'Mmm.' Ferren could see difficulties in the plan.

'Or trick him into telling us,' Tadge put in.

'Let's worry about that later,' said Kiet practically. 'It's going to be hard enough getting in.' She turned to Ferren. 'Why don't you tell us everything you remember about the Camp?'

So Ferren told them everything he remembered. He'd only seen a fraction of the total complex, and he wasn't very sure about the location of what he'd seen. But he described the food stores and stockpiles, the barracks and furnaces, the mechanical monsters and the Pit.

He was aware of Kiet's eyes upon him as he talked. It was the most attention she'd paid him for days.

Afterwards, though, she went back to avoiding him. As soon as the gathering broke up, she moved off in a hurry and became deeply involved in a conversation with Ethamy. He wished he could talk to her in the old way. But she appeared to have forgotten they'd ever been friends.

There was no-one else with whom he could share his doubts and worries. He climbed up inside the tubular steel frame and reached a horizontal bar twenty metres above the ground. Perched on the bar, he could watch the activities of the Humen on the plain around the Camp.

The more he watched, the more he realised how highly organised it all was. Draglines and dredges wheeled, dug, emptied, wheeled again. Troops of Hypers marched this way and that at a frantic pace. Instead of chaos, there was a remarkable degree of coordination.

Observing the areas of most activity, he calculated the least risky route to the moat. He also noted some patches of oil and grime, which could be used for purposes of disguise. As for a way of crossing the moat . . . he fixed eventually on a large powerline that passed over the water on metal supports. Much better than the bridges . . .

He planned everything he could plan. Then stayed on his perch, going over and over it in his mind. He could only pray that the rescue attempt wasn't already too late. He waited impatiently for the hours to pass.

3

At night, the activity in and around the Camp continued under arc-lights. The lights shed pools of intense blue-white brilliance. Between the pools was darkness and shadow.

The team advanced to the moat. They had blackened themselves in oil and grime, imitating the black rubber suits of the Hypers. They tried to imitate the gait of Hypers too, marching along like a regular work-party. Ferren steered them clear of the real Hypers.

Close up, the constant dull rumble of the Camp turned into something more distinguishable. There was a rhythm to it – or rather, a multitude of related rhythms. Every booming, clanging or hammering had its place in the design. Once again, Ferren had a sense of extraordinary coordination. It was as though the entire Camp moved to the thoughts of a single mind.

They marched along by the side of the moat. The water was murky, the banks were in darkness. Directly ahead, the powerline crossed the water in a succession of loops, hanging down between its supports. It crossed at a much lower level than the bridges.

A few metres away, Ferren gave the signal. They dropped to the ground and rolled over the lip of the bank. Hidden from view, they scuffled over soft earth and gathered by the side of the powerline.

It was as thick as a tree trunk, sheathed in grey plastic. When Ferren touched it, it seemed to thrum under his hand. He had a sense of energy streaming from the Camp to the machines outside.

He climbed up onto it, gripping tight with arms and legs. The thrumming also had a rhythm of its own. He worked his way forward, little by little, over the water.

There were lights in the distance, but none shone towards him. The difficulty was in staying on top of the powerline. The smooth plastic and the oil on his body made a treacherous combination.

He passed the first support and half slid down the loop that followed. The supports swayed alarmingly. They looked like temporary structures held together with clamps and butterfly nuts. He signalled to the rest of the team: only one at a time.

Then he continued on his way. At one point, the powerline sagged down until it was almost touching the water. But at last he reached the other side.

He waited while the others followed. Crossing one at a time, it seemed to take forever. But no-one was observed and no-one fell off.

When the team had reassembled, Ferren led them up the embankment. The embankment was an artificial rampart of compressed cinders, twenty metres higher than the opposite bank. They pressed themselves flat against the slope, trusting that their blackened bodies would merge with the black of the cinders. The cinders crunched under them as they climbed.

At the top was a wire fence. Here they had a stroke of luck. The fence had been cut and parted so that the powerline could pass through. No-one had bothered to seal up the gap around the powerline afterwards.

Through the fence and into the Camp. Now they were in an area of stacked building materials. Stack after stack in row after row, mostly large rectangular slabs of composite. The composite looked like crushed rock and rubbish bonded with plastic fibre.

They veered away from the powerline and threaded between the stacks in single file. Somewhere ahead they could hear loudspeaker announcements.

Build it, build it, for the great offensive!

Faster, faster, faster for your Doctor!

It was the recorded voice of Doctor Saniette, amplified and echoing. The rhythm was urgent but the tone was lifeless.

They kept going until they came to the end of the stacks. Now they looked out over an area of open ground.

On the right, huge earthmoving machines roared and charged. They were demolishing a cluster of U-shaped huts. Corrugated roofs crumpled like paper under their scoops and shovels.

On the left, a new building was rising up. The building-plan was already marked out with blue lines in the air, a diagram formed by intersecting lasers. A non-stop stream of slabs converged towards the site on overhead cables. Gangs of Hypers manoeuvred and locked each slab into place according to the diagram.

Ferren watched in amazement. The diagram was filling up and becoming solid before his eyes. The Hypers drilled and riveted and welded as if choreographed. Showers of sparks flew over them as they worked.

Further loudspeaker announcements pushed them to greater efforts:

How are you working, Troop 223?

Are you in rhythm, are you focussed?

Do it, do it, do it for your Doctor!

There was also a gigantic electronic signboard with words in flashing red lights:

OFFENSIVE BEGINS IN 28 HOURS 32 MINUTES!

And, a moment later:

OFFENSIVE BEGINS IN 28 HOURS 31 MINUTES!

A whisper in his ear brought Ferren back to the immediate problem.

'What do you think?' asked Rhinn. 'Can we get across?'

'It'll take ages if we don't,' whispered Flens in his other ear.

Ferren nodded. It would require a long detour to go around to the right or the left. Whereas here in the middle it was relatively dark and not very far to the other side. But it was still risky. Unless . . .

He swung and stared at the stacks of building materials. He snapped his fingers.

'Okay. Here's how we do it.'

The team nodded agreement as he explained his idea.

'As long as the slabs aren't too heavy,' said Bross. 'I mean, for Tadge and Gibby.'

'Don't worry about us!' snorted Gibby.

Each member of the team collected a slab. They carried them in front of their chests, hooking their fingers under the lower edge. The tops of the slabs came up over their heads and hid their faces from view.

'They'll never see us like this!' cried Tadge, staggering a little under the weight.

'Let's go,' said Ferren.

They marched out across the open space. On the right was the roar of earthmoving machines, on the left the racket of drills and riveters. The Hypers were absorbed in their own tasks. They were all at least thirty metres away.

Ferren took a peep forward around the side of his slab. The team was approaching an array of tall torpedo-shaped cylinders, painted red and white, standing vertically in racks. They were halfway there already.

Then he heard a sound of crying and whimpering. Wretched hopeless voices – where?

He came to a sudden halt and the team halted behind him. Where, where, where?

Then he looked up and saw them. A group of terrified Residuals was passing across in a cage overhead. The cage glided along on a cable, the Residuals clutched at the bars.

He knew immediately where they were heading – to the Pit! Like the Residuals he had seen on his previous visit, like his own mother and father, like his sister Shanna! Condemned to the same unspeakable death in the Pit!

He forgot everything. He even forgot to keep his face hidden. His heart went out to the victims in the cage. He turned to watch as they passed overhead. There must be a way to help . . .

'Keep moving!' hissed Kiet. 'We can't stand here!'

But it was already too late. They had drawn attention to themselves: the only motionless figures in a scene of universal activity.

'You there!' A shout rang out from the direction of the earthmoving machines. 'Where you going with those slabs?'

They started forward again. But another shout rang out.

'Whose command are you under?'

Then a shout in a different tone.

'Stop where you are!'

They dropped their slabs to the ground and ran.

4

They ran in among the racks of cylinders. A dozen voices were now shouting, a dozen Hypers in pursuit.

A blast of cold air struck them. The cylinders were icy and coated with frost. Tendrils of white vapour drifted around like frozen steam.

Behind them, new announcements were already blaring forth on the loudspeakers.

Troop 229 alert! Troop 223 alert! Troop 341 alert! Troop 58 alert!

Search for unidentified fugitives in Industrial Zone 8C! Report all sightings to Doctor Saniette!

They arrived at a line of steel rails and a procession of slowly-moving buckets on wheels. Ferren led the team over the rails, between the buckets.

On the other side were huge hulking units of heavy machinery. Gleaming pistons rose and fell, parallel shunts slid back and forth. The ground was covered with metal gratings, a slippery surface thick with grease. They had to duck and weave their way around whizzing belts and spinning axles.

Whumpp! Ussh! Whumpp! Ussh! Whumpp! Ussh!

Ferren could hear the heaving and panting of Plasmatics labouring away inside the machinery. But he knew from his previous visit to the Camp that they were no danger. Even if they could see or hear, they could only act under direct mathematical orders.

The loudspeaker announcements seemed to come from all sides. So did the shouts of Hypers. The dozen chasing behind weren't the only danger. Other troops were entering the industrial zone from other directions.

They scuttled along, half sliding and skidding on the grease. Then suddenly Tadge cried out.

'Ow-ow!'

He had fallen through a hole in one of the gratings. His foot was trapped up to the ankle. The team skidded to a halt.

Bross grabbed him round the waist and hoisted him into the air. The entire grating lifted up from the ground. Kiet and Ethamy manipulated his foot and twisted the grating. In a moment he was free.

'Wait!' hissed Ferren, as the grating dropped back. 'What's down there?'

They pulled the grating aside and stared into a dark hole. There was an echoing emptiness and a glint of water two metres below.

'Quick!' said Ferren.

No need for further instructions. One by one, they jumped down into the hole, then moved aside to make room for the next person. The emptiness seemed to extend on all sides. The water was only a few centimetres deep.

Ferren was last down. He reached up and dragged the grating back into place. It slotted home with a dull clang.

Had they been spotted? Had they been heard? The first wave of boots approached, pounding on the metal overhead. They held their breath.

The first wave of boots passed over and dwindled away.

Still there were more to come. They waited as a second wave passed over in a different direction. Then a third, then a fourth. They heard shouting and cursing and voices reporting into microphones.

Then silence. They grinned with relief. Their faces were pale blurs in the darkness.

But it wasn't completely dark. Faint light seeped down through a hundred gratings. They surveyed their surroundings: a vast subterranean world. Rows of piers stretched endlessly into the dim distance.

'How far does it go?' whispered Flens, in wonder.

'Let's find out,' said Ferren. 'How's your ankle, Tadge?'

'Sore. Not sprained.'

'Good. We'll walk as far as we can before climbing out.'

Kiet whirled suddenly. 'What was that?'

'What?'

'I thought I heard a splash.'

'Where?'

'I don't know. Not close. Over there perhaps?'

She pointed. But nothing could be seen in the faint light. She shrugged.

'Maybe I imagined it. Let's go.'

'Stay close together,' Ferren warned.

He set off and the team followed, sloshing along through slimy water. In some places the water rose as high as their knees. After stubbing his toes a few times, Ferren soon learned to walk carefully. There were hidden sills between the piers.

Their progress was accompanied by the constant drumming of machinery overhead. Now and then they heard sharper clanks and rattles. But was there another noise as well?

Kiet tapped Ferren on the shoulder.

'Did you hear it?' she whispered. 'Did you hear it that time?'

Ferren nodded. 'I heard something.'

Flens joined in over Ferren's other shoulder. 'Perhaps we're being followed? Perhaps a Hyper came down after us?'

Ferren was troubled. If a Hyper was following, he'd be able to summon help the moment they climbed back up to the surface.

'Let's keep moving for now,' he said. 'I don't think he intends to attack.'

They kept moving. In some places, the roof was hot from the machinery overhead, beating down in waves of warmth. In other places, hanging pipes dripped oily effluent all around them.

Ferren strained to hear the noise above the sound of their own splashing. A gentle swish of water, always exactly the same distance behind . . .

Something had to be done. He remembered Flens's idea of capturing a single Hyper and forcing him to reveal the location of the surgeries. Maybe the situation could be turned to advantage?

He signalled a halt and the team clustered around.

'Okay, we'll have to attack him. We'll work a trap.'

He spoke in a whisper. The swish had ceased as soon as their own splashing ceased.

'Here's the plan. As soon as we come to somewhere dark, four of us will split off and hide behind the piers. The rest keep going as if they were the whole team. Lots of noise and splashing. Then the four of us leap out as he passes.'

'Good,' said Bross.

Ferren named Flens, Kiet, Bross and himself as the four to leap out. Then they all turned and walked on as before.

After a while, Ferren saw an area where the light was blocked by an especially large unit of machinery above. He changed direction towards it. As they came under the shadow, he slipped off suddenly to the left. Flens slipped off to the right. They took up position behind a pair of piers. Kiet and Bross followed suit at the next pair of piers.

The rest of the team went on ahead. They made so much noise and splashing that Ferren could no longer hear the following swish. He measured out the time. Coming closer, coming level, passing in front . . .

'Now!'

There was a wild commotion as the trap sprang closed. Flens, Kiet and Bross dashed forward, kicking up water, yelling in the dark.

'Get him!'

'Bring him down!'

Only Ferren didn't dash forward. As he went to move, a strong sinewy hand clamped over his mouth. Something cold and thin pressed against his throat.

'This is a knife,' murmured a menacing voice in his ear.

He froze. Gradually the commotion between the piers died down.

'Have you got him?'

'That's me you're holding!'

'Where's the Hyper?'

The hand came away from Ferren's mouth, but not the knife from his throat. His captor pushed him half a pace forward, out at the side of the pier.

'Trying to catch me, hey?' The voice was hard and mocking. 'But you weren't quick enough. And now here's one of you caught instead.'

A torch snapped on and a beam of light shot forth. The beam was focussed upon Ferren, upon the knife under his chin. Blinded by the dazzle, he screwed up his eyes. His captor remained hidden behind the pier.

'You want to watch him die?' asked the voice.

'No!' Kiet's face darkened. 'You touch him and I'll kill you!'

'You think so? Then watch me do it.'

Kiet took a step forward. Ferren gurgled as the knife bit into his skin. Kiet halted, in an agony of indecision.

'One more step and he's dead.'

'You won't.' Kiet was beside herself.

'I will. Fond of him, are you?'

Ferren's mind was beginning to work again. The

voice behind the knife was hard and mocking, but not in the way of a Hyper. He struggled to speak.

'You're – not – a Hyper!'

A humorless laugh. 'No. I'm much more dangerous.'

'Who – are – you?'

'No, you tell me. Who are *you*?'

'Ferren.'

There was a sudden gasp. 'What? What did you say?'

Again the knife bit into Ferren's skin. Again he could only gurgle.

'He's Ferren,' said Kiet quickly. 'I'm Kiet. We're all from the tribe of the Nesters. Except him.'

'Where's *he* from?'

'A tribe called the People.'

'You're lying!'

Ferren breathed more easily as the knife shifted away from his throat. The threat was starting to go out of the situation.

'I'm Ferren of the People,' he said.

The knife dropped to the ground with a splash and a clatter. The sinewy hand seized him by the shoulder and turned him around. The torch shone full on his face. He was being inspected. Still he couldn't see for the dazzle.

'Ferren! It can't be!'

The tone had changed to a kind of incredulous wonder. The voice was beginning to sound familiar. The torchbeam trembled.

'Ferren! Ferren of the People! My own little brother!'

5

Ferren couldn't adjust. Shanna? His sister? His sister who had been taken away two years ago? He stood there thunderstruck.

The others gathered around, plying Shanna with questions. After the fear and tension of the last few minutes, they were wild with relief. Shanna didn't seem to hear the questions. She had eyes only for Ferren.

'You've grown up, little brother,' she said at last. 'But I'd still recognise you anywhere. Your face hasn't changed so much.'

Ferren found his voice. 'Let me see you.'

Shanna laughed and turned the torchbeam on herself. Ferren drank in her features with devouring intensity. He hardly noticed her stained and ragged clothes. A wetness came to his eyes.

Shanna had grown up too. She appeared much older than her eighteen years. There were furrows on her forehead, lines around her mouth and nose. A scar ran down on the left of her chin. With her hair pulled back in a tight knot, she looked very grim and warrior-like.

But her eyes were exactly as he remembered. Deep hazel eyes, full of care and understanding – and at the same time, keen and probing. Ferren had never been able to keep secrets from his older sister.

He opened his mouth to speak. But Shanna moved first. She sprang forward, pounced upon him, seized him in a hard fierce hug. Ferren wrapped his arms around her, hugging just as hard.

For a long time, they made only stifled inarticulate sounds as they clung to each other. The young Nesters backed away a little, respecting the moment.

But, eventually, Tadge grew restless. 'I don't get it,' he complained. 'What's his sister doing here?'

Kiet explained. 'Her name's Shanna. The Selectors took her for military service. He thought she was dead.'

'They seem very close,' commented Gibby. 'I wouldn't hug any of *my* brothers like that.'

'The Selectors took both parents when they were young. They only had each other.'

'How come she survived in the Humen Camp?' asked Tadge.

Kiet shrugged. 'Maybe she'll tell us when she can.'

Shanna disengaged herself gently from Ferren's arms. She had caught the last part of the conversation.

'Yes, I'll tell you everything,' she said. 'But not here.'

She rubbed at her eyes and sniffed. For a moment, she seemed less like a miraculous mythical being, more like an ordinary eighteen-year-old. Then she bent and recovered her knife from the water. She slipped it into a sheath that hung from a strap at her waist.

'Come this way,' she said. 'We'll sit where it's dry.'

She led them off in a new direction. The beam of her torch reflected from the ripples and cast wavery lines over the roof and piers.

Eventually, the piers ended and they came up against a blank brick wall. They splashed along parallel to the wall until they arrived at a gaping hole. The bricks had been pulled away and a large rounded cavity hollowed out in the earth behind.

'It's like a nest!' cried Ethamy.

'Climb inside,' said Shanna. Her voice had recovered its crisp tone of command.

It was a squeeze for them all to fit. They sat shoulder to shoulder, with their knees under their chins and their heads tucked forward under the low roof.

'Is this where you sleep?' asked Tadge.

'Sometimes.' Shanna nodded. 'One of my safe-holes. I have dozens of them, all over the Camp.'

'All underground?'

'Yes. I keep underground most of the time.'

'Wow! What a life!'

They gazed at her in amazement. A grin formed slowly on her face. It was as though her face wasn't used to the expression, as though she hadn't grinned in a very long while.

'Tell us how you survived,' said Kiet.

Shanna's grin faded. 'It's a long story,' she said. 'Let me remember . . .'

They waited in silence, swallowing their impatience.

'I escaped from the compound,' she began at last. 'When the Selectors brought me here, they put me in a compound with people from other tribes. Suddenly it was no longer military service they were talking about. They jeered at us and threw us food like animals.

'I knew I had to get out during the night. I tried to dig a hole under the wire, but there were steel rods going down far below the ground. None of the others would help. They'd given up hope.

'Then I had another plan. I lay down in the hole I'd dug and covered myself with earth. When the Hypers came in the morning, they didn't see me. I suppose they weren't used to the idea of Residuals trying to get away. They didn't even count numbers – just herded everyone out through the gate. After they'd gone, I jumped up and escaped. They hadn't bothered to re-lock the gate.'

She spoke slowly, gathering her thoughts between sentences. Gibby broke in with a question.

'But you stayed in the Camp! Couldn't you find a way out?'

'Oh yes.' Shanna agreed. 'I could have found a way. But I was curious. I wanted to know what the Humen did to Residuals. I wanted to know what they'd done with my mother and father.' She flicked a glance towards Ferren. 'Our mother and father.'

Ferren nodded unhappily. 'You discovered the Pit,' he said.

For a moment, Shanna looked surprised. But when he added nothing more, she went on with her story.

'Yes, I saw the psychic jelly drawn off. I saw the bits of bodies taken to be made into Plasmatics. Then I vowed revenge. I swore to kill as many Hypers as possible, to keep on killing until I was caught.

'I had to wait to find them alone, where I could creep

up from behind. I learned secret underground routes. I killed fifteen of them. But I got sick of killing in the end.'

Her voice wound down to a halt. She cupped her chin in her hands and stared at nothing in particular.

'So what have you been doing since?' asked Kiet.

'Sabotage. Wrecking their machines.'

'All by yourself?'

'Yes.'

'All this time?'

'Yes.'

She seemed worn and drawn, her features fleshless in the yellow torchlight. So familiar and yet so strange, thought Ferren. He'd experienced exile from his tribe – but nothing like Shanna's terrible isolation. Her strength of will was almost frightening.

But now she turned to him with a sad smile on her face.

'There was something else,' she said. 'I always hoped I might find the Plasmatics that had been made from the bodies of our mother and father. I thought I might be able to communicate with them.'

Ferren shook his head. 'No-one can communicate with Plasmatics.'

She studied him curiously. 'What do you know about Plasmatics?'

'I know enough.'

'Do you? How long have you been here in the Camp?'

'Not this time. I was here once before. This time it's a special mission.'

'What sort of special mission?'

'There's someone we have to rescue. Miriael.'

'Miriael? Strange name.'

'She's an angel.'

'Residuals rescuing angels? Are you serious?'

'She's on our side.'

Shanna's eyebrows shot up. 'Things must have changed if angels can be on the same side as Residuals.'

'Yes, big changes. You wouldn't believe. You have to come and help with the Residual Alliance.'

'The what?'

'Residual Alliance. You'll find out. There's going to be a meeting with representatives from all the tribes. We're joining together to fight against the Humen.'

'Ah, fighting against the Humen. That's good.'

'So you'll come with us?'

'I'll come with my little brother. Of course I will.'

Ferren's face broke into a broad grin. Then he became serious again.

'But first we have to rescue Miriael. Do you know where the surgeries are?'

'Yes.' Now it was Shanna's turn to grin. 'I did a little sabotage there, just the other day. I rewired their power supply.'

She seemed ready to give further details. But Ferren cut in.

'Can you take us there?'

'Right now?'

'We're in a hurry.'

'Okay. Let's go.'

6

Before setting off, Shanna distributed the small stock of weapons that she kept in her safe-hole. There was a clasp-knife for Ferren, a serrated blade for Kiet. Then they waded on through the water, keeping parallel with the brick wall.

After a while they came to a tunnel where pipes ran through the earth. Shanna led the way forward, wriggling along at the side of the pipes. It was closed in and airless, with a choking smell of moist clay. Ethamy could barely squeeze her roly-poly shape through the narrowest parts.

They left the tunnel by a vertical shaft. Shanna had gouged secret handholds and footholds into the sides of the shaft. There was a climb of a few metres, then a manhole cover at the top.

Shanna lifted the manhole cover and checked in all directions. Then she sprang out and vanished into the night. When Ferren came to the top, he saw a long khaki-coloured shed with panes of mirror-glass leaning against one wall. Shanna was in the triangular space between the panes and the wall, beckoning for the team to follow.

It was like another kind of tunnel. The panes of mirror-glass were stacked along the entire length of the wall. The team crawled through on their hands and knees.

At the other end, they looked out on more khaki-coloured sheds. Somewhere ahead was a grinding rumbling noise.

'Hear that?' Shanna asked. 'That's the Main Belt.'

She offered no further explanation. Instead she darted out from the mirror-glass, sprinted five paces and jumped down into a ditch. One by one, the team came after her. The ditch was chest-deep, with a mound of earth providing additional cover at the side.

They ducked down and scuttled along for almost a hundred metres. The grinding and rumbling grew to a loud continuous thunder. They didn't raise their heads until the ditch came to an end. Then they peered out at the Main Belt.

It was a conveyor belt, a ten metre wide surface of black rubber. It looked like an enormous river rolling along. There were even tributary belts feeding in and branching out. It carried an extraordinary variety of cargoes: bales of plastic, bundles of wire, coils of strip metal, machine parts, crates, drums, canisters.

And not only cargoes. Also riding on the black surface were Hypers with long hooked poles. They used their poles to shift and reposition the cargoes.

Ferren's spirits sank. 'We have to get across that?'

Shanna nodded. 'It's far worse than usual. It's

because of this offensive that's about to be launched.'

She pointed to an electronic signboard that spanned the Main Belt like an overhead bridge. Flashing red lights spelt out the message:

OFFENSIVE BEGINS IN 27 HOURS 41 MINUTES!

'My secret routes have all been disturbed since the arrival of this new Doctor,' she went on. 'New constructions everywhere, everyone working day and night.'

'So what do we do now?'

Shanna gave a shrug. 'We wait. There'll be a gap eventually.'

She squatted down in the bottom of the ditch. Ferren and the team did the same. The signboard clicked over minute after minute. The cargoes and Hypers continued to pass by in a never-ending flow.

Whispered conversations started up along the line. Shanna raised her head to check the Main Belt from time to time. Then her gaze returned automatically to her brother's face. It was a while before she spoke.

'You know what you said about no-one being able to communicate with Plasmatics?'

'Except for the Hypers with their mathematical commands.'

'Yes, well, it's nearly true. The Humen don't know any other way to communicate with Plasmatics. But I do.'

'You do? You've done it?'

'Yes, with a few of them. It's only possible if they include some of the original nervous system. Then they're not totally mindless. Some of them even have traces of personal memory left.'

'How do you communicate?'

'I transfer my thoughts by touch.'

'By touch!' Ferren shook his head.

'You don't believe me?'

Ferren stopped shaking his head. 'Of course I believe you. If you say it, I believe it. You're clever enough to do anything.'

Shanna dropped her eyes in the face of his sudden intensity.

'Ah, not clever enough to find any traces of our mother or father,' she said.

There was a long silence. Ferren was still adjusting to the idea that Plasmatics weren't totally mindless. Then Shanna changed the subject.

'Tell me about your friend.'

Ferren was taken aback. 'Who? Kiet?'

'Yes. Tell me about her,' said Shanna.

'What's to tell?'

'I don't know. Call it a sisterly hunch.'

'She's just one of the team.'

'She seems to look at you in a particular way.'

'Not that I've noticed.'

'And you look at her in a particular way.'

'No I don't. I don't look at her at all.'

'Okay. You have a particular way of *not* looking at her.'

'One of the team,' Ferren repeated.

'Mmm. But the only one of the team who knew my name. You told her a lot about me. You didn't tell the others.'

'It doesn't mean anything.'

'I think it does. I know you, Ferren. You'd only talk about me to someone special.'

Ferren wished she'd drop the subject. He felt uncomfortable with her eyes upon him.

'We're hardly even friends any more,' he said.

'Ah. You had a falling out?'

Ferren shrugged. 'I don't know what we had.'

'And yet she was desperate when I had my knife to your throat.'

'Was she?'

'I saw the expression on her face. That wasn't just team loyalty.'

Ferren couldn't help looking in Kiet's direction. She was at the other end of the line, engaged in a conversation with Bross. He looked quickly away again.

'Anyway, she's going to be mated with Bross,' he said.

'Mated?'

'It's what they do in her tribe. Partners for life.'

'Oh. Is that Bross she's talking to now?'

'Yes.'

'Hmm. They seem very close. Pity.'

'Why do you say that?'

'I was hoping you might get lucky yourself.' Shanna studied Bross for a moment. 'He's a fine well-built fellow. Very muscular. But not up to her standard.'

'What do you mean?'

Shanna grinned. 'Of course, as a sister, I might be biased. But I think you're better looking. Or more interesting looking, at least.'

'What do you mean, *her standard*?'

'Her standard? I mean, she's amazingly attractive.

Don't tell me you haven't noticed?'

'Is she?'

'With that hair. Those eyes. Probably even too good for you.'

'She's still not as beautiful as . . . as . . .'

Ferren faltered. Obviously no human being could be as beautiful as an angel. He wanted to explain that Miriael was his ideal, that he was hopelessly in love with her. But face to face with his older sister, it seemed a ridiculous thing to say. How could he make such a claim? A hopeless devotion to the unattainable – it would sound stupid. She'd pull him down to earth at once.

'Not as beautiful as you,' he finished lamely.

Shanna laughed. 'I may have brains, little brother, but we both know beauty isn't my strong point.'

He had the feeling she could see right through him. He didn't know what to say. He was saved when her attention was suddenly deflected to the Main Belt.

'What's *that*?' she muttered.

Ferren raised his head and looked out. Approaching along the Main Belt was a hospital trolley, accompanied by an augmented Queen-Hyper and a pair of ordinary Hypers in gauze masks. On the trolley lay a long rounded shape like a body bound in silvery tape. The tape had been snipped open at one end only.

Ferren gasped as he caught a glimpse of bright golden hair.

The whole team rose to look. Shanna gestured with both hands.

'Stay down!' she hissed. 'You'll be seen!'

The hospital trolley came level with their hiding-place. There was no longer any doubt. Miriael's face was clearly visible.

'It's her!' exclaimed Ferren in a stunned voice. 'Miriael!'

'So she's out of the surgeries.' Shanna's brisk efficiency cut through his amazement. 'Do we follow?'

'Yes,' answered Ferren. 'Yes, yes, *yes*!'

7

They couldn't follow close to the Belt itself. They retreated a short distance along the ditch, then leaped out and ran in the shadows of the khaki-coloured sheds. They were taking risks now.

'We'll make for the next major junction!' cried Shanna. 'Find out where she's headed!'

They met no Hypers on the way. Instead they came to a flat concrete area dotted with mushroom-shaped caps of white enamel. The air was thick with a cloud of yellow vapour. It smelt foul and bit into their skin like a corrosive spray. But it hid them from view.

The vapour came from puddles of liquid on the ground, the puddles came from the mushroom-shaped caps. They heard loud gurgles under the concrete, then the caps disgorged a scummy yellow overflow. Then more gurgles and the overflow was sucked back in. Vomiting and swallowing, vomiting and swallowing, over and over again.

They arrived back at the Main Belt just in time. Peering out through the vapour, they saw the hospital trolley already coming towards the junction. At the junction, the conveyor divided into two separate belts, branching left and right. The Hypers and Queen-Hyper were busy manoeuvering the trolley over towards the left.

Shanna cursed under her breath.

'What is it?' asked Ferren anxiously.

'The left belt leads straight to Doctor Saniette's headquarters.'

'Why would they be taking her to him?'

'I don't know. I hate to think.'

'We'll have to rescue her there.'

Shanna stood watching as the trolley passed over the junction and continued along the branch to the left. Her mouth was a hard tight line.

'I don't like to go near Doctor Saniette's headquarters,' she said.

'Why? Is it heavily guarded?'

'It's not that. There's something evil about the place.'

'Give us directions then.'

'No, I'll come with you. I just don't like it.'

She turned and ran back through the vapour in a different direction. They left the concrete area behind and entered a construction site. There were excavations, half-built towers and great sloping ramps of earth. The site was in darkness, temporarily deserted.

They clambered over ramps and swerved around excavations. Loudspeakers blared announcements in the distance: different announcements from different loudspeakers. As they came to the top of one ramp, Shanna suddenly stopped and pointed.

'There! That's him!'

They followed the line of her arm and saw a bell-shaped dome like a hill. It rose fifty metres high, with a smaller bell-shaped turret on top. The turret was transparent and illuminated from within. Inside was a head, the upper part of a head, silhouetted in profile. They could see the steep forehead and the bulge of a giant eye. Doctor Saniette's eye! Fortunately it wasn't looking in their direction.

'The dome was erected when Doctor Saniette arrived,' said Shanna. 'It's inflatable plastic. Can you see those smaller domes attached?'

They all nodded.

'That's the front entrance, where messengers come and go. The headquarters staff occupy the smaller domes. Doctor Saniette occupies the big dome.'

Ferren was puzzled. 'Doesn't he move around?'

'He doesn't need to. He controls everything through reports and signals.'

They stood gazing for a moment. A great deal of activity was going on around the front entrance: lights flashing, voices calling, Hypers running.

'We'll try to sneak in at the back,' said Shanna.

They continued on by a looping route. The back of the dome was surrounded by a host of small hump-like tents. They left the construction site and plunged in among the tents.

Cables snaked across the ground, hundreds and hundreds of them. The tents were made of plastic, supported on blown-up plastic ribs. Electrical equipment gave off a continuous hum.

As they crept and darted from the shadow of one tent to another, Ferren began to experience a curious pressure on his skull. At first he thought it was the hum. But it grew stronger and stronger as they approached the dome.

'You feel it?' Shanna turned to him. 'That's why I don't like this place.'

Then Ferren remembered. He remembered the sense of an evil presence when Doctor Saniette had passed over on top of the overbridge. The same pressure bearing down, as though the air was resonating with a million thoughts.

But it was no worse than a low-level headache. He focussed his mind on the job in hand. Shanna had now advanced to the back of the dome. He came up and stood beside her.

The dome was like a larger version of the tents: panels of flexible plastic stretched out between ribs of blown-up plastic. But these ribs were the size of tree-trunks.

Shanna waited for the whole team to reassemble. Then she bent down to the nearest panel and raised the bottom edge. She peered underneath.

'Okay. Follow me. Stay behind cover.'

In the next moment she was flat on her belly and wriggling in under the plastic. As her feet disappeared from sight, Ferren dropped down and wriggled after her.

The temperature in the dome was excessively warm and a sickly-sweet medicinal smell hung in the air. Ferren gazed around in wonder.

On all sides of the dome was a kind of scaffolding. It rose up in level upon level of galleries and walkways, ladders and railings. Light filtered down from high above.

A sharp thrust against the soles of his feet reminded him to keep moving. He crawled on to where Shanna was hiding behind a massive square duct. The duct ran at ground level all around the interior of the dome. He could feel hot air streaming from its louvres.

Shanna peered cautiously over the top of the duct. She was watching activities on the other side of the dome. Ferren watched too. Although his view was partly obscured by two colossal pillars, he could see a network of wires and black boxes set up on the scaffolding. Doors opened and closed, Queen-Hypers strode out onto the scaffolding, tap-tapped on the black boxes, strode back in again. Everything seemed to take place with a maximum of efficiency and a minimum of noise.

The whole interior space was weighed down under a solemn hush. There were no loudspeakers in here. Again Ferren experienced the pressure on his skull.

Then he realised. The two colossal pillars weren't pillars at all, but the trousered legs of the Doctor himself. They terminated in shiny cylinders, more like hooves than feet. Doctor Saniette was standing perfectly motionless, as though he'd gone to sleep standing up.

Ferren raised his eyes and took in the white medical coat. It shimmered where patches of light fell on it from above. Higher again were the arms, stretched out in front. Above that, the head and shoulders disappeared into the top of the dome. It was impossible to get a clear view of Doctor Saniette's face.

'Look! There's the trolley!'

The whispered exclamation came from Rhinn. All the members of the team had now come up behind the duct.

Ferren lowered his gaze to the hospital trolley. It had just entered the dome through a ground-level door. It was wheeled by the same two medical assistants, but now surrounded by no less than five Queen-Hypers.

The medical assistants manoeuvred the trolley onto a metal plate, not far from the Doctor's strange feet. Miriael's tape-swathed body lay motionless. One of the Queen-Hypers moved across to the scaffolding at the side, unhooked a long hanging chain with a ring on the end and carried it back to the trolley.

The other Queen-Hypers lifted four ropes attached to the corners of the metal plate. They fastened the ropes to the ring, then signalled to someone on the scaffolding behind the black boxes.

In the next moment, the chain jerked upwards and the ropes went taut. The metal plate creaked as it left the ground.

Ferren stared in horror. The trolley was being winched to the top of the dome!

His eyes followed it slowly higher and higher. Dangling in mid-air, it began to rotate in ever-increasing arcs, first clockwise, then anti-clockwise. It looked very tiny against the vast white bulk of Doctor Saniette's medical coat.

When it came to the level of the Doctor's arms, the silvery cocoon was no longer visible from below. Everyone watched as if in a trance.

Then Shanna broke the trance. 'Are you still determined to rescue her? You know it's almost certain death?'

'Yes,' said Ferren.

'Yes,' said the rest of the team.

'How about you?' Ferren asked Shanna.

'Oh, I'm used to almost certain death.' She smiled grimly. 'Okay. Let's work out how to do it.'

8

Dangling and rotating, clockwise and anti-clockwise. Miriael was dizzy and disoriented. Doctor Saniette's dazzlingly white medical coat shimmered before her eyes.

She rose up slowly past his arms. His hands rested on two huge control panels. There were a dozen sockets and screens on each panel, and each of his fingers was plugged into a socket. The sickly-sweet medicinal smell intensified as she approached his face.

She was just below his chin when the chain ground to a halt. The skin of his face was evenly textured and evenly flesh-coloured. A number of wires looped down over his chin and across to the scaffolding. They seemed to be clipped to the underside of his lip. Microphones? The lip moved in constant rapid motion, as if speaking.

Then the speaking stopped and the gigantic face tilted down towards her. In the centre of the face was a single bulging eye. Her mind swam at the sight of her own reflection magnified and distorted on the gelatinous surface.

'Well, here you are. The angel Miriael.'

His voice was very gentle, deliberately gentle, as though held carefully under control.

There was a stir of movement, a vast brushing and swooshing. Miriael swivelled her eyes and saw a hand rise up from below. A giant thumb and forefinger closed in on either side of the metal plate. The trolley stopped rotating.

She stared at the tips of the thumb and forefinger. They weren't covered in skin but in leathery-looking pads like an animal's paw. Sprouting from each pad were thousands of black vibrating bristles. They must be nerve-endings, Miriael thought, nerve-endings that engaged directly with receptors in the sockets.

'And now we have the opportunity to talk,' the voice went on. 'Bridging the unfortunate gulf between Humen and Celestial.'

'I've got nothing to say to you.'

'Ah, surely you have, Miriael. I was talking to another angel recently, you know. He had plenty to say.'

'Who? Asmodai? He's a traitor!'

'Traitor from the Heavenly point of view. But he was able to understand *my* point of view.'

'You're mad if you think you can trust him.'

'Mad? No, I could never be mad, Miriael. I represent reason. I'm the supreme example of rationality. That's what I want to explain to you.'

'You want to explain yourself *to me*?'

'I want to offer you the possibility of an alternative point of you. Is it so hard for you to listen?'

His voice fluctuated strangely in volume, sometimes

louder and sometimes softer. He continued on in his softest tone.

'My only goal is a better world. A peaceful ordered world without risks or dangers, where everyone can be watched over and kept safe. Isn't that desirable?'

'Except that it's the Doctors who decide what's safe.'

'Doctor Saniette decides. One overarching mind. Otherwise clashes and contradictions arise.'

'Not even the other Doctors?'

'I am the ultimate of my kind. I alone have the mental capacity to maintain a perfect peace.'

'After you've fought a perfect war, of course. After all the slaughter and destruction of your great offensive against Heaven.'

'Commencing in twenty-seven hours, fifteen minutes.' His giant features hovered above her. 'Yes, Miriael, it *will* be the perfect war. I have calculated the exact application of force necessary to produce the required result.'

'You think like a computer.'

'Not at all. A computer calculates only along a single track, whereas I hold a million things in mind simultaneously. I can coordinate the interaction of a million factors. No-one else has ever come close to my capacity.'

'Spoken like a typical megalomaniac.'

'You think it is a pleasure to have this capacity?'

Miriael contented herself with a contemptuous snort.

'No, Miriael, it is not a pleasure. I do not enjoy my existence. How could you imagine? It is an agony, this infinite consciousness. I can never sleep, not in the way that you know sleep. Eternal vigilance is the price I pay for my infallibility.'

'You never make a mistake?'

'It is an ongoing struggle. Unpredictable factors are always appearing. Even in the last few days, the last few hours ... There is always something else to be conscious of. I can never relax. Such stress, such strain, such weariness. But I have to bear the burden.'

'No you don't.'

'Yes, because I'm the only one who can. No other mind is capable of taking on so much responsibility.'

'I don't think it's responsibility. I think it's fear.'

'Fear? What does fear have to do with reason?'

'I think you calculate so much because you're afraid. You have to be conscious of everything because you can't stand the tiniest bit of risk or uncertainty.'

'You have not understood. You have not tried to understand. Is it so hard for you to listen?'

'You said that before.'

His whole body quivered. It was as though he was being pulled in different directions, barely balancing under a multitude of tensions.

'I could crush you in an instant! But I remain under control! Objective, impartial, rational! See how rational I am!'

The wind of his breath blew over her. She had the impression of a volcano about to erupt.

'Whereas you – you are limited! You don't make sense! You are a nonsense!'

His face had come down very close. But suddenly he drew away. His hand released the metal plate and dropped back down towards the control panels. Miriael said nothing.

After a few moments, there was a clanking sound from far below. Then she noticed a chain moving in front of the Doctor's other shoulder. It seemed that something else was being winched up.

When he spoke again, the deliberate gentleness was back in his voice.

'A pity you couldn't take in an alternative point of view. I had hoped you might rise above your limited perspective.'

'You didn't take in *my* point of view either.'

'No, but I don't need to. I'm going to extract it from you in slices. I shall examine and analyse it, along with every other memory in your mind.'

As he spoke, a large white kidney-shaped basin came slowly into view. Inside were various shining stainless steel instruments. They had long handles and sockets on the ends of the handles.

The basin came up as high as Miriael's trolley, then halted. The huge eye rotated towards it.

'Now I shall perform the operation that could not be performed in the surgeries,' he said.

Then stopped. His voice started to fluctuate again.

'What's that shouting? Who is it? What's going on down there?'

9

'Ya-a-ah! Ya-a-ah! Ya-a-ah!'

Ferren stared down from his position high in the scaffolding. He watched as Flens ran across towards the Queen-Hypers and black boxes, jeering and waving his arms. Crazy daredevil Flens! Ferren's own role was dangerous enough, but Flens's role was almost suicidal.

Everything depended on split-second timing. Each member of the team knew exactly what to do and when to do it.

It had taken Ferren five minutes to climb to the top of the scaffolding. The Queen-Hypers were all on the other side of the dome, but he'd still had to keep stopping and hiding until he was sure they weren't looking. Now he lay stretched out on the deck of the uppermost gallery.

The winch that supported Miriael's trolley was right beside him. The chain ran from the winch up to a pulley in the roof, then down to the ring to which the four ropes were attached. The trolley dangled close to the giant head of Doctor Saniette.

Looking at the head from behind, Ferren could see a

mass of perfectly cropped hair rising out above the collar of the white medical coat. It looked more like an artificial mat than real hair. What *was* Doctor Saniette?

But there was no time to ponder the question. Flens had successfully attracted the attention of the Queen-Hypers, and the Doctor too. Now he ran back under the scaffolding, still yelling at the top of his voice. The Queen-Hypers left their posts and came after him. It was Flens's role to act as a diversion.

Ferren felt for the clasp-knife that Shanna had given him. Still there in his belt – okay! He took a deep breath, jumped to his feet, then sprang on top of the winch. Taking hold of the chain, he began to climb.

No-one was facing in his direction, only Miriael. Lying flat on her back on the trolley, her eyes went suddenly wide as she caught sight of him. *Don't make a sound,* he willed silently. *Trust me!*

The chain sloped at a forty-five degree angle. He hauled himself higher and higher, hand over hand, gripping and propelling with his feet. He came up under the pulley in a matter of seconds.

Now he had to get across to the vertical chain on the other side of the pulley. He reached out with his right hand. Too far away!

He let go with his legs as well. A wrenching pain shot through his joints as he hung dangling by a single hand. But, finally, he reefed in the chain with his outstretched fingers.

He transferred himself across. Then he half-slid, half-clambered down to the ring. He put his feet through the ring and paused for a moment.

He was very close to Doctor Saniette's left ear. If the great eye swivelled just a fraction, he was doomed. But at present the eye was still focussed downwards.

'Yah! Yah! Yaa-aah!'

Flens was creating a wonderful distraction. He had to draw attention away from Ferren, but without coming close to the five members of the team who were hidden behind the duct. He darted this way and that, popping out his head and jeering from time to time. The Queen-Hypers were working to encircle him. Fortunately they were unarmed.

Then the Doctor began stamping with the hoof-like columns of his feet. Up and down, up and down, always over the same spot.

Thumm! Thumm! Thumm! Thumm!

It was as though he was terrified of some tiny insect. But his attempts to trample it to death were slow and clumsy.

Ferren pulled out his clasp-knife, opened the blade and bent down to the ropes below the ring. He needed to sever only two of the four: the two that held up the foot of the trolley. He sawed away at the polymer fibre.

It took only a few seconds, though it seemed to last for hours. The polymer was tough, but the edge of his blade was sharper. He sawed away until both ropes were reduced to a strand. A single final slash would do it.

He checked around. The hiss of escaping air was now audible even above the sound of the Doctor's stamping. Shanna and Kiet must have punctured several of the dome's ribs. Was the roof a little lower already?

He looked towards the other five hidden behind the

duct: Bross, Rhinn, Gibby, Tadge and Ethamy. They carried the circle of flexible plastic cut out from the wall of the dome. They were staring up at him, waiting for his signal.

But even as he gave the signal, a troop of Hypers rushed in through the ground-level door. They were armed with short-nosed triple-barrelled pistols. As the Queen-Hypers shouted orders, they raised their pistols, aiming at Flens.

Ferren slashed down with his knife. The final strands of rope parted, the foot of the trolley dropped instantly. The group below ran forward with the circle of plastic stretched out between them like a trampoline. Miriael's tape-bound body slid off the trolley and plummeted fifty metres.

Ferren's heart was in his mouth. The stretched-out plastic looked so impossibly tiny! Desperately, the group below adjusted position to catch her.

The cocoon-like shape hit the plastic and bounced up. Then landed again and came to rest.

Neither the Hypers nor Queen-Hypers had noticed. The pistols of the Hypers spat tracers of light. Ferren couldn't see Flens's position in the scaffolding. But he heard the gasp of pain and the curse. The Hypers ran forward.

The group below had rolled Miriael off to the side. Now they stood with the circle of plastic stretched out again. It was Ferren's turn to jump.

The Hypers fired a second volley. This time there was a shriek – a shriek that died away into silence. The Hypers cheered and ran forward again.

Ferren was stunned. For one moment he couldn't move. When he went to jump, it was too late. Doctor Saniette had seen him.

Stamping his feet up and down, the Doctor rotated. The expression on his face was unreadable. Anger? Fear? The giant eye wasn't even remotely human.

In desperation, Ferren launched himself into space. But he never reached the ground. As Doctor Saniette turned, Ferren landed on the sleeve of his white medical coat. He slid into a crease as big as a trough.

The Doctor let forth a bellow, a mighty roaring wind. There were words in it – *Control*! and *Not allowed*! and many more. But the words were garbled and mixed up together.

Then the great arm began to swing back and forth, back and forth. It seemed that the Doctor was frantic to dislodge this new insect that had landed on him. But still his movements were slow and clumsy. Ferren clung on for grim life, gripping the white material between hands and knees. The folds of the sleeve changed around him like the waves of a sea.

It couldn't last. At any moment, he would be thrown off. But suddenly the swinging stopped.

Ferren looked up and discovered the reason for his salvation. The roof of the dome had come down around the Doctor's shoulders. His huge head was trapped and blinded.

Ferren rose on his knees. The curve of the sleeve obscured his view. Was the group still there with the plastic trampoline? At least he seemed to be facing in the right direction.

Now or never. He let go of the material and slid down the curve, over the edge.

Everything happened as if in slow motion. He was falling, spinning, tumbling . . . He heard shouting, caught a momentary glimpse of upturned faces.

'Quick!'

'To the left!'

Thwackk!

The impact drove the breath out of his body. He landed, bounced up into the air, dropped back onto the stretched-out plastic.

Made it!

Bross, Rhinn, Gibby, Tadge and Ethamy lowered the trampoline and turned to Miriael. Shanna and Kiet came running up with their knives in their hands. As Ferren scrambled to his feet, another volley of shots rang out on the other side of the dome.

'Let's go!' cried Shanna.

'Flens!' Ferren had to know. 'What's happened to him?'

Shanna merely pointed.

Beyond the Doctor's hoof-like feet, the Hypers and Queen-Hypers stood round a blood-soaked patch of ground. All that remained of Flens was a scattering of smashed flesh and bone. They had blasted his body to pieces.

'Let's go!' Shanna repeated.

The team headed towards the plastic wall of the tent, which now sagged heavily earthwards. Bross, Rhinn and Ethamy took hold of Miriael's cocoon by some loose ends of tape and hauled her over the ground.

They had gone no more than a dozen paces when the Hypers and Queen-Hypers spotted them. There were shouts of command from the Queen-Hypers. The ordinary Hypers raised their pistols.

But they had to hold their fire when Doctor Saniette's legs suddenly moved across their line of vision. The Doctor was no longer stamping up and down on the same spot, but lurching, lumbering forward. As he moved, he dragged the entire dome with him.

Shouts of command turned into shouts of alarm. The bellying plastic pulled against the scaffolding, which started to tilt and topple. Unsecured equipment came crashing down, then ladders and railings, then the entire structure. The Hypers and Queen-Hypers were directly below the main collapse.

It was a scene of chaos. From high above came another thunderous bellow.

'*I will – I will keep – control – control – control*!'

Doctor Saniette seemed to have gone berserk.

'Let's go!' shouted Shanna for the third time.

10

They crawled out from under the plastic, into the area of hump-like tents. Ferren, Bross and Rhinn hoisted Miriael's cocoon onto their shoulders. Swerving around tents, stumbling over cables, they barely managed to keep their feet as they ran.

No-one was chasing after them. The dome was now a shapeless lumpish mound. Muffled sounds came from within, sudden swellings bulged out here and there. The giant Doctor continued to wallow around, unable to break free. It seemed that the plastic was anchored by the secondary domes at the front entrance.

They emerged from the tents and re-entered the construction site. Kiet shouted to Shanna as she ran. 'Where are we going? Back underground?'

Shanna shook her head. 'Not possible here. I've got a better idea. Very close.'

She was leading them in a new direction. They came out of the construction site onto a wide area of tarmac. Thirty or forty transport machines sat parked between white lines. There was nobody around.

Shanna knew exactly where she was going. She dodged between the machines until she came to a particular snub-nosed traction engine. She heaved herself up behind the engine and squatted on a small footplate. Steel baffles at the sides half hid her from view. Attached to the engine was a train of four hoppers on wheels.

Ferren nodded as understanding dawned. 'Plasmatics?'

'Yes.' She unsheathed her knife. 'I told you I'd managed to communicate with some of them. I can communicate with the one in this engine.'

She applied the tip of her knife to a screw at the back of the engine housing. She unscrewed one screw after another, six screws in all.

A flare shot high in the air, painting the night sky pink and green. There was a growing volume of noise beyond the parking area. Sirens wailed, voices shouted, loudspeakers boomed. The whole Camp would be hunting for them now.

The team were very quiet. For the first time, they had a moment to grieve for their missing member. Then suddenly Tadge spoke up.

'Hey! Where's the Doctor?'

He pointed in the direction of the dome. But the dome was no longer there.

'Perhaps he's fallen over,' said Gibby, without much hope.

Shanna removed the final screw and lifted out the whole bulkhead. Now the engine's machinery lay fully exposed. There were muscles packed behind pistons, chambers filled with red and pink tissue. Ferren had seen such things before, but the rest of the team shuddered.

Shanna reached in with the fingers of one hand. Ignoring the chambers and pistons, she touched the thin glistening strings that connected across at the top of the machinery.

'The nervous system,' Ferren commented.

'Yes.' Shanna nodded. 'This is the part I communicate with. But I need to communicate without distractions.' She directed a glance at the tape-swathed figure on their shoulders. 'Do something useful. Cut your angel free.'

She turned back to her task. Ferren, Bross and Rhinn slid Miriael from their shoulders and placed her gently on the ground. Miriael smiled as she looked up into their faces.

'I can't believe it. Ferren . . . Bross . . . Rhinn . . .'

'And Kiet,' said Kiet, pushing forward to the front.

Ferren had lost the knife that Shanna had given him. But Kiet had kept hers. She went down on one knee beside the angel.

'Hold still please,' she said.

She began cutting through the silvery ribbons of tape. She started from around the neck and worked methodically downwards. Other hands pulled away the loosened tape.

Miriael held still. But her blue eyes shone, her whole body trembled with anticipation. When Kiet cut the last strip around her ankles, she couldn't hold still any longer.

She sprang to her feet with the remaining bits of tape

flapping around her. She flexed her limbs and stretched her wings.

'Alleluia!' she sang out. 'Alleluia!'

'Be quiet!' snapped Shanna, without turning round.

Miriael stopped flexing and stretching. Everyone waited in silence for Shanna to finish.

She was muttering words as she pressed on the glistening strings. Her fingers moved as though tapping out a message. Certainly the Plasmatic couldn't have heard the words in the ordinary way. Shanna seemed to be somehow willing her thoughts across.

At last came the movement they'd been waiting for. The tissues and muscles heaved in the metal chambers, the pistons slid back and forth.

'Ready to go,' Shanna announced.

She withdrew her hand, swung around – and gasped. It was her first sight of a real live angel. She stared in wonder at the long slim legs, the white-feathered wings, the golden hair.

'This is Miriael, this is Shanna,' said Ferren.

Miriael studied Shanna with almost equal curiosity.

'You can communicate with a Plasmatic? No-one's ever done that before.'

Shanna looked away. Her normal gruff manner returned.

'Yes, and if we're lucky, it'll help get us out of this place.' She addressed the team from the footplate. 'Listen up. You're all going to hide in the hoppers, while I direct the Plasmatic from here. If the Humen don't see us, they'll think it's just one of their machines following Humen orders.'

Everyone nodded as the plan sank home.

'Okay,' said Shanna. 'Climb in. Two to a hopper.'

They hurried to climb in, shuffling round on either side of the engine. Ferren swung himself up on the hopper immediately behind Shanna. He assumed Miriael would join him. But Miriael kept going to the very back of the train. Instead, it was Kiet who swung herself up on the other side of his hopper. For a moment their eyes met. Then they continued to climb in.

The hopper was empty except for a few leftover chunks of rock. The floor was curved like the inside of a barrel, the walls came up to their chests.

Shanna reached into the engine once again. She tapped on the glistening strings and the engine leaped forward with a jerk. Then she sat back while the Plasmatic steered its own way round the other transport machines. Evidently it didn't need detailed instructions.

Bross and Rhinn were in the second hopper, Ethamy and Tadge in the third, Gibby and Miriael in the last. Shanna gestured sharply, ordering them all to duck down.

'Stay hidden now. We're heading for the nearest bridge over the moat.'

The engine rattled along at a steady pace. The rattle changed when they left the tarmac and rolled across loose grit. Gazing skyward over the rim of their hopper, Ferren and Kiet could see the tops of small cone-shaped hills. It was a depot area for coal, sand, gravel and lime.

Ferren seemed to remember a similar area from his previous visit. Perhaps it was even the same? But he couldn't be sure.

After a while, the cones disappeared and the rattle changed again to a smooth drumming. They must have come out onto a larger road. There were overhead lights and sounds of marching Hypers. It was a ragged sort of marching, out of step and out of rhythm.

Further again, they passed under a huge board sign spanning the road. Its red lights spelt out an incomprehensible message:

OFFENS IN MIN 26 41!

The messages booming out from the loudspeakers were equally senseless. It was as though they were caught in an endless loop, repeating themselves over and over:

Ready ready ready ready ready ready ready

or

Do it do it do it do it do it do it do it do it

Still the engine rolled steadily forward, still no-one had challenged them. Sometimes the hoppers passed so close to marching Hypers that Ferren and Kiet could hear every word of their rasping speech.

'What's happening?'

'Some kind of enemies.'

'Inside the Camp?'

'Everything's going crazy.'

'What's the Doctor doing about it?'

'Going crazy too.'

'What about his great offensive?'

Ferren and Kiet flattened themselves against the curving sides of their hopper. If some Hyper took it into his head to peer over the rim . . .

But the voices faded and the train advanced into yet

another new area. Now they were travelling between tall beehive structures. There were rows and rows of them, all coated with soot. Ferren and Kiet unflattened themselves.

'It seems almost too easy,' said Kiet.

She was right. In the next moment, trouble struck.

'Hey!' came the sudden shout of a Hyper. 'Where's that train going?'

A second voice joined in. 'Empty, is it? Send it back.'

'No, there's something strange. I want to take a look.'

The voices came from directly ahead.

'$4pq$ minus $2x^3$!'

As the mathematical command rang out, the engine faltered. But only for a moment. Then it returned to its previous speed. Another command rang out.

'$4pq$ minus 9.5 times $8xy$!'

This time the engine didn't even falter. There were cries of surprise from the Hypers.

'It must be Shanna!' Ferren whispered. 'She's overriding their commands.'

'What'll they do now?' Kiet whispered back.

Her question was answered by a sharp clang. It seemed to come from the front of the engine.

'Did we hit one of them?' asked Kiet.

Then they saw the top of a head looming up – a black rubber-clad head. One of the Hypers had jumped onto the nose of the engine. He rose up balancing on hands and knees. He didn't look into the hoppers, but down at the footplate where Shanna was trying to hide.

'Res-s-s-s-idual!'

A murderous hiss. He reached round to unsling a

long tubular gun that he carried on his back.

Ferren grabbed two chunks of rock from the floor of the hopper and jumped to his feet. The Hyper had disengaged his gun but hadn't yet turned it on Shanna. For one moment, his glaring eyeslits confronted Ferren.

Then Ferren leaned forward and swung both arms simultaneously. As his fists came together, the two chunks of rock smashed against both sides of the black rubber-clad head.

The Hyper lost his grip on the nose of the engine. The speed of the train carried him backwards and he fell down sprawling on top of Shanna.

Ferren drew back his arm and dealt another rock-weighted blow to the side of the Hyper's head. Kiet stretched forward and grabbed at his gun. Shanna rolled onto her back and kicked out with both legs.

It was all over in an instant. The Hyper was propelled from the footplate, thrown out sideways. Limbs flailing helplessly, he sailed through the air and crashed to the ground.

The gun remained in Kiet's hands. It had a bulbous magazine like a many-celled seed-pod. She flourished it in triumph.

But her triumph was short-lived. From all around came a roar of voices. Dozens of Hypers had halted, dozens of Hypers were staring at the train in amazement.

'That's them!'

'Enemies in the Camp!'

'Gettem!'

There was no hiding now. Once more Shanna

reached into the engine, tapped on the glistening strings. The pistons whizzed back and forth, the train accelerated to maximum speed.

The Hypers were too slow to catch them. But already some were reporting into tiny wrist-microphones. The train rounded a curve and came into a broad concrete road.

'Nearly there!' cried Shanna.

The bridge was straight ahead, only a hundred metres away. But in that hundred metres were gangs of Hypers, transport machines and half a dozen augmented Queen-Hypers.

Shanna kept tapping and muttering. The engine swerved from side to side of the road. The Hypers were in a state of rage and confusion. But the Queen-Hypers knew exactly what to do. They crouched like cats, following every swerve.

Then the first of them sprang. Like a black missile, she arrowed a full fifteen metres through the air. She latched onto the side of the third hopper.

Tadge cried out as an arm reached over the rim and clamped over his shoulder.

Ethamy threw herself forward, yelling at the top of her voice. With bare hands, she tore at the copper circuitry on the Queen-Hyper's face. The Queen-Hyper transferred her grip from Tadge's shoulder to Ethamy's neck. Ethamy gasped as the long black fingers began to squeeze.

'Use the gun!' Shanna yelled at Kiet.

'I don't know how!'

'The trigger! Aim and pull!'

Ethamy's face was dark with blood, her eyes popping. She tried to poke her fingers into the Queen-Hyper's eyes. But her fingers went all the way in through the eyeslits. There were no eyes to poke.

Kiet aimed the gun but couldn't find the trigger.

The black hand closed like a vise, crushing Ethamy's neck back to the bone. Then a sudden twist, a sickening crack. Ethamy's head flopped over sideways like a broken doll.

Kiet shrieked. In the same moment, she found the trigger and pulled.

Something shot spinning from the barrel of the gun. It drilled into the Queen-Hyper and burst open inside her like flowering steel. Spikes exploded outwards through chest, groin, back and shoulders. The Queen-Hyper was transformed into a kind of metal hedgehog.

She fell away from the hopper, dragging Ethamy's lifeless body with her. When the spikes hit the concrete, her own body broke apart. There was a loud *Whumffff!* as multi-coloured psychic deposits volatilised.

'Keep shooting!' cried Ferren.

Kiet only wanted to weep for Ethamy. But there was no time. Already other Queen-Hypers were launching themselves at the train.

Ferren hurled one of his two chunks of rock at the first attacker. He struck her in mid-air and deflected her flight. She failed to latch on and dropped back onto the road.

Another Queen-Hyper caught hold of the last hopper, containing Gibby and Miriael. Kiet took aim.

'Out of the way!' she shouted.

As Gibby and Miriael flung themselves against the other side of the hopper, Kiet fired. Again the projectile drilled into the rubber-clad body and exploded in metal spikes.

Ferren hurled his second chunk of rock. Kiet shot at a Queen-Hyper who was poised to spring, destroying her before she'd even left the ground.

For the moment there were no more attackers. But a groan from Shanna made them turn.

Two machines were converging to form a barrier across the road. On one side was a bulldozer, on the other a mobile crane. Hypers screamed mathematical orders as Shanna aimed for the rapidly-diminishing gap.

With a final spurt of acceleration, the traction engine thrust its nose into the gap. The first hopper squeezed through, then the second. Mere millimetres on either side. The third hopper barely made it. Then the jaws closed. The fourth and final hopper was trapped.

There was a rending screech of metal on metal. The wheels of the engine spun round and round. The whole train skidded to a halt.

Ferren and Kiet could only watch in frozen horror. The bulldozer's shunt ground forward on one side, the crane's caterpillar tracks on the other. Sparks flew everywhere. Gibby and Miriael retreated to the middle of the hopper as the walls buckled in around them.

Then the grinding stopped. The two machines had also come to a halt. Shanna redoubled her efforts, shouting aloud as she urged on the Plasmatic-powered engine.

Slowly, incredibly, the train started to inch forward

again. The walls of the last hopper buckled even further – but pulled free at the same time. More scraping of metal on metal. Then the last hopper emerged, still upright on its wheels.

Ferren and Kiet recovered their voices. 'We did it! We did it!'

But even as they cheered, a dull thunder vibrated in the ground.

Thumm! Thumm! Thumm! Thumm!

They looked around and their hopes collapsed. There ahead was the gigantic figure of Doctor Saniette. He was lumbering forward to block their way to the bridge.

11

His head had come out at the top of the dome, which trailed behind him like a long billowing gown. He tilted back his head and gave a great bellow.

'*I – con – keep – con – must – con – trol*!'

It was like a hundred voices all trying to speak at once. Something very strange seemed to be happening to Doctor Saniette.

Shanna brought the train to a stop. On the right stood a forest of plastic pipes, a crisscross lattice between stainless steel tanks and columns of glass. On the left stood a row of masts and aerials, winking with lights like electrical trees. Hypers and Queen-Hypers were advancing behind the masts. Shanna slewed the engine to the right.

'We'll try for another bridge!' she shouted.

The hoppers swung out, teetered, almost over-balanced, recovered. The nose of the engine smashed into the pipes, which shattered like brittle twigs. Lengths of pipe cascaded all around. Ferren and Kiet held their arms over their heads and shook fragments out of their hair.

Shanna kept the train heading parallel to the moat. The engine veered around steel tanks and glass columns. The columns were like tall measuring jars filled with pink or purple liquid.

Doctor Saniette came after them. His movements were slow but his strides were enormous. He didn't bother to veer, but crashed through everything in his way. His hoof-like feet stomped down on steel and smashed through glass. The air was heavy with the smell of chemicals.

Kiet tried to aim her gun at him. But it was impossible. Bits of pipe kept falling on top of her, knocking her this way and that. Their hopper was half-filled with a litter of plastic.

Suddenly they burst out onto a wide square of bitumen. A dozen turntables rotated slowly in the ground, batteries of lights shone from above. On the opposite side of the square was an industrial zone of huge iron mills and rollers. On the right was a mountain of crushed scrap, held back by a wire mesh fence. On the left was the moat – and a bridge over the moat.

But Doctor Saniette had also seen the bridge. Even before Shanna could communicate new instructions to the engine, he had swung across to the left. There was no way they could reach the bridge before he cut them off.

Shanna cursed and let the engine run on ahead. They passed the rotating turntables and entered the industrial zone. They hurtled along a passage between throbbing pounding machinery.

'He's not coming after us!' cried Ferren in surprise.

They found out why a moment later. The passage was blocked by a troop of armed Hypers. Shanna tried to charge them.

The Hypers carried cone-shaped weapons like the Selector's flamethrower. As the engine rushed towards them, they bunched up in formation. The Hypers at the front dropped down on one knee, the Hypers behind aimed over their shoulders.

Jets of foam shot from the nozzles of their weapons and burst into flame. Streams of fire played onto the nose of the engine.

Ferren and Kiet ducked down below the rim of their hopper. Red and orange flames made a sizzling canopy over their heads. A tiny spot of foam fell on Kiet's shoulder and ignited with an agonising blaze. Ferren smothered it instantly with his hands. Another spot fell on the litter of plastic around their feet. One length of pipe caught fire and burned with a thick black smoke.

Still the train moved forward. But it was rapidly losing speed. Ferren and Kiet could feel the walls of their hopper warming up. The nose of the engine must be burning hot.

Ghaaaghaaa-ghaaahhhhh!

It was the sound of a Plasmatic in extreme pain. A kind of bubbling whimper, like the cry of an animal.

'We can't go on!' gasped Kiet.

Shanna must have come to the same conclusion. She pulled up short of the Hypers and swung the engine around. There was just enough room to make a U-turn. The hoppers wheeled round behind and the train headed back in the opposite direction.

Escaping from the flames, the engine rapidly picked up speed. In no time at all, they were out on the bitumen square again. Ferren and Kiet looked out over the rim.

Their routes were closed off on all sides. Doctor Saniette had taken up a position in front of the bridge. The mountain of scrap was completely impassable. And hundreds of Hypers and Queen-Hypers were rushing towards them through the smashed chemicals area.

Shanna called out over her shoulder. 'I'm going straight at him! It's our only chance! Hang on!'

Ferren and Kiet relayed the message to the other hoppers. The train clattered between turntables, heading towards the bridge. Everyone braced and stared ahead.

The deflated plastic dome still hung from Doctor Saniette's shoulders, but most of the trailing material had now fallen away. The white medical coat showed through rips and rents in the plastic.

The Doctor uttered a maddened stutter of rage. 'I – I – I – I – I – I – I – I – I – I – I – !'

Kiet sighted her gun and fired at him. Once, twice, three times. Metal spikes flowered in the folds of the plastic. But they couldn't penetrate through to his body. Useless!

As they approached, he began to stamp his feet. Up and down, side to side, like an ungainly dance.

Shanna swerved as if to go around him to the right. The ground shook as his hoof-like foot came down. But the swerve was only a feint. Already Shanna had switched direction, now racing to the left.

With a ponderous shuffle, the Doctor readjusted. His

other foot slammed down three metres in front of them. The way was blocked. The engine jerked to a halt.

They stared at a shiny cylindrical hoof, at a white trousered leg. So close, so huge. The plastic material of the dome was like a curtain hanging above their heads. The material was drenched in liquid chemicals, the trousers were spattered with pink and purple stains.

Shanna tried to reverse direction. Doctor Saniette bent at the waist and lowered his face for a closer look. His single bulging eye was as vast as a planet rushing towards them. His hand descended too, curved in a scoop to gather them up.

'Yow!'

Taking an instinctive step backwards, Ferren had trodden on something burning. The length of pipe that had caught fire was still blazing away at the bottom of the hopper.

He stooped and snatched it up, drew back his arm to throw.

For a fraction of a second, Doctor Saniette's eye reflected the bright yellow flame on the tip of the pipe. Then the eye lifted away. With all his might, Ferren threw.

The length of pipe soared in an arc. It missed the eye and landed on the chemical-drenched material of the deflated dome.

The effect was spectacular. There was a tremendous *whoooooosh*! as the material went up in a sheet of fire. A blast of heat radiated downwards.

Doctor Saniette hardly moved. Instead of beating at the fire, his arms could only make ineffectual back-

and-forth movements. His whole body quivered in a halo of flame.

Shanna had finally managed to reverse direction. The engine turned away from the hoof-like foot and began to go round in a wider loop to the left.

The Doctor straightened to stand upright again. Black burning scraps of material floated in the air. The inflammable plastic dome had disintegrated, revealing the white medical coat underneath. Lines of red fire smouldered on the coat and trousers.

Everyone in the hoppers stared upwards in amazement. Out on the square, the Hypers and Queen-Hypers also stared. It was a frozen picture – except for the flames. Then Kiet pointed and cried out.

'Look! Look! *Look*!'

The Doctor's clothing was peeling away. Now they could see right through to the body beneath. Only it wasn't exactly a body. The giant Doctor was composed of hundreds of ordinary doctors, all fastened together.

It was an incredible sight. The individual figures were bound in with straps and harnesses, side by side, one on top of the other. Interconnecting wires ran from the backs of their skulls. They all wore their own white medical coats.

The train circled around the Doctor, now travelling beside the moat, behind the foot. The foot shifted unsteadily on the ground.

Everywhere, more and more doctors were exposed. They were like the living cells of a mighty organism. A dozen were visible in the region of the right kneecap, twenty in the right hip. Flames licked at their medical coats. They too were starting to burn.

All over the body, tiny mouths shrieked, tiny 'O's of fear and pain. The doctors kicked and struggled, trying to break free. But they couldn't escape from the straps and harnesses. Ominous ripples ran through the towering limbs. Here and there, a few doctors hung limp and motionless. They appeared to have fainted from sheer terror.

The colossus swayed and sagged. The separate cells were no longer cooperating. Suddenly, the members of the team realised their own danger.

'He'll fall on top of us!' cried Ferren.

The engine made a sharp turn onto the bridge. It was a single arched span of thirty metres. Rattling and wobbling, the train went up over the arch.

Doctor Saniette no longer retained even the outward form of a human being. His body had distorted into impossible bulges and hollows. He staggered a step closer to the bridge.

The train came to the top of the arch and rushed down on the other side. The Doctor toppled slowly backwards, toppling towards them. Time seemed to stand still. They had almost reached the outer bank –

Klunnnnch!

The giant body fell back onto the bridge with a bursting, splitting sound. The monstrous head smashed down just two metres short of the last hopper. The bridge leaped beneath them, the whole train was tossed high in the air.

Ferren flew upwards, grabbed at the rim of the

hopper, managed to keep his feet.

Amazingly, every hopper landed upright on its wheels. As the bridge sank down under the Doctor's weight, the engine continued to race forward. Gaining a purchase on the bank beyond the moat, it towed the rest of the train onto solid ground.

Ferren stood staring out at the back of the hopper. Doctor Saniette's head had cracked wide open. Inside were dozens of tightly strapped figures wriggling like maggots. A dark red colour seeped and spread across the white of their medical coats.

'The end of Doctor Saniette,' Ferren breathed in wonder.

All that remained of the Doctor was a shapeless mass, like a vast promontory in the water. Parts of the mass heaved spasmodically, others were completely still. Fires continued to burn here and there, sending up wisps of smoke.

'I wonder what the other Humen will do now,' Ferren said.

There was no answer from Kiet. But a growing clamour of sound rose up on the opposite side of the moat. A multitude of harsh voices cried out in rage and lamentation.

'They'll have to go round by other bridges,' said Ferren. 'At least we've got a start on them.'

Still no reply. He turned his head, expecting to see Kiet right behind him. But she wasn't there.

He gaped at the empty hopper. 'Where is she?'

He had to repeat the question before anyone heard him. Then they all started talking at once.

'I was looking the other way!'

'Me too!'

'She must've been thrown out!'

'When the Doctor hit the bridge!'

Ferren recovered from his state of shock. 'We'll have to go back and search for her!'

But even as he spoke, searchlights shot out from the Humen Camp, sweeping across the surrounding plain. They located the train in a matter of seconds.

The members of the team stared at one another in the stark blue light.

'No going back now,' said Shanna grimly.

'We have to!'

'Impossible.'

Ferren was frantic. 'If you won't, I'll go by myself!'

'Don't be a fool, little brother.'

But Ferren was already starting to clamber out of his hopper. Shanna jumped up, stretched out, grabbed him by the leg.

'No!' she shouted. 'I'm not going to lose you too!'

Ferren tried to pull away. Shanna's grip slid down his leg and locked around his ankle. She was using both hands now.

'Help me!' she appealed to the rest of the team. 'Don't let him do this!'

Ferren used both hands too. He twisted around and prised Shanna's hands away from his ankle. Finger by finger, he unlocked her grip.

The rest of the team tried to dissuade him.

'Ferren, you can't do anything for her now!'

'There are Hypers watching from the bank!'

'The Humen are crossing on the other bridges!'

'There are Queen-Hypers coming out!'

Ferren had the vague impression of someone climbing into his own hopper from the hopper behind. But he didn't look round. He prised away the last of Shanna's fingers and jerked his leg free.

'Do something, Bross!' shouted Shanna.

Ferren never saw the blow coming down. There was an explosive impact on the side of his skull. Then nothingness. Consciousness went out like a light.

12

Where was he? He forced his eyelids open. There was a throbbing pain across the side of his skull. He seemed to be lying on bare earth.

At first, he could see nothing in the darkness. But he could hear familiar voices: not only the rescue team but also the base party that had stayed behind. Somehow he had returned to their refuge outside the Camp.

He began to see it as his eyes adjusted: huge steel tubes and panels of sheet metal. A faint glimmer of light was visible in the gaps between the panels. Perhaps dawn was approaching?

Soon he could distinguish the forms of the speakers too. Some stood peering out between the panels, others sat in small groups on the ground. Their voices were low and serious.

The only one he could recognise was Miriael. Even in the dimness, her height and golden hair gave her away.

So they were back at the base with Miriael. The rescue had been successful. But he didn't feel successful.

He remembered Flens blasted to small pieces of flesh and bone. He remembered Ethamy with her neck broken. And worst of all –

He groaned aloud. The memory of Kiet weighed down on him like a lump of lead. Kiet thrown out of the hopper – and he hadn't even noticed! Kiet abandoned and left to die! Kiet, Kiet, Kiet!

'Hi! How are you feeling?'

Someone had come across, someone was speaking to him. An athletic male figure. Bross.

'I heard you groan,' Bross squatted down beside him. 'You've been out for ages. I didn't mean to hit you so hard.'

'Doesn't matter.' So far as Ferren was concerned, nothing mattered any more.

'It was the only way I could stop you. You wanted to go back looking for Kiet.'

Ferren said nothing. He was beyond arguing. Bross sucked in his cheeks, then blew them out again.

'We're half of us carrying injuries,' he commented. 'Rhinn has a huge gash in her leg. Tadge has a broken arm. I've got burns all over my back and chest.'

'Not to mention the ones who died,' said Ferren bitterly.

'Yes, Kiet and Flens and Ethamy.' Bross seemed puzzled by the bitterness. 'I'm sorry.'

'Me too.'

'You mustn't blame yourself. We all accepted the risks. We all knew we might not survive.'

'But you and I survived. Kiet didn't.'

'Nor Flens and Ethamy. Three lives lost for the sake

of the Residual Alliance.' Bross sighed heavily. 'It was a terrible price to pay.'

Ferren looked away with a sudden stab of guilt. *For the sake of the Residual Alliance.* Bross didn't question it, of course. But was that the real reason for the rescue mission?

The words he'd once spoken to Kiet came back to him. *She's the one special person in the world for me . . . I'd do anything for her . . .* The memory made him wince. Had he risked other people's lives because he thought he was in love with an angel? Had he launched an almost suicidal rescue mission for the sake of his own daydreams?

Again he gazed across at Miriael. The light had grown a fraction stronger and he could see her clear pale features under the golden hair. Very, very beautiful – but also very remote. Suddenly it seemed that her beauty had nothing to do with him.

Stupid, stupid daydreams! Anger and misery knotted in his stomach. How could he ever be close to an angel in the way he'd imagined? He could never share with Miriael the things he'd shared with Kiet!

The things he'd shared with Kiet . . . Like the afternoon by the secret pool, lying side by side on the warm sandstone, watching the dragonflies . . . or the meeting under the rhododendron bush, when she shook rainwater down on his head . . . or the hours on top of Allan Kor, leaning back in their seaweed throne, smelling the salt of the sea . . .

And now? How could she be gone? He couldn't bear to lose her. He'd never guessed, never realised. He wanted her back. He ached with a deep-down ache.

A hundred images flooded through his mind. Kiet smiling, Kiet thoughtful, Kiet in a temper. Her dark red hair, wide mouth, white teeth. Kiet bringing him an armful of pears, Kiet tightrope-walking between the islands, Kiet dancing her wild flinging dance –

'No-o!' The groan burst out of him, louder than before.

Bross glanced down in surprise. Other glances came from other corners of the refuge.

'Is he awake?' Miriael called out.

'Yes,' answered Bross. 'Since a few minutes ago.'

Miriael rose to her feet. So did the person she'd been talking to. It was Ferren's sister, Shanna.

Ferren closed his eyes. He didn't want to speak with anyone – least of all Miriael. He wanted to be left alone. Perhaps if he pretended to fall back asleep . . .

Miriael and Shanna never reached him. halfway across, they were halted by an urgent cry.

'Hey! Somebody approaching!'

The cry came from one of the base party who'd been keeping watch between the panels.

'Who?'

'Heading straight here! I think it's – it can't be!'

Ferren opened his eyes and sat instantly upright. The sudden wild leap of hope was almost more than he could stand.

The watcher was stuttering with excitement. 'It is! It's her! It's Kiet!'

13

Everyone gathered around the moment she stepped inside the refuge. Kiet was as surprised to see the rest of the rescue team as they were surprised to see her.

'How did you get here?' she gasped.

But her question was drowned out by a dozen voices all asking her the same thing. She stood covered in mud, half laughing and half crying with relief.

'I got thrown out of the hopper,' she brought out at last. 'So I had to make my own way back.'

'But the Humen! What about the Humen!'

She grinned. 'I was too smart for them. I landed in shallow water beside the bank. When the searchlights came on, I knew I'd be spotted. So I slid out into deeper water. I kept totally submerged, all except my nose.'

She tilted her head and demonstrated breathing through her nose, leaning backwards.

'See? Like that. If they saw my nose, they probably thought it was just something floating on the water. They stood on the inner bank staring across the moat. It was you and the train they were looking at. Then gangs of Hypers came round on the outer bank to inspect the Doctor.'

'Wow! They still didn't see you?'

'They waded out in the water, coming close. So I stayed submerged and moved away backwards. Very very carefully, so as not to make a ripple. I kept on backing away for ages. I went under one bridge, but it still wasn't safe to come out on the bank. Then the next bridge was an overbridge with high pylons. No-one could see when I crawled out between the pylons. I knew I had to get back here before daylight.'

'You only just made it,' commented Miriael.

'Yes. I crept around for a while before I could recognise where I was. And all the time the searchlights were sweeping out and the Hypers and Queen-Hypers were chasing after the train.' A puzzled expression came over her face. 'That's why I didn't expect you back here. I thought you were still in the hoppers.'

'So did the Hypers,' said Miriael. 'That was the plan – Shanna's plan. She told the Plasmatic in the engine to keep dodging around at top speed.'

'We jumped off where the Humen couldn't see us,' added Rhinn. She had a strip of bloodstained cloth bandaged around her leg. 'We jumped into a trench while they kept chasing after the train.'

'I think it must have circled the whole Camp,' said Kiet.

'I'd have liked to see their faces when they finally caught it,' said Shanna.

Kiet laughed at the idea. 'So when did you get back?' she asked.

'Half an hour ago. We'd have been sooner, but we had to carry Ferren.'

'Ferren?' Kiet scanned around with a frown. 'Where is he? What's wrong with him?'

'He, er, got a nasty blow on the side of the head,' explained Shanna.

'He's over here,' said one of the base party.

The crowd parted to reveal Ferren standing quietly at the back. They opened a way for him to come forward. But he didn't move. He was gazing at Kiet with a broad foolish smile on his face.

'What's wrong with him?' Kiet asked again.

'Perhaps he's still a bit dopey in the head,' suggested Tadge.

Ferren said nothing. He stood as if fixed to the spot, just smiling and smiling.

14

Morning sunlight came angling in between the steel tubes and panels of sheet metal. The rescue party had divided out into smaller groups again. Miriael and Shanna went back to the discussion they'd been having before Kiet's miraculous return.

Miriael was curious to hear Shanna's personal history, and Shanna was curious to hear the whole past history of the Millennial War. As they talked, Shanna kept casting secret glances at Miriael's long legs, white wings, blue eyes. Obviously she couldn't get used to the sight of a real live angel.

But her secret glances didn't stop her asking questions. As Miriael had already learned, Shanna had a sharp intelligence. Once she'd learned about the past, she wanted to think ahead to the future.

'Doctor Saniette *is* destroyed, isn't he?' she asked.

Miriael nodded. 'As a single being. Some of the individual doctors probably survived. But not enough to recreate another Doctor Saniette.'

'What does that mean for us?'

'The threat is over for a while. But the Doctor's secret weapons still remain. Also, there's Asmodai and his flying wing of Morphs. He could be a new force in the future.'

Shanna snorted. 'So could we. The Residual Alliance.'

Miriael grinned. 'I still can't believe what you've done. A tiny group of Residuals has knocked out the most dangerous attack on Heaven for centuries. A hundred battalions of angels could hardly have defeated Doctor Saniette. But you did.'

'By accident.'

'Yes, I know, the mission was to rescue me. Nonetheless. The Residual Alliance has already changed the history of the world. And this is only the start.'

'What next?'

'The meeting of representatives from all the tribes. We go ahead with that as planned.'

'Right. Ferren said something about it. He's been helping you organise this Alliance, hasn't he?'

'More than helping. He's been the key to it all.'

Shanna couldn't hold back a flush of pride. 'Ah, he's something special, my little brother!'

Her eyes scanned the refuge, looking for Ferren. Miriael studied her in silence.

And you're something special too, she thought. A solitary Residual surviving for two years in the Humen Camp. No support, no-one to talk to – only a burning desire for revenge. It seemed almost incredible.

Miriael couldn't help making comparisons to her own situation. She too had been cut off from the society of her kind. She too knew the experience of being alone. If Shanna had survived, then she would too.

I wonder if we'll get used to each other, she mused. A strange sort of angel and a strange sort of Residual. Both in the habit of being alone . . .

Shanna suddenly snapped her fingers.

'There he is!' She pointed. 'With Kiet.'

Ferren and Kiet were almost hidden from view in a quiet corner of the refuge. Bright sunlight fell across Kiet's hair and Ferren's shoulders. Their heads were close together as they talked.

Miriael smiled. 'What do you think? Should we call him across to discuss the meeting of representatives?'

Shanna shook her head. 'I think it'd be a shame to distract him now.'

They both laughed and turned their eyes away.

'Ah, little brother,' murmured Shanna under her breath. 'Perhaps you'll get lucky after all.'

TRADITIONAL ANGELOLOGY

Anael	Head of the Order of Principalities, Anael is one of the seven Angels of Creation and ruler of the Second Altitude of Heaven. Also known under the names of Haniel and Hamiel.
Anaitis	A high-ranking female angel, also called Anahita.
Archon	Any very powerful angel may be described as an Archon.
Berial	Once an angel in the order of Virtues, Berial rebelled and was cast down with Satan.
Meresin	One of the Fallen Angels, and a lord of thunder and lightning in Hell.
Miriael	A minor angel, known as a warrior.
Orders of Angels	Traditionally, there are nine orders of angels. In descending rank they are: Seraphim, Cherubim, Ofanim (or Thrones), Dominions, Virtues, Powers, Principalities, Archangels and Angels. Confusingly, the

term 'archangels' can also be used for the very highest princes of Heaven. In this book, angels of the eighth order have been given the name of 'Junior Archangels', angels of the ninth order have been given the name of 'Junior Angels'.

Samael

According to many authorities, Samael was the original name of Satan, the mighty angel who led a rebellion against God and was driven out from Heaven. (Satan was never called Lucifer: only a mistaken interpretation of the Bible connected that name to him.) Even as an angel in Heaven, Samael was associated with poison and served in the dark role of an angel of death.

Early Church fathers such as St. Jerome believed that Satan and his followers would eventually repent and be forgiven. As Samael, Satan would then return to his original position in Heaven.

Uriel

Uriel is an Angel of the Presence and one of the four greatest archangels, along with Michael, Gabriel and Raphael. He controls the South and is also commonly included among the Angels of Destruction.

And now a preview of

FERREN AND THE
INVASION OF HEAVEN

the final book in the HEAVEN AND EARTH
TRILOGY

1

Ferren woke up with a shudder.

'What is it?' His voice was thick with sleep. 'What's happening?'

There was no reply. He was alone in the nest. Of course, Miriael and Shanna had gone off on their reconnaissance mission two days ago.

He struggled to shake off the furriness in his mind. Something was wrong, but he couldn't work out what.

Then the light started to return. Cool blue moonlight, filtering in through the entrance hole, growing rapidly brighter.

So *that* was it! Some kind of obstruction had blotted out the moon. A cloud? But his skin was crawling, the hairs stood up on the back of his neck. Instinct told him it was something much larger, much blacker, much more sinister than a cloud.

He rolled over, got up on all fours and headed for the entrance-hole. He was still half asleep. But he was desperate to look at the thing in the sky.

Too late. When he came out into the open, the full

moon was shining and the sky was clear. He gazed up through the twigs and leaves overhead. Nothing. Whatever it was had gone.

He stood frowning and troubled. Had anyone else woken up? The Nesters' settlement seemed quiet and peaceful. Or wait! Was that someone speaking in the distance?

He strode along the tunnels between overhanging lantana bushes. The moonlight cast a network of stark black and white over everything. He came towards a small clearing in front of Kiet's nest.

There were half a dozen people there. Ferren recognised Kiet and her family: her mother Nettish and her brother Tadge. It was Tadge who was doing all the talking.

'It was so big, you wouldn't believe! From there to there it was!'

He gestured from one side of the sky to the other. He was spluttering with nervous excitement. His mother tried to soothe him with frantic pats to the head and shoulders.

'There, there! It's all right! Don't scare us! Don't scare yourself! Hush, hush, *hush*!'

'What did you see?' Ferren demanded, hurrying up.

'I'm telling you,' spluttered Tadge. 'It was black with crisscross lines. Shaped like this.' He drew a triangle in the air.

'Did anyone else see it?' asked Ferren.

Kiet shook her head. 'We were too slow. Do you know what I think?'

'*No!*' cried Nettish.

But she didn't mean it as an answer to Kiet. She had her hands raised as if to ward something away. Everyone followed the line of her gaze.

'Here it comes again!' cried Tadge.

A tidal wave of blackness was advancing over the sky. It was in the form of a vast delta, spreading wider and wider. One by one the stars went out.

They ran for the shelter of the bushes. Nettish flung herself to the ground and wrapped her arms over her head.

It created no wind but passed through the air with a thin high hiss. It cut across the disc of the moon like a diagonal blade. Suddenly they were under its shadow, and the world was dark and chill.

Cries and moans and whimpers rose from the nests all around. More and more people were waking up.

Ferren resisted the urge to cower. He observed the crisscross structure of the delta, black on black. In the centre of the structure was a pale glowing oval like an eye.

The oval hovered above their heads. For a few moments, the delta seemed to pause, swinging a little to the left, a little to the right. Then it glided off on its smooth silent way. As its trailing edge uncovered the sky, the stars reappeared and the moon shone forth again.

Ferren realised he was shivering. He looked at Kiet and saw she was shivering too. She turned to face him.

'I thought so!' she cried. 'Asmodai! Did you see him in his globe?'

'I saw the purple of his robe.'

'That was him. Asmodai and his flying wing of Morphs.' Her eyebrows formed a straight black line, her white teeth gleamed in the moonlight. 'He must have captured many more colonies of Morphs.'

Ferren nodded. 'I never thought his wing could be so big. And he's done something to the Morphs. They were always transparent and invisible before.'

'Why was he flying over our territory? Was he searching for something?'

Ferren didn't answer. He was listening to the clamour of voices across the settlement. Voices raised in alarm, voices on the edge of panic.

Nettish lifted herself up off the ground. 'What do we do now?' she flustered. 'What? What do we *do*?'

'We calm everyone down,' said Ferren. 'We go and talk to them in their nests. Me and Kiet.' He turned to Kiet. 'If you talk to the Nesters, I'll talk to the representatives from other tribes.'

'What shall we tell them?'

'As much as they want to know. The Nesters know half the story already.'

'The representatives don't.'

'So I'll tell them. Let's go.'

'Can I come?' asked Tadge.

'No, you go back to sleep,' said Kiet sternly.

'What if the thing comes again?'

Kiet shrugged. 'You'll just have to hope it doesn't.'

Also available from Penguin

FERREN AND THE ANGEL

RICHARD HARLAND

What if the Third Millennium began with the ultimate medical discovery – a way to bring the dead back to life?

What if the dead reported the existence of a real Heaven, with Blessed Souls and nine Orders of angels?

What if scientific attempts to explore the heavenly realm led to an ultimate war between Heaven and Earth?

What if Earth ended up under the control of a new evil species?

This is the kind of world that Ferren has been born into. Only he doesn't know it yet . . .

'A marvellously imaginative concoction.'
The West Australian

FOREST

Sonya Hartnett

The forest is earth and leaves,
sun and shade, feather and blood and bone.
It is the old way, the true way,
the wild way to live.

But, for Kian, wilderness is not home.

'Sonya Hartnett is creating new literary territory.'
Australian Book Review

Also available from Penguin

THE MUSIC OF RAZORS

CAMERON ROGERS

Desperate to escape his past, Henry Lockrose – dead two hundred years – has trapped little Walter inside the shell of his own body. Now he's after Walter's sister, Hope, who must make a choice between holding on to a shattered childhood, or losing whatever it is that makes her human.

Only the creature Walter has become can save Hope. But is it too late to save himself?

'A nightmarishly imaginative debut from a writer of real assurance and vision. Watch him: he's going to go places.'
Neil Gaiman

Come exploring at

www.penguin.com.au

and

www.puffin.com.au

for

Author and illustrator profiles

Book extracts

Reviews

Competitions

Activities, games and puzzles

Advice for budding authors

Tips for parents

Teacher resources